BLUE SKY GONE

ANCIENT
CITY
PRESS

Ancient City Press

Blue Sky Gone
Copyright © 2021 by J.S. Farmer
All rights reserved

First Edition
ISBN: 978-1-7373074-1-9

jsfarmerauthor.com

BLUE SKY GONE

J. S. FARMER

PART ONE

CHAPTER 1

September 2019

It was a bright and sunny September afternoon in Greenport, a small New England town tucked away in the quiet southwest corner of Connecticut. Audrey had just finished wiping down all of the counters in the kitchen. Feeling the familiar tightness in her chest, she quickly sat down on a trendy lime-green kitchen island stool to catch her breath. Audrey took a puff of her inhaler and concentrated on steady breathing. It didn't take much for her to get winded these days.

Once a decorated police officer, Audrey had been forced to leave the job due to progressive respiratory illness. It was no mystery where the illness came from, but Audrey never dwelled on that. She instead looked at it as an opportunity to be home for her two daughters, Addelyn and Hope. Even though they were both in school, Audrey was grateful to be home each day when they got off the bus—something she would have missed working second shift at the police department.

It was the calm before the storm. Any minute, two kids full of pent-up energy from their day at school would come barreling into the house.

Right on cue, the big yellow bus pulled up in front of the house with flashing red lights. The bus doors had barely opened as Addelyn and Hope burst free, stomping down the steep, awkward bus steps. Audrey watched from the window of their colonial New England home as the girls ran up the driveway. She took a quick puff of her inhaler before they reached the house. She didn't want them to know just how bad her health had become.

The door flung open, and Addelyn came running in first, waving a flyer wildly high above her head. "Mommy!!" she exclaimed excitedly. "I want to do this! Can I? Can I?"

Audrey stopped the flyer from waving in front of her face to read it.

SCOUT RANGERS: HIKING, FISHING, CAMPFIRES, SURVIVAL SKILLS, the flyer read in big bold letters.

It was right up her daughter's alley and she knew it. So what was the uneasy feeling she had in her stomach?

She looked down at her daughter and saw the light of excitement in her eyes. Addeyln was a striking seven-year-old little girl with long sun-kissed blonde curls and eyes as green as a leprechaun's. Looking at her, you would never suspect that her favorite things in the world were sharks, bugs, and snakes.

"Is this really what you want to do Addelyn?" Audrey asked.

"Yes, yes, yes!" Addelyn replied.

She took Addelyn's delicate little hands in her own and kneeled down to her eye level.

"I think this would be perfect for you. I just want you to know that you may be the only girl. I don't want you to be surprised," Audrey gently said.

Suddenly, Audrey realized what her uneasy feeling was about. Her time in the police academy many years before as the only female in the academy class came flooding back.

There was so much her daughters didn't know about her. She feared that if she were to reveal glimpses into her past it would lead to telling of that day— September 11, 2001. But her illness was getting more noticeable, and she knew that one day she would have to reveal the dark truth about how and why she was so sick. Not only would she have to face the horrors of that day all over again, she would have to share that darkness with her daughters. They were still too young to know.

Addeyln thought for a moment.

"I'm not scared. I want to do it," Addelyn said definitively.

Audrey smiled and pulled her close.

Like mother, like daughter…

———

"Let's go, girls! You are going to miss the bus!" Audrey yelled from the kitchen, her morning coffee getting cold on the counter.

Two backpacks perfectly packed with lunches, completed homework, and endless forms to return to school were staged upon the counter. Next to the backpacks, Audrey noticed a yellow sticky note stuck to the counter.

SIGN ADDY UP FOR SCOUT RANGERS was scribbled in Addelyn's second-grade handwriting on the note.

Hope and Addelyn came running down the stairs into the kitchen. Hope, a carefree five-year-old girl with short blonde curls, was dressed in pink, sparkly leggings and a purple unicorn shirt. Addelyn was garbed in much more subdued tones—camouflage leggings and a black T-shirt.

Audrey felt strong enough that morning to walk the girls down the end of the driveway to catch the bus. She never knew when she would feel well enough to do anything. There was no pattern to her illness except that it was getting worse.

As they climbed onto the bus, Addelyn yelled over her shoulder, "Don't forget, Mommy! Scout Rangers!"

Audrey waved as the bus pulled away, their little faces in the windows of the big yellow bus disappearing into the distance. She had only made it halfway back up the driveway, when she felt her chest tighten and her head get light.

It's getting worse.

She paused to catch her breath and steady herself.

Audrey slowly made her way into the house to retrieve the flyer Addelyn had brought home. Searching the flyer for the email and contact name, she plopped down in front of the computer and started typing.

> *Good morning, Blair,*
> *My daughter Addelyn would like to join Scout Rangers. She is really looking forward to it. Please let me know how to sign her up. Thank you.*
> *Audrey*

Send.

The day flew by in a flash, so much so that she didn't notice she hadn't received a response about Scout Rangers. It wasn't until the bus came and Audrey saw the look on Addelyn's face that she knew something was wrong.

Audrey sat on the front steps feeling fatigued and lethargic. Hope jumped off the bus in front of Addelyn, flying a paper unicorn she'd made at school, cheerily singing a song she had learned in music class that day. Hope floated on air as she skipped up the driveway, while Addelyn walked sullenly behind. Addelyn reached the steps and stood with her head hung low.

"What's the matter?" Audrey gently asked.

"The boys at school said I can't be a Scout Ranger. They said it's only for boys," Addelyn said with tears in her eyes.

Just then, a notification chimed on Audrey's phone. She glimpsed quickly at the screen to read the notification. What she saw made her jaw muscles clench with anger.

If there are any **BOYS** *who would like to join Scout Rangers, please let me know! All* **BOYS** *are welcome. Contact me, Blair, to sign your sons up!*

Audrey reeled. **BOYS**. Written in capital letters and in bold nonetheless!

Audrey's eyes narrowed as she pulled Addelyn toward her. The fierce look that often flashed in Audrey's eyes met Addelyn's forlorn face.

"Listen to me," Audrey said, lifting Addelyn's chin. "You can be *anything* you want to be, no matter how hard someone may try to stop you," Audrey said as she wiped a tear from Addelyn's cheek. "Now, let's go get you signed up for Scout Rangers."

Addelyn's face brightened, and the sparkle returned to her green eyes.

They have no idea who they are dealing with.

That night as Audrey lay in bed, her memory drifted back eighteen years earlier, to a time she so often tried to forget.

CHAPTER 2

Eighteen years earlier...Monday, April 23, 2001
7:50 a.m.

"*Breathe!*" Audrey quietly scolded herself.

It was the first day of the police academy, and Audrey's lifelong dream of becoming a police officer was coming true. All she had to do was get through the grueling six months ahead of her.

Audrey peered through the windshield of her parked car, studying the old brick academy building in front of her. She took a deep breath and pushed the car door open. Stepping out onto the asphalt, Audrey looked down at her freshly polished black boots, double-checking that she didn't get even the slightest scuff mark on them. Then, she did one last nervous check of herself in the reflection of the car window.

Audrey had ironed her khaki recruit uniform a hundred times in the days leading up to that morning. There was not a wrinkle to be found. The American flag pin was straight above her chest pocket, and patches were sewn just right on her sleeves. Her name badge, which spelled out **MORETTI** in bold letters, was pinned strategically under the flag. Not a strand of hair was astray from her tightly wound bun. She was ready.

Audrey reminded herself again to breathe. She put one foot in front of the other until she was standing at the front entrance of the academy building. Audrey pulled open the heavy wooden door and entered the lobby. She was the first one there. The old lights above were harsh on her eyes, and the air smelled musty. Audrey claimed her spot on the old wooden bench in the lobby and sat quietly observing the woodwork and outdated decor of the old building. After a few moments, the front door opened, and a nervous young man walked in. His boots were shiny, uniform pressed perfectly, and he carried a stiff black duty bag, much like hers. It was clear by the way it swung when he walked that it was empty.

One by one each nervous recruit pulled open the same heavy door and found a spot to sit in the old lobby. Soon, the foyer was almost full, and Audrey had counted ten new recruits. As she looked around the room, she came to a sinking realization that she had never considered before.

I can't be the only female recruit in the entire academy class…

Audrey looked at her watch that was set to military time. Her heart sank. It was 0759 hours, only leaving one more minute for a fellow female recruit to walk through the door. Deep in her heart, she knew no one would dare show up at the last minute. Just then, the sound of a lock releasing from the rear door of the lobby made the recruits straighten their postures.

The door swung open, and a police officer in full uniform appeared in the doorway. He was an average-sized man, in his midfifties, with pale skin, and a clean-shaven face. His gray hair was just long enough on top to reveal that it was on the verge of turning white. With a hardened look on his face, he began to slowly make his way around the room, puffing out his arms in an attempt to look bigger and more intimidating than he actually was. He stopped and stood in front of each recruit, staring down at them without saying a word. Finally after several awkward moments, he began to bark out his introduction.

"I am Sergeant Gaston. I am a police officer and you are *not*. Some of you, *not all* of you, will graduate this academy. Only those who make it through will hold the honorable title of police officer. While in this academy, you will stand at attention in the hallways when a real police officer walks by. You will address me as 'sir' at all times. Do you understand?" Sergeant Gaston barked.

"Yes, sir," the group collectively replied in their bravest voices.

"Look around this room. The people standing here are your future backup and your fellow officers one day, *if* you pass this academy. When one of you screws up, you all screw up," Sergeant Gaston finished.

Audrey looked around the room, and for the first time in her life, she felt part of something big, a sense of belonging she'd never experienced before.

Sergeant Gaston spun on his heel. With his back turned, he instructed the group to follow him.

"First we get changed into our physical training uniform. I want to see how many push-ups you can do, how strong you are, and how much you can take," Sergeant Gaston sneered. He held open the heavy wood door at the back of the lobby, leading to the hallway of the academy building. "The locker room is at the end of the hall," he informed them, pointing left down the long corridor.

As Audrey filed into the hallway with the other recruits, Sergeant Gaston stepped in front of her.

"Except you," he glared down at her. "Your locker room is that way." He pointed in the opposite direction.

Suddenly, the feeling of solidarity Audrey had felt just moments before disappeared. She was reminded that she was, in fact, the only female in the entire academy class. She walked down the hall, glancing over her shoulder. The rest of her classmates were entering the men's locker room, politely holding the door for each other and patting each other on the shoulder as they passed by.

The women's locker room was desolate and painfully quiet. As she changed into her navy-blue shorts and academy T-shirt in silence, she imagined her male classmates down the hall, breaking the ice and getting to know each other as they got dressed. She sat down on the bench by herself, hearing only the buzzing of the old fluorescent lights above.

This is going to be a long six months...

———

It had felt like the first day of the academy would never end. Audrey barely had enough strength to turn the key to her tiny apartment. Her small six-hundred-square-foot apartment was just enough for her and Lucy, her red tabby kitten. Audrey stumbled in and collapsed onto the futon. She could feel every muscle in her body aching from the day. There had been never-ending reasons to make the class do push-ups throughout the day. A shoelace untied or a question answered too slowly. Any excuse prompted the instructor to scream, "Drop and give me fifty!" If the class didn't stay in sync, the instructor waited until they reached forty-nine push-ups to make them start again at zero. By dismissal time, each fresh and hopeful face from that morning was pale with exhaustion.

Lucy hopped up onto Audrey's lap and looked at her with a mix of curiosity and indifference. Audrey tried to reach out to pet her, but she could not lift her arms. She wondered how she would do it all again the next day. She wished someone were there to carry her to her comfortable bed. Unable to move, she sprawled out across the futon and closed her eyes. As she drifted into a deep sleep for what only felt like minutes, day two of the academy came all too fast.

———

Five months later... Thursday, August 30, 2001
11:00 a.m.
Audrey had survived five long, grueling months of the police academy. That morning, she stood on the grassy field behind the academy building on a blazing hot, late August day. The police academy had started on a cool morning back in April. As the months passed, the sun had become stronger, and the air became heavy with humidity. She never imagined just how

intense physical training would be under the pounding summer sun of late August in Connecticut.

With their bodies, the class formed a wide circle where they usually did their daily physical training. However, that morning was different. It was Baton Training Certification.

They had been training for months with the baton, a cylindrical club made of heavy plastic and metal, used by police officers as a defensive tool. A young man stood in the middle of the circle, dressed in a full padded suit, ready to test each recruit's practical application. Audrey could barely make him out under the padded helmet, but she was sure she had never seen him before. He looked young, almost too young to be a police officer. He seemed inexperienced and anxious, shifting back and forth from one foot to the other inside the safety of the padded suit.

Sergeant Gaston stood on the sidelines with a clipboard in one hand and a stopwatch in the other.

"This is Officer Riccio," Gaston announced, introducing the nervous young man to the class. "Officer Riccio graduated from the previous academy class. Since he has the least amount of seniority on shift today, he will be our test dummy, no pun intended of course." Sergeant Gaston glanced over at Officer Riccio with a look of annoyance, and disappointment in his eyes.

It was clear that Sergeant Gaston didn't think very highly of Officer Riccio.

With a hint of satisfaction in his voice, Sergeant Gaston said, "Officer Riccio will be on the receiving end of your baton strikes today."

The panic in Officer Riccio's eyes was evident, even through the wire barrier that protected his face. In addition to his nervous demeanor, he was also clumsy and awkward. Audrey wondered if he had picked the wrong profession altogether.

"You'll have three minutes in the ring to demonstrate what you have learned in baton training," Sergeant Gaston continued. "If I feel your strikes have been satisfactory, *and* you complete three full minutes in the ring, you will pass." He acknowledged each recruit as he spoke, but his eyes skipped over Audrey completely.

Sergeant Gaston had not been conspicuous with his distaste for Audrey. She knew by his countless snide comments over the course of five months that he wasn't thrilled with females in police work. Audrey naively thought in the year 2001, those biases wouldn't still exist, but she was wrong.

But Audrey had stayed focused on her dream of becoming a police officer, and refused to let anyone stand in her way. For five months, the class had been vigorously trained on firearms, pepper spray, taser, and baton. Audrey was excited to finally apply what she had learned in a practical setting. She had made it to the final month of the academy and was confident that she would pass all of the certifications. Baton was the first practical test in the coming weeks and she was ready. During the test, the recruits would not wear any protective padding, a sobering example of what it would be like on the street.

First up was a wide-shouldered, towering young man named Preston Briggs. His intimidating appearance was no indication of his kind and gentle heart. Though most of the men in her class had become like brothers to her, she had a special relationship with Preston. He was her best friend. She noticed him always checking in on her without ever making her feel like she was less capable. Despite the fact that Preston was brute and strong, he had a calm and gentle demeanor. Audrey worried greatly for him when the day came that he'd be on the street. She worried that a cold-hearted criminal might detect his inner gentle nature.

Preston stepped into the ring. His black hair, shaved in the back, shimmered with sweat. Sergeant Gaston started the timer. With the sound of the buzzer, Officer Riccio awkwardly jerked his arm in the air, allowing Preston to perform his first strike. He moved to the left, then right, stumbling over his own feet several times, but allowing Preston the opportunity to perform all of the correct strikes. The awkward, uncoordinated dance continued for several minutes until the buzzer rang.

"Well done, Recruit Briggs! You have passed Baton Certification," Sergeant Gaston boasted proudly.

High fives and cheers rang out from the classmates. Preston made his way back to his spot right next to Audrey.

"Great job." Audrey patted his back.

Slightly out of breath, Preston gave her a relieved smile. "It wasn't nearly as bad as I—"

"Recruit Moretti!" Sergeant Gaston barked out. "You're up!"

There was a noticeable change in his voice from moments before. It was deeper, angrier, and bitter.

There was no such thing as privacy in a police department. Personal business flies through the channels faster than wildfire, and it was no secret that Sergeant Gaston was having issues in his personal life. He had been more surly than usual lately, and Audrey noticed an elevated level of hostility toward her.

Regardless, she was ready, having trained hard to learn all of the baton strikes and when to use them. She was confident that she would pass with no problem. Audrey stepped into the ring and stood in front of Officer Riccio, who was sweating profusely under his helmet.

"You have three minutes on the clock," Sergeant Gaston growled at Audrey. "Three...two...one...begin!"

Officer Riccio jerked his left arm up into the air. He was unsteady on his feet. Audrey knew he must have been sweltering inside the heavy padded suit. She went in confidently to demonstrate her first strike, the hard baton landing solidly on the padding. Audrey struck again, confident with her form. She knew her perfect execution was irking Sergeant Gaston. She had the distinct feeling he wanted to fail her. Audrey advanced toward Officer Riccio, causing him to retreat backwards towards the perimeter of the ring. Feeling strong and confident, she lunged forward with all of her momentum. Halfway through her strike, Officer Riccio tripped over his clunky padded feet. Falling backwards, his foot swung up into the air, striking Audrey's face as she came down with her strike.

Audrey heard a crack, and felt a sudden rush of pain flood her brain. Before she could even process what happened, she was stumbling backward trying not to fall. The intense pain in her face made her feel dizzy, and disoriented. Her eyes were blurry and her nose throbbed. She quickly realized that her nose was broken.

Audrey briefly caught her balance and tried to focus. Through double vision, she saw Officer Riccio struggling to get up off the ground, hindered by the cumbersome suit.

Officer Riccio pushed up onto his feet and pulled the sweaty helmet off his head. His eyes flew open when he saw the immediate swelling in Audrey's face.

"I'm so sorry! Are you okay?" he stammered, wide eyed and mortified.

"Next up!" Sergeant Gaston barked. "Clear the ring, Recruit Moretti."

Audrey would be damned! She had three minutes in that ring, and she would finish it. She could still fight broken nose and all. There was no way she was going to let him fail her.

"Three minutes!" Audrey growled in a voice she had never heard from herself before, as she advanced toward Officer Riccio, giving him no time to put his helmet back on. She struck the baton down on the padding with perfect form.

Dizzy and disoriented, she thought she was standing upright. When her left hand grazed the ground, she realized she was falling sideways.

I am not going down.

Audrey refused to let her feet come off the ground. She knew that was exactly what Sergeant wanted to see—expected to see.

But the throbbing in her face was so intense that she worried she would pass out. Stars buzzed around in front of her eyes as if she could reach out and touch them. She could hardly hear anything over the ringing in her ears.

Audrey imagined herself falling to the ground in front of Sergeant Gaston and the satisfaction that would give him. She refused to let her legs give out.

I will not fail.

Suddenly, a jolt of adrenaline flooded her veins. Audrey rushed toward Officer Riccio with her baton, envisioning Sergeant Gaston inside of the padded suit. She struck him repeatedly, demonstrating perfect form with every strike she had learned. Adrenaline had numbed the pain of her broken nose. She felt nothing but the desire to prevail.

It was a fight for everything she had worked for and the respect that she deserved.

The buzzer finally rang out but Audrey was so focused that she didn't hear it. Officer Riccio was cowering down, shielding his head with his padded arms while Audrey continued to strike past the buzzer.

Suddenly, she heard Preston's voice. "It's over, Audrey. Let me look at your face," he said gently.

Preston took the baton from her hand. Tears of anger stung her eyes as she looked up at him.

"It's definitely broken," Preston said softly.

Audrey pressed her hand to her cheek, feeling the swelling that was rising in her face. She looked around the circle to see her fellow recruits' faces frozen in horror.

Audrey turned to look at Sergeant Gaston who was angrily scribbling notes on the clipboard. There was no way he could fail her, and she knew it was killing him. She had finished her three minutes in the ring and demonstrated perfect application of her strikes. Sergeant Gaston glanced up from the clipboard to see that most of the class had huddled around Audrey, a look of disgust in his eyes.

"Are you okay, Audrey?" one of her classmates asked.

Audrey's eyes narrowed as she looked deep into Sergeant Gaston's heartless soul.

"Never been better," she replied.

CHAPTER 3

Thursday, August 30, 2001
4:30 p.m.

Audrey's reflection in the mirror of her tiny apartment's bathroom looked like someone else's. She was unrecognizable to her own self. Her eyes had begun to turn black and blue, and her face was swollen all over. Every single movement she made caused a jolt of pain from her nose directly into her brain. Lucy sat on the vanity counter, looking up at Audrey.

"It feels as bad as it looks," Audrey said, patting the top of Lucy's head.

There was nothing the doctor could do until the swelling came down. He wanted her to refrain from all physical activity and gave her a note to be excused from the police academy for the rest of the week. But no matter how bad she looked, and despite how much pain she was in, she would stand in front of Sergeant Gaston first thing the next morning. He expected her not to be there; he was hoping she would never come back.

The flip phone on the kitchen counter buzzed. In bold-faced, all caps letters, the word SIS was displayed across the little screen. It hurt to hold the phone up near her face.

"Hey, Hannah, what's--"

"You know you can sue, right?" Hannah cut her off. "First, I hope you kicked some ass, but someone needs to be fired, and you need to sue. I know a guy here in the city that would take this on in a heartbeat. I already told him about it. You'll never have to work another day--"

"Hannah," Audrey tried to interrupt, but Hannah kept talking a mile a minute.

"Hannah!" Audrey said louder.

Hannah finally stopped talking.

"I am not interested in a lawsuit. I knew what I was getting myself into. I mean, I thought I knew what I was getting into, but this is the career I have always wanted. Anyway, that is exactly what they are expecting me to do." Pausing, Audrey reflected back on the incident earlier that day before continuing. "I am going to do something much better. I'm going to walk into that building tomorrow, and then, I am going to finish this academy."

There was silence on the phone for a few seconds and then a sigh. "You are so stubborn, just like Mom," Hannah said.

Between the two of them, Audrey was the most like their mother. Audrey had inherited her street smarts, grit, and strong personality. Their mother was also fanatic about emergency preparedness. While Audrey was growing up, lectures on finding the nearest exit and always being aware of their surroundings were common conversations at the dinner table. At the end of every lecture, the girls would finish with, "We know, we know…and always trust your gut."

Audrey followed in her mother's footsteps, checking smoke detectors every three months instead of six, flashlights always on hand, and a three-month supply of bottled water stashed away just in case. Audrey worried about everything, while Hannah floated along with much less concern.

When Hannah had moved to New York City, Audrey's going-away gift for her was a small emergency kit she had put together for her briefcase. She made it according to Hannah's style—a cute little pink satchel containing a whistle, face mask, protein bar, mini flashlight, and a map of New York City.

"What the heck do you think is going to happen in New York?" Hannah had burst out with laughter after she opened it.

Audrey had been affronted. "You never know what can happen anywhere at any time! One day you just may thank me."

Hannah and Audrey accepted that they were as different as sisters could be, but they loved each other more than anyone in the world, despite their differences.

"Does Mom know by the way?" Hannah asked.

"Heck no!" Audrey exclaimed. "You know she would be down here tomorrow with someone up against the wall. She would get me fired."

They both laughed, which sent another jolt of pain to Audrey's head.

"Okay, I'm going to try and get some sleep. It is a big day tomorrow—Shotgun Certification. The goggles don't even fit over my face," Audrey said.

"I have an early meeting for a new hedge fund merger. I'll touch the sky for you from the eighty-fourth floor!" Hannah said.

Hannah had been working in Manhattan for almost two years at Berkley and Stanton Financial. She had scored an internship right out of college and quickly began to work her way up. Recently, she had been offered a full-time position as a junior research associate.

Her job mainly entailed preparing market reports, doing financial research, and documenting meeting notes. The entry-level nature of her position had her also getting coffee, lunch, and just about any other frivolous requests for the higher-ups. It didn't matter to her though. She would do whatever it took to establish her career and move up in the company.

Audrey worried about her sister working in the World Trade Center. Since the bombing of the North Tower in 1993, the World Trade Center had given Audrey an uneasy feeling. She didn't feel comfortable with her sister working on the eighty-fourth floor of the South Tower.

"Could our lives be any more different?" Hannah asked with a laugh.

Audrey tried to smile, but it ended up as a wince from the pain.

"Good night, Sis. I love you," Audrey said in a sleepy voice.

"Nighty night," Hannah said, the way she always did when they were little. "I love you too. Show them who you are tomorrow."

Audrey docked the phone into the charger station and picked up the prescription bottle from the doctor. TAKE ONE

PILL EVERY SIX HOURS, the label read. She had to qualify
with a shotgun first thing in the morning. There was no way
she could have narcotics in her system.

Audrey slowly shuffled to her bedroom, with Lucy trailing
behind her. Every step she took caused her face to throb. She
propped up every pillow she had against the headboard and
tried to get comfortable. One hour turned into another hour
as she restlessly waited for the pain to subside. Finally, her body
gave in, and she dozed uncomfortably off to sleep.

CHAPTER 4

Friday, August 31, 2001
7:45 a.m.

Elbowing her way through the crowd, Hannah pushed and weaved through thousands of people also trying to get to the subway station. She held her briefcase tightly in her hand as it bounced off each body she passed. The early morning air in late August in the city provided only minimal relief from the sweltering daytime temperatures. The air quickly turned stuffy and unpleasant as she descended into the subway station.

The odor in the subway was something she still hadn't become adjusted to. The humid, stuffy air only exacerbated the smell of urine and body odor from too many people crammed below street level. She loved the energy in the city though—so alive and full of promise. After all, she was living her dream, working for one of the largest and most powerful financial institutions in the world.

Hannah had done the morning routine so many times that she had it perfected. Her Tribeca apartment was just around the corner from the Franklin Street train station. Each morning she took the 1 train on the red line, two stops to the World Trade Center.

Hannah glanced at her watch. She knew she had to get to the train station every morning by 7:50 a.m. to catch her train in time. She was a few minutes ahead of schedule. Steve Berkley, the cofounder of Berkley and Stanton, was in the office every morning at 6:30 a.m., sharp. In the short time Hannah had worked there, she had witnessed a dozen people get fired publicly on the spot for being late. She didn't ever want to face the same fate.

With her platform in sight, she took a breath of relief and slowed her pace a bit. Hannah reached into her pocket for her cell phone. Flipping the phone open, she found AUDREY in her recent calls. Still walking, she pressed the call button. She knew Audrey was on her way to the academy, but she wanted to leave her a voicemail to wish her luck.

The voicemail answered as expected. *"Hi, this is Audrey. My life is completely consumed by the police academy right now. Please leave a message, and I will call you back in six months."* Beep...

"Show them who you are today, Sis!" Hannah said. "I love you."

As Hannah went to flip the phone shut, something suddenly crashed into her body with such force that her feet came off the ground. The impact sent her phone flying through the air. Somehow she managed to hang on to her briefcase as she violently landed on her left side, knocking the wind out of her lungs and causing her briefcase to unlatch, the contents scattering out onto the dirty subway floor.

"Ow! What the—" Hannah was just about to curse, when she noticed someone suddenly hovering over her with their arm extended down to help.

"I'm so sorry! Are you okay? I thought I was going to miss my train, and I didn't see you—I mean you weren't exactly paying attention either, but never mind, it was my fault... and...I'm rambling. Are you hurt? Please let me help you up," the stranger said.

The pain in Hannah's hip was so intense that she could hardly move. She reached out and felt the stranger's strong grip pull her to her feet in an instant. She was suddenly standing face to face with a tall, handsome young man, with perfectly styled golden-brown hair. His bright blue eyes studied her, making sure she could stand. Smoothing her long blonde hair away from her face, she tried not to notice his broad shoulders and sculpted muscles underneath his dress shirt. The thought of her phone suddenly jolted Hannah from her gaze.

"Oh crap! My phone! It flew out of my hand!" She started searching along the ground, knowing it had been shuffled around by hundreds of passing feet. "That jerk could help me look. It is the least he could do," she grumbled to herself. Finally, she spotted her phone in the distance. It had been kicked up against a bright yellow, painted pillar.

Cursing to herself, she brushed the dust off her phone and made her way back to pick up her briefcase. The handsome young man who had tackled her moments earlier had picked up all of her belongings and put them back into the briefcase.

He stood there with the briefcase in one hand and a small, pink zippered pouch in the other.

"What should I do with your uh…emergency kit?" he asked with a wry smile, holding up the pink pouch. HANNAH'S EMERGENCY KIT was written in her sister's handwriting across the front.

Hannah snatched the pouch from his hand, with a look of pure annoyance. She reached for her briefcase and then checked her outfit, brushing the gray dust off of her left side. In all of the commotion, she hadn't even thought about her train. She looked up toward her platform to find that no one was standing there.

"I missed my train!" Hannah turned to him. "*You* made me miss my train!" she said angrily. She then started to panic. "I'm going to get fired." Hannah paced while she tried to think of what to do next. The next train would get her there too late, a taxi would take forever with traffic, and she didn't know the city on foot that well.

"Where are you headed?" he asked.

"The World Trade Center, South Tower; I work at Berkley and Stanton. Well, I did at least until I met you," Hannah grumbled.

A smile spread across his face, annoying Hannah even more.

"Why are you smiling?" she snapped.

"North Tower here," he said, raising his hand in the air. "*We* actually missed *our* train."

"Great," Hannah said sarcastically.

"Can you run in those?" he asked, looking down at her feet.

She had forgotten what shoes she had put on that morning. She looked down at her light pink patent leather flats. Not ideal, but doable.

"Yeah, if it means keeping my job," Hannah responded with desperation in her voice.

"What if I promise I can get you there on time?" he asked with confidence.

Hannah brushed off her gray pantsuit again, the stubborn dust still visible on her outfit.

"I *might* forgive you for almost killing me in the subway station just now," she replied.

"Come on," he said, grabbing her hand. He weaved her through the packed subway station, up the stairs and back out into the summer air.

"My name is Travis by the way!" he shouted over his shoulder.

"Hannah," she called out as he led the way.

"I know!" he yelled over the sound of horns honking and people bustling by. "Hannah with the pink emergency kit." He flashed a charming smile.

Hannah wanted to be annoyed, but there was something about him that drew her in.

They scrambled through the crowded sidewalks, turning onto a quiet side street. Suddenly they were free from the sea of people, running straight ahead and unobstructed. Travis led Hannah through a maze of side streets, each leading to a busy city street packed with shoulder to shoulder people and cars that weren't moving. He turned right, then left, crossing streets and weaving in and out of cars.

Hannah had absolutely no idea where she was. Suddenly she realized that she had put her trust in a complete stranger. What if he were some kind of crazy killer who had targeted her and purposely tackled her? Pretending to save the day, he was really leading her to his torture chamber.

Just as she was about to pull her hand away, he yanked her left around the corner. There they were, standing at the entrance of the plaza in front of the enormous Twin Towers. She looked at her watch. 8:20 a.m. Ten minutes early! They stood at the edge of the plaza, catching their breath for a moment.

"So, now that I got you here on time, and you have forgiven me, how about I make it up to you? You know, the whole knocking you down and missing our train thing? Dinner tonight?" Travis asked with a hopeful smile, showing off his perfectly aligned, bright white teeth.

"Umm…I said I *might* forgive you, and I haven't decided yet if I have. How do you know the city so well anyway?" Hannah asked, aware of the miracle he'd just pulled off.

"I'm a pretty interesting guy, full of interesting surprises, but you'll never know, unless you have dinner with me tonight. It is your one and only chance. One of those once-in-a-lifetime opportunities you always hear about."

Travis pretended to be very impressed with himself, placing one fist on his hip and the other under his chin.

Hannah couldn't help but chuckle at his absurd pose. There was just something about him that continued to captivate her. Hannah let Travis stand locked in his pose for a moment before responding. Finally she said, "I get off at five. I'll meet you in front of the fountain in the plaza."

"Thank goodness! I couldn't hold that ridiculous pose much longer."

Hannah laughed out loud, surprising herself with her unhindered reaction. She turned and walked toward the entrance of the South Tower, glancing over her shoulder before she reached the large glass doors. As Travis walked toward the North Tower entrance, he jumped up and kicked his feet to the side, clicking his heels together.

What did I just get myself into?

While Hannah waited in front of the stainless steel doors for her elevator to arrive in the lobby of the South Tower, she replayed the entire morning in her head. She had the overwhelming feeling that her life had just somehow changed forever.

———

Friday August 31, 2001
8:00 a.m.

Her face was hideous. Audrey buzzed into the academy building, aware of the stares and gasps as she walked by. She knew the mere sight of her was shocking. Audrey walked down the hall toward the classroom, like she did every morning, but something caused her to stop midstep. A boisterous conversation traveled from the conference room at the end of the adjacent corridor. Audrey very clearly heard her name.

Every morning the instructors gathered in the conference room before the day started. They casually sat around, drinking coffee, talking about the plan for the day, and of course any latest gossip. That day, Audrey knew that she was the latest

J . S .   F A R M E R

gossip. She turned down the corridor, and slowly approached the open conference room door. Standing off to the side, and out of sight, she listened.

"What the hell is wrong with that Riccio kid? How did he even make it through the academy?" one of the instructors in the room asked.

Someone in the room snorted.

"No kidding. I heard he barely passed field training too. That girl though, I heard she didn't go down. That's pretty impressive," someone else in the room said.

That girl… the reference made Audrey cringe.

Suddenly, she heard the unmistakable voice of Sergeant Gaston.

"Impressive my ass. There's no way she is coming in today. She'll milk this for all it's worth," Sergeant Gaston sneered, his voice filled with abhorrence. "I'd be surprised if she ever comes back."

Audrey felt the blood rise to her head, causing her broken nose to pulsate with each beat of her heart.

"Hey, Gaston, don't be jealous that she has more balls than you," someone taunted.

The entire room bellowed with laughter.

"Whatever," Sergeant Gaston scoffed. "You'll see. She doesn't have what it takes."

Audrey had heard enough. She presented herself in the doorway, squaring her shoulders to the room so that her face was in full view. Her back was straight, chin held high, and her eyes pierced across the room at Sergeant Gaston.

You could hear a pin drop. Everyone in the room nervously averted their eyes, except for Sergeant Gaston. He sat with his jaw slightly open, the look on his face of shock and embarrassment.

Audrey cleared her throat.

"I thought you might want a status update," Audrey spoke loudly and clearly, pointing to her nose. "It's broken in two places…and I am here."

She let the awkward silence fill the room.

Sergeant Gaston tried to speak, but it came out as pathetic stutter. "I…uh…didn't mean—"

"Yes, you did," Audrey cut him off.

She glared at him, causing him to squirm in front of his peers.

Audrey turned to walk back down the hallway. "Oh, and I am ready to pass Shotgun Certification today too," she said over her shoulder.

Not a sound came from the conference room behind her as she rounded the corner to the classroom.

Audrey peeked through the slim glass window of the door into the classroom. The guys were already seated, using the few minutes before the day started to brush up on motor vehicle law. She took a deep breath and courageously entered the room, once again with her chin held high, displaying her two large black eyes and swollen nose.

"Holy crap!" Ray exclaimed, dropping his pencil.

Suddenly all heads lifted in Audrey's direction.

"I don't want to be the fashion police here, but you went a little heavy on the purple makeup today, Audrey," Ray said, breaking the tension in the room. Ray was always ready with jokes and harmless sarcasm. It was one of the things that had kept her going through the tough, long months of the academy. She had never been more grateful for his lighthearted humor as she was in that moment.

A couple of the guys nervously laughed, while others waited with baited breath to see how she would respond.

"I look super-hot, right?" Audrey replied.

The guys erupted with relieved laughter, but it was short-lived. It got awkwardly silent again as they all nervously glanced at each other.

Jonathan, a short, stocky twenty-three-year-old ex-football player, from a small farm town, broke the silence. "You really rocked it yesterday, Audrey. You never gave up." His voice cracked with emotion. He stopped for a second to collect himself. "I will take you any day as backup," he finished.

Audrey tried to smile, but it was of no use. Her face was too swollen. She saw Preston staring at her from across the room. When their eyes met, he smiled and winked. She knew exactly what he was thinking. As awful as it was for him to watch the day before, it gave him reassurance that she could physically handle herself on the street.

"That kid is a clumsy oaf," Ethan said, as he sat leaning back in his chair, with one arm over the back of his seat. Ethan was a muscular, rough-around-the-edges kind of guy who grew up in a tough neighborhood in the Bronx. Audrey often wondered if he chose to become a cop to keep himself out of trouble. He rode that fine line between good and bad, but he had a heart of gold if you earned his respect.

"I kicked his ass during my turn. I think he soiled his pants," Ethan said with a proud, crooked smile.

Audrey had missed the rest of the day while she was at the emergency clinic.

"It was great, Audrey," Jonathan said. "We all gave it to him good."

The guys started to ramp up, recounting their time in the ring with Officer Riccio.

Just then, Firearms Instructor Diaz walked into the room. "All right, class. Settle down. I'll be taking you down to the range for Shotgun Certification today," he announced.

Sergeant Gaston was nowhere to be found. The fact that he couldn't show his face or look at Audrey's gave her an immense feeling of victory. *What a coward,* Audrey thought to herself as the class walked single file down the stairs to the shooting range.

They had been training with the shotgun for months. The first time Audrey had fired the shotgun, the violent thrust to her shoulder had knocked her off balance, causing her to completely miss the target. By now, she could hit the target from any position with steady precision. However, that morning, her eyes were half-swollen shut, and the pain in her head was debilitating. Since she could not take her prescribed pain medication before handling a firearm, she was forced to suffer through the raw pain.

Audrey put the goggles on as best she could, but her nose was so swollen that the goggles sat crookedly on her face. In order to pass the shotgun certification test, she would have to rely mostly on muscle memory. Her vision was blurry, and the pain in her head was as excruciating as it had been earlier in the morning. Looking through the bulletproof window into the range, she observed an obstacle course set up with six targets hanging at the back wall.

Failure is not an option, she gave herself a little pep talk.

She was disappointed that Sergeant Gaston was not there to watch her pass another certification against the odds.

Two instructors were inside the range to demonstrate each requirement. They were to fire six shots from six different positions, a combination of standing and kneeling. The final shot was from the prone position, lying flat on the floor with chest down. Audrey couldn't lean forward or backward without feeling a knifing pain in her head. Just the thought of lying flat on the ground hurt, but she refused to fail.

"Who's up first?" Instructor Diaz asked the class.

"I am," Audrey said, stepping forward to grab a handful of buckshot and a shotgun from the rack.

No one dared argue. Preston nodded at her with encouragement. "You got this, girl," he whispered as she passed by.

Standing at the first station, Audrey positioned the stock to her shoulder. She remembered the early days of shotgun training. Big purple bruises covered the front of her shoulder. Through her training, she had perfected her technique. Audrey took a deep breath, lined up the barrel to the target, and steadied herself.

"Begin!" Instructor Diaz yelled, standing with a clipboard at the back of the range.

In the left-kneeling position, she pulled the trigger. The target exploded, leaving a large, gaping hole directly in the center. She moved methodically to the next station—right-kneeling position. Another perfect shot. Every explosion of the firearm caused intense pounding in her head. She had completed each shot, demonstrating how well she had mastered her training. Finally, she stood at the last station—the prone position shot. Audrey slowly lowered herself to the floor. The pressure in her face was so intense that it felt like her head would explode. She wanted to quit; the pain was just too much.

"Failure is not an option," she scolded herself out loud as she painfully positioned the shotgun to her shoulder. She tried to focus on the target downrange, but her eyes had begun to tear up from the pain. She blinked, trying to clear her focus, the goggles still crooked on her face. Audrey couldn't even see the target anymore. Suddenly, her sister's voicemail message that morning ran through her mind. *Show them who you are today, Sis.*

There was no better way to prove herself to Sergeant Gaston than to pass that certification. She *had* to make that shot.

Audrey closed her eyes, took a deep breath, opened them again, and fired, hitting the last target dead center.

CHAPTER 5

Friday, August 31, 2001
8:25 a.m.

Hannah stood, looking up at the red numbers above the elevator doors, her hip still throbbing from the fall in the subway. She couldn't believe she had just agreed to dinner with the very guy who had slammed into her.

Floor Seventy-Eight was lit up in bold red for what felt like forever. Hannah knew it was stopped at the sky lobby, letting off dozens of people to then board the local elevators up to their upper floors. There were a total of 110 floors in each of the towers. The express elevators ran directly to the forty-fourth- or seventy-eighth-floor sky lobbies. Local elevators accessed each floor in between. Finally the elevator descended seventy-eight flights in a matter of seconds. The chime sounded, letting people know the doors were about to open, and the crowd began to move forward. People shuffled into the roomy elevator until they were packed shoulder to shoulder.

Hannah hated elevators. She had an intense fear of getting stuck, or worse, plummeting to the ground. Ever since she'd started working at the World Trade Center, she had recurring dreams about the cables breaking right before she reached the sky lobby on the seventy-eighth floor. She would feel herself free-falling and crashing to the ground, jolting her awake from a dead sleep.

The elevator rose up with such intensity that it caused her ears to pop and her belly to flip-flop. When the doors opened at the seventy-eighth-floor sky lobby, Hannah shuffled out, along with the others in the elevator. The door opened opposite of where they entered, keeping them moving in an orderly fashion.

Hannah finally reached the eighty-fourth floor of Berkley and Stanton. She weaved through the remaining people who were making their way to the floors above.

Berkley and Stanton occupied most of the eighty-fourth floor. The towers were designed with an open floor plan, making the office space feel wide open. A large conference room was located along the north-facing windows. Offices lined the rest of the perimeter windows, giving the higher-ups their own personal aerial view of the city. An open trading area and a colony of cubicles comprised the large center space.

Marilyn usually buzzed Hannah in, but she was busy on the phone, behind the ostentatious reception desk, which was made of Bocote wood and black marble countertop. It was rumored that Mr. Berkley had personally traveled to the West Indies to pick out authentic Bocote and had hired a top designer in the city to create the most magnificent desk for the entryway. He was not a modest man by any means, and image was everything to him.

Hannah reached into the side pocket of her briefcase and pulled out her employee badge. The picture taken two years before could have been someone else completely. Back then, she'd been new to the city, having come from a small Connecticut town, so she hadn't found yet her New York City fashion sense.

She saw her reflection in the tempered glass door as she held the badge up to the card reader. A twenty-five-year-old junior research associate with a paycheck, she finally had extra money for blonde highlights, new clothes, and fancy shoes. Every morning she wrapped chunks of long blonde hair around the curling iron to create loose, flowing curls that fell over her shoulders. Hannah never left the apartment she shared with two other roommates without applying mascara to her long, black eyelashes.

Attention from men was not unfamiliar to Hannah, but she found most of them shallow and uninteresting.

Marilyn was just hanging up the phone as Hannah walked through the door. "These banking executives, let me tell you. I should get hazard pay just for dealing with their enormous egos!" Marilyn grumbled as she scribbled a note down on her notepad. She looked up to see Hannah strolling in, with a smile plastered across her face and seemingly lost in thought.

Rising up from behind the desk, Marilyn looked at her suspiciously. "Mmm hmmm…spill it…who is he?"

Hannah snapped out of her trance. "Huh? Oh, nothing. I mean no one. I met a guy this morning." Hannah stumbled over her words.

Marilyn raised her eyebrows with interest.

"Actually, he knocked me down in the subway," Hannah continued, trying to explain the unusual encounter.

Marilyn's face dropped in disappointment. It was not the kind of juicy romantic story she was hoping for.

"Anyway, I agreed to have dinner with him tonight. I don't know why. I mean, I'm still really annoyed, but he made me laugh."

Marilyn's interest suddenly came back. "Ohhh, girl, you know what they say about a guy who can make a girl laugh?" Marilyn asked with a lascivious smile.

"Marilyn!" Hannah exclaimed. She felt her cheeks turn slightly red. She looked around, ducking her head in embarrassment. "It's just dinner, and anyway, I am not looking to date anyone right now," she whispered.

"Mmm hmm," Marilyn nodded her head knowingly, turning back to her desk.

"It's not like that." Hannah shook her head. "Well, I'd better go before Berkley catches us having a moment of joy in our day."

"Wait! Before you go, let me show you some pictures of my grandbabies from last weekend." Marilyn pulled out an envelope of four-by-six-inch pictures from her pocketbook. "I took my babies to the South Street Seaport. Little Jeffrey loves bridges. He got such a kick out of seeing the Brooklyn Bridge up close. Look at that smile." She held up the picture, her face beaming.

Hannah could feel the love radiate from Marilyn's heart when she talked about her grandchildren. There was nothing in the world Marilyn loved more than being a grandmother.

It made Hannah think of her own grandmother. She'd passed away when Hannah was just six years old, but she remembered her vividly. Even though she had been taken from Hannah far too early in life, she knew how much her grandmother loved her. She wanted to believe that she was always watching over her, but she often struggled with that belief.

Marilyn flipped through the pictures quickly, looking for a specific one. Kyra, Marilyn's five-year-old granddaughter, was notorious for refusing to have her picture taken. "Here it is!" She triumphantly held up the picture.

Marilyn was crouched down between Jeffrey and Kyra in the picture, their tiny arms wrapped lovingly around her neck. All three were smiling, hair blowing gently in the warm August air. The deep blue water of the seaport was sparkling in the background, and the late afternoon sun lit up their faces.

"I am going to make copies of this one and put them in frames for my babies to keep in their bedrooms. I'll be putting one right here on my desk, so they are always with me."

"I am surprised Kyra agreed to be in the picture," Hannah said.

"I couldn't believe it either. She didn't even protest. There must be a reason, but I suppose we will never know." Marilyn shrugged her shoulders.

"I'll see you on break." Hannah waved over her shoulder as she walked toward her cubicle.

Weaving through the rows of cubicles, Hannah finally reached her desk. It wasn't glamorous, but it was an upgrade from the large, oval conference table she'd shared with eight other interns the year before. At least she had her own space to put her coffee mug and a couple of pictures. She could even kick off her shoes for a few minutes without anyone noticing. She placed her briefcase down on the side of her chair and sat down. The armrest of the chair brushed up against the bruise forming on her hip. Travis was still so much on her mind that she forgot what she even had to do that morning when she got into the office.

She looked over at one of the framed pictures on her desk. It was a close-up of her and Audrey at the Jersey Shore. They were wearing matching red sweatshirts they had bought at a small gift shop on the boardwalk. Hannah and Audrey had taken a last-minute weekend trip to the shore, right before Audrey had started the police academy. It had been a chilly March day with gray skies and a cold, biting air, but that was one of Hannah's favorite times to visit the shore. After a long, grueling New England winter, it was nice just to see the ocean, even if they had to bundle up. Audrey had asked the only passerby on the beach to snap a picture. Their matching blonde hair flew wildly in the cold ocean breeze. The huge waves crashed in the background, and their red sweatshirts popped in contrast to the ocean's gray backdrop.

Audrey and Hannah had been inseparable growing up. In adulthood they were still just as close, separated only by physical distance.

Hannah sat at her cubicle desk, wondering how Audrey's morning was going. She pictured her firing a shotgun with goggles that didn't fit over her face.

"Morning!" a head suddenly popped out from the cubicle next to her.

Hannah jumped, bumping her sore hip against the armrest again. "Geez, Miles!" Hannah said, trying to catch her breath. "You don't have to be so perky in the morning! You need to cut down your coffee intake."

"Oh, I haven't had any coffee yet," Miles replied energetically.

"No human is naturally that perky in the morning, Miles. What do you need?" she asked, trying to discreetly shuffle her flats back onto her aching feet.

"I have something important to ask you," Miles said anxiously.

"If it is a market research briefing, can I read it after the 9:00 meeting? I have had one hell of a morning and I—"

"No, it's not anything like that. It's…uh…personal," he stuttered nervously.

Suddenly, Hannah noticed Mile's right hand was hidden behind his back, and he was wringing his left hand anxiously by his side. Hannah turned her chair to face him with her full attention. From behind his back, he pulled out a small black box. He opened the box, displaying a gorgeous solitaire diamond ring in a platinum-gold setting.

Hannah gasped.

"I'm going to do it. I'm going to propose to Stephanie this weekend!"

"Miles!" Hannah jumped up to hug him, knocking his glasses slightly off his face. "I'm so happy for you! She's a very lucky lady."

Miles blushed, straightening his glasses. "I'm so nervous. What if she doesn't say yes?" he asked worriedly.

"Of course she will say yes. You are a catch." Hannah gave him a reassuring smile.

Miles took a deep breath to calm his nerves. "Thanks, Hannah. Now I just have to keep it a secret until tomorrow. I hope I don't blow it. I am going to propose up on the observation deck."

"That is absolutely perfect, Miles. I can't think of a more magical place to get engaged," Hannah said, successfully hiding the fact that she was terrified of the observation deck on top of the South Tower. In the two years she had worked at the World Trade Center, she'd never once considered venturing up there to top of the building. The eighty-fourth floor was high enough.

"Thanks, Hannah," Miles said graciously. He shoved the black box into his dress pants pocket and returned to the other side of their cubicle wall.

Hannah sat back down in her office chair, imagining what it would feel like to find the person she wanted to spend the rest of her life with. Miles was twenty-nine years old and had been dating Stephanie for just about a year. Hannah had met her at the Christmas party the year before. When Miles introduced her, he beamed. They both looked so happy. For a moment, Hannah secretly longed to find the same thing, but she quickly pushed the thought out of her head. She wasn't ready to find that person yet anyway. She was focused solely on her career.

Gathering up her materials for the meeting, she made her way to the large conference room. Hannah had been working at Berkley and Stanton for almost two years. She loved that she always met someone new. There were about six-hundred Berkley and Stanton employees on the eighty-fourth floor, not counting the endless flow of interns, consultants, and banking executives that came and went.

Hannah spotted one of her friends, Don, up ahead. He was a broad-shouldered man in his early sixties, with a nicely manicured salt-and-pepper beard. Don was leaning up against a cubicle wall, drinking from an extra-large coffee mug, grumbling to the person on the other side. Don had been on a special assignment at the New Jersey office run by Stanton for a few months and had recently returned to the city.

"Good morning, Don!" Hannah said cheerily. "It is nice to see you. How have you been?"

"Well, I just sent my second daughter off to college two weeks ago, so I'm totally broke. I'll probably be living in a cardboard box soon, but things are great!" he sarcastically replied.

Hannah chuckled. "Now you really do sound like my dad," she said, patting him on the shoulder.

Living in the city away from her family had been hard on Hannah, especially in the beginning. Don had taken her under his wing when she was an intern. He had two daughters of his own and naturally felt protective of Hannah. As independent as she was, she appreciated being looked out for in a big city. She was often able to give him some helpful father-daughter advice in return.

"I have the 9:00 merger meeting with Goldstar and Rush, wish me luck," Hannah said crossing her fingers.

"You have no worries, kid; you will be vice president here in no time, maybe even the next Berkley," he winked.

Hannah nudged him with her elbow before continuing toward the conference room. She arrived at the large, empty conference room before anyone else. There was a lot of preparation to do before the meeting. The projector had to be set up and ready to go, coffee made, and cream and sugar restocked. It was her job to make sure the entire meeting went smoothly from beginning to end. Hannah would also take meeting minutes, and if called upon, recite any pertinent data she had come up with during her research.

Though the two towers were approximately two-hundred feet apart, Hannah never really paid much attention to the identical structure just outside the windows of the conference room. In fact, she avoided the windows altogether, fearful of the view below. But that morning she was curious and feeling braver than usual. She approached the windows, peering all the way up to the top of the North Tower. Hannah felt her stomach flip-flop the way it did in the elevator. The height of the buildings seemed impossible.

She suddenly thought of her mother's constant teachings about nearest exits and having an escape route. Hannah came to the sobering realization that 168 flights of stairs were between her and the exit to safety. She tried to clear the worry from her mind. If there were a fire, there were sprinklers. Plus, the building was made of pure steel. Security had been beefed up since the bombing of the North Tower in 1993. Nothing that bad could happen again, anyway, she convinced herself, turning away from the window.

CHAPTER 6

Friday August 31, 2001
3:00 p.m.

All ten recruits in Audrey's academy class passed Shotgun Certification that morning. The rest of the day was spent learning about crime scene photography and how to take fingerprints. As the academy stretched into its final weeks, they had moved into more hands-on learning.

The last hour of the day the class got to practice rolling each other's fingerprints. They were partnered up by number, and Audrey's bad luck struck again when she was paired with Scott. There was always one in every group, and Scott was that person.

He was an older recruit, in his midforties, with shifty eyes and a smarmy personality. He was like the arrogant uncle who thought he was really funny and didn't know that the family secretly couldn't stand him. It didn't take long for the class to adopt the name "Uncle Scott" unbeknownst to him.

He was also the only classmate who never asked if she was okay after she got her face busted in the day before. It was clear to Audrey that he had a problem with her. She could only assume he shared the same sentiment as Gaston about women in police work.

Audrey began to roll Scott's index finger on the ink pad.

"Well, you pretty much have a free ride the rest of the way," he said flippantly.

Audrey's blood pressure began to rise. "What exactly do you mean by that, Scott?" Audrey asked, even though she knew exactly what he meant.

Scott let out an arrogant, dismissive laugh. "Oh come on, you know. They are afraid you're going to sue them. They will just give you whatever you want the rest of the way," he said in a tone as haughty as the look on his face. "Pass you even if you fail, give you some kind of award, or say that you have the highest average, who knows?" he continued, never having the guts to look up at her.

Audrey squeezed his index finger hard and torqued it all the way to one side, causing him to wince. "Maybe they should be afraid of me," she replied, cutting off the circulation in his index finger.

Scott kept his head lowered, never looking up to meet her eyes.

Just another big mouth coward, she thought.

People had underestimated Audrey her whole life. She was often mistaken as weak because she was a young, blonde female with a petite frame. Anyone who made the mistake of underestimating her always learned the hard way.

Four o'clock on Friday felt like it would never come. Staring at the ancient round clock on the wall, the hands seemed to be stuck forever on 3:59. Finally the long hand reached the top of the hour, and they were dismissed not one second sooner.

"Hey, Audrey, want to come out for happy hour with us?" Jonathan asked as they gathered up their things. She sometimes wondered if the guys were just being polite by inviting her. Did they actually want her around, or was it obligation?

Ethan leaned in as he walked past her. "We're starting at The Pub and then ending at The Painted Lady, "he emphasized with his best debaucherous voice.

Audrey appreciated the invite, but she was just not up for a night out.

"Sounds fun and all," Audrey said, "but I am in no shape to be anyone's wing woman tonight. In fact, I think I might scare your prospects off with this face."

"Just slap some sunglasses on, and no one will notice," Ethan said, unable to hold back his laughter.

"I don't think they make sunglasses big enough to fit over all that face!" Jonathan hooted, putting his arm around Audrey.

"Very funny." Audrey playfully shrugged Jonathan off. "Thanks, anyway, but I am going home. Have fun," she said, slinging her heavy duty bag over her shoulder.

The class shuffled out of the building together, Preston walking next to Audrey as he did everyday. The guys stood in a group in the parking lot, while Preston walked Audrey to her car. A bad feeling was plaguing her. Before getting into her car, she turned to Preston and said, "Don't get in trouble tonight."

—————

Friday August 31, 2001
4:45 P.M

Hannah logged out of her computer and checked the time on her watch. She still couldn't believe she had agreed to meet Travis at the fountain at five o'clock. She peeked around her cubicle to say goodbye to Miles. He was down on his knee, practicing proposing to his computer.

Hannah smiled. "Good luck tomorrow, Miles. It's in the bag."

"Thanks, Hannah. When you see me Tuesday morning, I may be a betrothed man," he said, straightening up, trying to sound confident.

"Oh, are you taking Monday off?" Hannah asked, confused.

"No, it's a holiday, silly. No one will be here Monday."

Still seeing the blank look on her face, he continued, "Labor Day..."

"Oh! Yes, Labor Day!" she exclaimed.

Hannah had completely forgotten about the long weekend—not that the time off mattered much to her. She still had not exactly established a social life in the city. Her two other roommates were a matter of necessity, not at all friend matches. They were never there anyway. Tamara traveled to Europe often for work, and Christina went back to New Jersey every weekend. With the thought of the long weekend in mind, Hannah came up with a tentative plan to go back to Connecticut to visit Audrey.

On her way to the elevator, she ducked into the woman's bathroom to freshen up her mascara and tousle her big curls.

She did one final check in the mirror. It took her a minute to identify how she was feeling. She was *nervous*! She didn't even know this guy, and besides she would probably never see him again after dinner. For all she knew, knocking girls down in the subway to get them into bed was his modus operandi.

The elevator stopped several times on the way down to pick people up on the way to the sky lobby express elevator on the seventy-eighth floor. Hundreds of people were all trying to get to the freedom of their weekend below. It always amazed her that so many people could be crammed in one spot on an elevator and not say a word to each other. Some had their headphones on, while others were scrolling through their BlackBerries, a new handheld electronic device that allowed executives to view emails and send messages. The rest just stared blankly ahead, thinking about their long commutes home and wishing they could teleport themselves to their living room couch.

The warm late August sun felt good on her body after a long day inside the chilly air-conditioned building. She often thought about getting fresh air on her lunch break, but the eighty-four floors to the exit below felt daunting. Instead she usually ate her lunch inside, meeting up with Marilyn, Miles, and Don in the conference room.

One sunny, warm spring day, Don had suggested they eat lunch outside, down in the plaza. Marilyn and Miles didn't feel like making the trek, but Hannah agreed to accompany him. It was a magnificent day. Birds were chirping cheerily at the return of spring, and there was a light breeze carrying the sounds of the city. They'd found an unoccupied bench in front of the glistening fountain in the plaza. Hannah had always been fascinated with the bronze sphere sculpture in the middle of the fountain. Don was a history buff with endless knowledge of New York City. That day Hannah had learned the meaning of the twenty-five-foot high bronze sphere. Built by German artist Fritz Koenig, the sphere symbolized world peace through world trade.

Hannah reflected on the memory as she made her way through the Austin J. Tobin Plaza to meet Travis at the fountain, dodging hundreds of scurrying bodies in every direction. She picked a spot in front of the fountain, taking a moment to look at her watch. It was 5:00 p.m on the dot. She nonchalantly scanned the crowd, trying to appear as though she didn't care if Travis showed up or not.

But what if he didn't show? What if he forgot? What if he changed his mind? Why did she care anyway? After all, she was still annoyed, her hip throbbing with soreness.

She looked at her watch. It was 5:05 p.m....5:08...5:10... She started to feel silly.

"What an idiot I am," she scolded herself out loud for wasting her own time. She was just about to turn and leave when suddenly she heard her name.

"Hannah!"

She saw Travis's head pop up over the crowd, his hand waving in the air. He looked ridiculous, jumping up and down to get her attention. Slightly embarrassed, Hannah stood waiting for him to reach her.

Out of breath, Travis stood in front of her with one hand behind his back.

"I'm so sorry I'm late. I was going to call you but...you know, I didn't have your number; that minor detail," he said, scratching his forehead awkwardly with his free hand.

Hannah couldn't help but be amused. "Is that your way of asking me for my number?"

"It's good, right?" Travis replied, lifting his head with pride.

"What is behind your back?" Hannah tried to peer around his side.

"Oh yeah. That's why I was late. Sorry…again, by the way," he said, pulling his arm from behind his back to reveal a large pretzel from a street vendor.

Hannah's eyebrows rose and a chuckle escaped. "A pretzel?"

"I didn't have time to get to the flower place down in the mall."

"So you opted for a street pretzel as your second choice?" Hannah giggled.

"I had to think fast, not too many options, you know," Travis explained. "It's my peace offering, New York City style."

"I'll take it. Flowers are overrated anyway," she said, taking hold of the paper-wrapped pretzel.

"So, where should we go?" Hannah asked.

"I know a place. It's a bit of a hole in the wall, but it's a local secret. You just have to promise to give it a chance. As in, don't judge by the outside. Deal?" Travis said, holding out his hand.

Hannah was hesitant, but she hadn't had much adventure in the city so far. "Deal." She shook his hand, not sure what she had just agreed to.

"We'll have to take the subway, unless you want to run through the city again, like this morning?" Travis joked.

Hannah looked at him unamused.

"Subway it is!" he said, leading the way down to the subway station underneath the North Tower.

Peak rush hour in the city was organized chaos. She let Travis lead the way. Hannah had mastered the subway only in a limited capacity. She knew how to get from her apartment in Tribeca to the World Trade Center for work. She also knew how to get to Grand Central Station for her visits back to Connecticut, but that was the extent of knowing her way around.

They reached the platform for the A train. Dozens of people had begun to push forward at the sight of the train coming. When the doors opened, a swell of people suddenly separated Travis from Hannah. He reached through the crowd and grabbed her hand, pulling her onto the train seconds before the doors closed. There was not enough room for all of the bodies crammed into the car.

"Here, stand in front of me and hold on," Travis said, pulling her between his body and the pole he had secured. He stood behind her holding on to the pole, each one of his arms at her sides. She felt his strong body behind her. He was steady and sure.

The train propelled forward with a sudden jolt, accelerating quickly. Travis tightened his grip with each bump and turn of the train, causing his chest muscles to flex. Hannah tried to ignore it. She didn't want to be attracted to him.

It was almost impossible to hear above the sound of the train's roaring and screeching over the tracks.

Travis leaned into her ear and asked, "Do you like seafood, by the way?"

"I love seafood," Hannah said loudly over the noise of the train. "There aren't too many types of food I don't like."

"Okay, good. Then you will be fine," Travis replied.

Hannah turned, looking up at him over her shoulder.

"What do you *mean* I will be fine?" she asked, her eyes narrowing suspiciously.

"Oh look, this is our stop," he said, conveniently dodging the question.

"Excuse me, pardon me, enjoy your weekend, have a good one," Travis said, greeting each person they passed as they pushed through to the open train door.

When they reached the street level from the subway stairs, they were in a neighborhood unfamiliar to Hannah.

"This seems a bit...um...sketchy," she said uneasily, trying not to offend him.

"Where are we?" she asked.

"Remember our deal," Travis reminded her. "Trust me."

"Well, in all fairness, I don't actually *know* you *to* trust you," Hannah stated. "You do remember that we just met this morning, right?"

"Fair enough, but in the short time you have known me— give or take nine hours—have I led you wrong?" Travis asked. "I picked this place because it's quiet. We may even be the only people there. No one is going to rush us out, and we can get to know each other," he said.

Hannah still wasn't convinced that he wasn't trying to pull a fast one on her, just to get her in bed.

"Okay," she said hesitantly.

Hannah studied the storefronts as they walked by. A pawn shop, then a small convenience store with a sign that read CHECKS CASHED and PHONE CARDS HERE. They had just passed a barber shop, when Travis stopped in front of a small restaurant under a striped awning. The red OPEN sign blinked in the window, and above it, another sign in big letters read HARU'S SUSHI PALACE. Travis held open the door and extended one arm, as though he were escorting her into a royal palace.

Hannah took one small step forward. "When you asked me if I liked seafood, I assumed you meant *cooked* seafood."

"Trust me," Travis said with confidence.

"What do I do with this?" Hannah asked, realizing she was still holding the pretzel he gave her.

"Put it in your briefcase as part of your emergency survival provisions," Travis teased.

"Very funny," Hannah said as she opened her briefcase and shoved the pretzel in.

She walked hesitantly past Travis, who was still holding the door. Entering Haru's Sushi Palace, Hannah felt like she had just been transported to a majestic royal palace somewhere far away. The interior was adorned with deep-red velvet swaths of fabric with black fringe, and gold accents hung on the red walls. Small tables were covered with shimmery gold tablecloths, and fancy gold-rimmed glasses were set on top.

Suddenly a middle-aged Asian man in a white chef's coat appeared from the back room. His face lit up with recognition. "Ah, Mr. Russell." He grabbed hold of Travis's hand, shaking it furiously. "I'm glad you are here. I have something new for you to try this week," he said with a heavy accent. He then turned his attention to Hannah and reached for her hand. "And who is this lovely young lady who accompanies you?" he asked.

"This is Hannah," Travis said, blushing slightly. "Hannah, this is Haru."

Hannah smiled politely. "It is nice to meet you."

"Come, I have a perfect spot for you. It is…how do you say? *Romantic?*" Haro said, nearly overrun with giddiness.

Hannah and Travis glanced at each other, slightly embarrassed by the awkward moment. Haru led them to a private and cozy corner table in the back of the room. Haru waited for Hannah to sit and pushed her chair in for her.

Travis looked up at Hannah nervously, trying to read her face as he unfolded his gold napkin and placed it on his lap.

"I'll bring over some of my homemade sake to get you started," Haru said. His face beamed. "It is five o'clock *somewhere!*" Haru said emphatically.

Travis chuckled. "Haru, it *is* actually five o'clock here, so…"

Haru looked confused.

"Never mind," Travis said.

Haru walked back to the kitchen, giggling wildly. He hadn't yet mastered his understanding of American sayings.

Hannah looked up and then around, scanning the room. "This is amazing. I feel like we stepped off the street into another world," she said in awe.

Haru came back in an instant with a large carafe of sake and two small ochoko cups. "My latest batch; it is strong, so take it slow," he said, still giddy.

Hannah was not a big drinker. As a young woman in the city, she wanted to be sure she was always in control. But for some reason, as she sat across from Travis, a person she hardly knew, she felt safe and protected.

Haru carefully poured the sake, filling the cups to the rim. Hannah quickly took a sip. The potent wine burned her throat as it went down, causing her to cringe and shudder. Within seconds, she felt her whole body get warm and her nerves begin to settle down. She took another sip.

"So, Travis *Russell*, now that I know your full name, tell me more about yourself," she said as she held the ochoko coyly in front of her, taking another sip.

"Well first, thank you for the open question," he said facetiously. "I am not sure exactly where to start with that so... um...well, I was born—"

Hannah cut him off. "Let's start with current day. What do you do for work in the North Tower?"

Hannah wasn't sure if it was the sake taking effect or Travis's easygoing nature, but she was starting to relax. She leaned back, settling more comfortably into her chair.

"I work at Garrett and Williams," Travis said.

Hannah recognized the name. "Isn't that the big fancy law firm up on the top floor?" she asked.

"104th floor, actually."

"Wow! I thought I was high up on the eighty-fourth. I was just looking up today from our conference room and realized how many more floors are above. Our conference room faces the North Tower," she informed him, starting to feel tipsy.

"Fun fact...the towers are actually a quarter of a mile high. Hey, next time you look up, maybe you will see me," Travis said jokingly.

The towers were designed with floor-to-ceiling windows to facilitate beautiful sweeping views of the city. Hannah had learned that the architect, Minoru Yamasaki, purposely designed the windows to be only eighteen-inches wide to prevent the feeling of acrophobia. Hannah appreciated the effort, since she surely had a fear of heights. From the outside, each tower had the appearance of an enormous steel grate, reaching high into the sky. Though the buildings stood adjacent to each other, it would be nearly impossible to look up and see Travis from her conference room.

Haru returned with a beautifully arranged platter, bursting with color. There were rows of orange, white, and pink perfectly sliced rectangles, arranged like fallen dominoes. The only items Hannah recognized on the plate were the neatly arranged slices of avocado and perfectly placed purple orchids among the rows of color. Off to the side was what she thought might have been a sushi roll, but there was something enormous sticking out of the top. It made quite a presentation, and Haru's face was beaming with pride.

"This is absolutely beautiful, Haru," Hannah said. "What exactly is everything?"

"Ah, sashimi, Mr. Russell's favorite," Haru said.

Hannah's eyes widened. "Sashimi is…raw fish?" she asked.

"Yes, Ms. Hannah," Haru replied. "Here we have yellowtail tuna, salmon, and white tuna," he explained row by row.

"And this is my new creation: Haru's Tempura Shrimp Mango Roll," Haru proudly announced, pointing to the enormous sushi roll.

"Enjoy!" Haru said excitedly, topping off their ochoko cups before disappearing back into the kitchen.

"Raw fish," Hannah said, apprehensively studying the colorful rectangles.

"You must learn to trust me," Travis said, using his chopsticks to grab a glob of wasabi. He dropped it into the small bowl of soy sauce and mixed it together. Carefully balancing a chunk of white fish between the chopsticks, he placed it in the mixture and tossed it over a few times until it was fully coated.

"Now close your eyes, and think only of the flavors in your mouth," Travis instructed.

Hannah never imagined that she would ever eat raw fish. She closed her eyes and tried to prepare herself for something awful. Instead the flavor exploded in her mouth. The buttery soft texture of the white tuna mixed with the salty soy sauce and the spicy wasabi was surprisingly delicious.

She opened her eyes to see Travis looking at her in anticipation.

"That was...delicious!" she said, picking up her own chopsticks to reach for another piece.

Travis let out a sigh of relief.

"So, man of mystery, how do you know the city so well?" Hannah asked. "I mean, the way you maneuvered us through the city this morning was pretty incredible, and now this place."

"Well, it's a long story and sort of...heavy. Maybe it's a conversation for another time," he said sheepishly, trying to avoid the conversation.

"No, it's okay. Really," Hannah assured him.

"Okay," Travis took a deep breath before beginning. "We moved here from New Jersey when I was fifteen. My little brother Eli was born with special needs. When he became school age, the school system in our town didn't exactly accommodate his needs. My mom fought with them for years until she was worn out. Then one day she found an amazing school here in the city for children with disabilities. They had great accommodations, so we moved here."

"Is your father here too?" Hannah asked.

Travis's face changed. Hannah immediately regretted asking the question.

"I guess that's where the story gets pretty deep. My dad, if you can call him that, bailed when Eli was born. He couldn't handle life with a special needs child and just left. I swore then I would never be like him. I can't wait to be a dad one day so that I can be everything he wasn't."

"I'm sorry. I didn't mean to—"

"No, it's okay. It has made me a better person. I know how *not* to be. There is something positive in every bad situation. That is just how I live my life," Travis said.

Hannah could tell Travis sensed her discomfort.

"That's not how I know the city so well though. When I turned eighteen, I became a bike courier to help put me through college. That's how I met Haru. I've delivered many packages to him over the years. I still courier sometimes, until I move up a little at the law firm and start making better money," he said.

"So you want to become a big fancy lawyer?" Hannah asked.

Travis laughed bashfully. "No, I am actually working in the Disability Law Department at Garrett and Williams. I want to represent the disability community to ensure inclusion in school systems, access to housing, and employment. I would eventually like to open my own disability advocacy agency to help families like ours. We sure could have used some extra support over the years, especially in those early days when my father left."

Hannah's heart fluttered. Earlier that morning she thought he was just some clumsy, self-absorbed jerk who had knocked her over in the subway. She was realizing she had him wrong.

"Enough about me," Travis said. "What made you want to go into finance?"

"Uh...well..." she stumbled. Suddenly all of her reasons for her chosen career seemed so selfish and greedy. The truth was money. Working on Wall Street was something that always fascinated her. She wanted the fancy clothes, expensive shoes, and lavish vacations. She searched helplessly for an answer that wouldn't make her sound like a shallow jerk.

"The stock market has always interested me. Being part of the finance world, I thought...you know...that I could..." she stumbled again, struggling to explain herself.

"I get it," he said, letting her off the hook. "There is nothing wrong with following the money. We struggled financially early on and it was hard. I don't wish that on anyone."

Hannah was relieved. She was surprised at how much she suddenly cared what he thought of her.

They had finished all of the sashimi. Looking down at the platter, Hannah said, "Let's tackle this roll now!"

After carefully peeling off the shrimp tail, they dipped the enormous circles of sushi in soy sauce.

"Ready? Go!" Travis said.

Feeling giddy from Haru's homemade sake, they giggled wildly as they shoved the giant roll of sushi into their mouths. Hannah unknowingly had soy sauce dripping down her chin. Travis grabbed the napkin from his lap, reached over, and wiped it away gently. Hannah's eyes met his as he leaned over the table. They were locked in a stare for a moment. His sparkling blue eyes gave her a full glimpse into his kind soul, making her heart flutter again.

Their gaze was interrupted by Haru, who had come from the kitchen to check on them. "Ah! You liked!" he exclaimed with delight, picking up the empty platter from the table.

Before Haru could walk away with the platter, Travis grabbed one of the flowers used for garnish. He leaned over the table and stuck the flower behind Hannah's ear. "Perfection," he said, sitting back down to look at her.

Hannah's head felt wonderfully fuzzy.

After a few minutes, Haru returned with another carafe of sake and was ready to fill their cups again.

"I think we are all set for tonight; just the check, please," Travis said.

"No charge for you, Mr. Travis. You do so much for me," Haru replied.

"Thank you, Haru, but I insist," Travis protested.

Haru dismissed his refusal with an animated swoop of his hand. He turned to Hannah and said, "Look over there." He pointed to a large gold dragon on the wall. "Travis hung that for me. It took both of us just to hold it up. He spent hours here until it was up on that wall." Haru then pointed up to the ceiling. "There. A bad leak ruined the entire ceiling. Travis replaced all of the old tiles with the new gold tiles."

Hannah's heart smiled. She looked over at Travis, who had his head lowered. She could tell the recognition was uncomfortable for him.

Hannah was listening to Haru, but did not take her eyes off Travis. *Who is this guy? Is he too good to be true?*

"You are a good man—a friend for life," Haru said, placing one hand on Travis's shoulder.

"Thanks, Haru; you are a good friend too. I'll be back next week." Travis discreetly placed a twenty-dollar bill on the table and then escorted Hannah to the door. As they stepped out onto the sidewalk, Travis took a deep breath of the warm evening air. "It's too nice out to get on that subway train. Where do you live, if you don't mind me asking?"

"By Pier 25," Hannah replied dreamily.

"That's not far from me. How about a nice late summer evening stroll through the city? I'll walk you home," Travis suggested.

"That has to be thirty blocks from here!" Hannah exclaimed.

"Do you have big Friday night plans or something?" Travis asked.

Hannah snorted. "Yeah, big Friday night plans. I'll probably eat ice cream by myself and watch David Letterman until I fall asleep on the couch."

Travis watched Hannah concentrate heavily on putting one foot in front of the other. "A nice long walk might help wear off some of Haru's sake."

She stumbled forward almost losing her balance on the uneven sidewalk.

"Easy there. Hold on to my arm so that you don't fall. You already did that today, remember?" Travis teased.

"How could I forget?" She smiled up at him with a drunken smile. She looped her arm through his, noticing his strong bicep muscle holding her up.

They walked arm in arm through the changing neighborhoods, past city parks and landmarks, many of which she had never seen before. There was a slight warm breeze, and the sun had fallen behind the buildings. The feeling in the air was magic.

Finally Hannah recognized where they were, taking the lead the rest of the way to her apartment. She stopped in front of her building's revolving door.

"Well, this is my stop," she said, digging in her briefcase for her apartment keys.

"Okay, well, enjoy your ice cream, and I hope Letterman is great," Travis said awkwardly. "Oh, and hey, maybe…I mean… if you want to…you know…get together again, I should probably get your number…so I can get in touch with you. I mean, if you want to. If not, it's—"

Her head still fuzzy, Hannah stopped his nervous rambling by leaning in to kiss Travis. His lips were perfectly soft and still had a hint of sake and soy sauce. She grabbed him by the hand and pulled him toward the revolving door.

"Come upstairs. My roommates are gone for the long weekend," Hannah said without looking back. She was sure of what she was doing. She didn't want ice cream; she didn't want to watch David Letterman. She wanted Travis.

"Umm, sure, I will come up…and make sure you get to your door safely," Travis stuttered, unsure of her expectations.

"That's not what I meant." She pulled him through the revolving doors, past the doorman, and straight to the elevator.

CHAPTER 7

Saturday, September 1, 2001
2:00 a.m.

The sudden buzzing on Audrey's nightstand woke her up from a dead sleep. Still unable to lie flat from her broken, throbbing nose, she rolled from the pillows, propping herself up in bed to see the red numbers on the clock. She squinted through her blurry eyes.

Two o'clock a.m.! Who is calling me in the middle of the night? This can't be good.

The caller ID slot on the front of the phone read PRESTON.

She flipped open the phone. "Preston, what is going on?" she answered, knowing something was terribly wrong.

"Audrey? Are you there?" Preston said.

"Yes, I'm here. What is wrong?" Audrey asked, confused.

"Audrey," he said, followed by a long pause, "I'm in trouble." His words were deliberate and slurred.

FARMER

He's drunk, Audrey realized. She had a bad feeling he would get in trouble that night. They were so close to graduating the academy.

"Where are you?" Audrey asked, her concern growing.

"At the police station. I punched that asshole in the face. He had it coming."

"What? Who? Preston, who did you punch? Oh my God! Are you under arrest?" she asked frantically.

"Scott...I punched Scott and he deserved it," Preston said, slurring his words so much that Audrey could barely understand him.

"Okay, we can talk about it later. Are you under arrest?" Audrey asked again.

"No, but they won't let me drive. I need a ride. I'm sorry to bother you—"

"I'll be right there," Audrey interrupted him as she jumped out of bed so fast that she forgot about her broken nose. It sent a shockwave to her face. She grabbed a pair of sweatpants from her drawer and quickly put a sports bra on under the T-shirt she had been sleeping in. She pulled her straggly blonde hair back into a ponytail and shoved it through the back of her Yankees baseball cap.

As she drove to the police department, she had a sinking feeling it all had to do with her. Audrey parked the car in the same parking lot she had left ten hours before. The police department was located directly next to the academy building, sharing the same parking lot. She recalled the last thing she'd said to Preston, just hours before.

Don't get in trouble tonight...

Audrey walked into the entrance of the police department. She didn't know the desk officer on duty. The academy was run by in-house officers and supervisors who worked the day shift. Unless one of the instructors was working a midnight overtime shift, she wouldn't know anyone, and no one would know her—so she naively thought. She was grateful for the anonymity, but her heart dropped when she realized the officer behind the desk unmistakably knew who she was. He jumped up from his chair.

"Recruit Moretti, right?" he asked.

"Uh...yes," she responded, caught off guard.

"Hang on; I'll be right out." He partially tripped over the rolling chair that he'd just stood up from and disappeared into the dispatch area. Then with a click of the door lock, he appeared in the lobby.

From behind the window, Audrey hadn't noticed how unkempt he was. He was a young cop. She guessed in his midtwenties. He had wavy black hair and dark brown eyes. He looked like he had only been on the job for a couple of years. As he walked toward her, she noticed his uniform hanging loosely over his overweight body. His gun belt was clearly not fastened with keepers, hanging crookedly off his hips. He walked awkwardly toward her, feet clunking on the floor with his heavy black boots.

"Nick Jebrowski," he said, jutting his hand forward to offer an introductory handshake. "You can call me Jeb."

"Audrey Moretti, but apparently you already know that," she replied.

Unlike Audrey, Jeb was wide awake and sprightly at the early hour.

"Hey." He looked over his shoulder briefly and then leaned forward. "It's messed up what happened to you during baton certification. Riccio is a total screw-up. Nice kid, but a walking disaster."

Jeb bent down to get a better look at her face under her hat. Wincing, he blurted out, "Man, I heard it was bad, but I didn't realize *that* bad." Realizing that came out wrong, he quickly corrected himself. "Not that you look bad, but wow, you know what I mean."

"I heard you didn't go down though," Jeb continued. "We need more guys; I mean…we need more cops like you. You wouldn't believe some of the wimps we have here—afraid of their own shadow. I'm not going to mention any names, but one time I was rolling around with this guy, high, out of his mind. I see my backup standing off to the side, afraid to jump in. I would take you any day over that guy."

"Uh, thanks, I think?" Audrey said, unsure if that was a compliment. She wondered if as a female officer she would only ever rank higher than the worst male officer.

"I'm here for Preston Briggs," she took the moment of opportunity to cut him off.

"Yeah, about that…" his face turned serious. "Listen," he said, leaning in again with a lowered voice, "we let him off the hook because he is a recruit here, but this is going to get back to the chief, if it hasn't already. Nothing stays quiet around here."

Audrey scoffed. "I'm picking up on that. Can I see him now?"

Jeb grabbed the microphone clipped to his uniform shirt and angled it toward his mouth.

"Uniform 192, you can bring that item out now," he said, overemphasizing a wink at Audrey.

He was a little much, Audrey thought, but he seemed like a good guy.

"Hey, it was nice meeting you," Jeb said cheerily. "You're almost there. I'll see you on your midnight rotation during field training. Let me know if you need anything."

"Thanks, Jeb," Audrey said, appreciating his genuine kindness.

Just then, Preston's face appeared in the small plexiglass window of the door. The door clicked open, and an officer tried to steady him as he escorted him out. Preston stumbled forward, avoiding looking Audrey in the eyes. He was highly intoxicated, embarrassed, and clearly still agitated.

The officer handed Audrey Preston's keys and wallet. "Get him home safe. He'll need to sleep it off. I'm not sure what will come of this for him. He clocked the guy really good. I guess he will find out on Tuesday," the officer said dolefully.

Audrey felt a pit in her stomach.

"Hey Audrey, at least you won't be the only recruit in class with a black eye anymore," Jeb blurted out in a failed attempt at a joke.

Audrey ignored him and concentrated on helping Preston to the door.

What the hell could possibly have happened?

Audrey helped him to the passenger seat of her car, reaching across his large body to click the seatbelt into the latch.

Audrey pulled out of the police department parking lot and headed back toward her apartment across town. In the condition he was in, she couldn't just dump him off at his place. She glanced over at the passenger seat. Preston's head was back on the headrest, eyes closed, completely passed out.

Her head was spinning the whole silent drive home. Preston was not an aggressive person. He was easygoing, calm, and collected. So what could have sparked him to turn physical, risking everything he had worked so hard for? The more she thought about it, the more the feeling in her gut solidified.

It definitely had something to do with me.

Audrey parked the car in her designated spot in front of her apartment. She walked around to the passenger side to open the door. "Hey," she said, shaking Preston gently to rouse him awake. "I need you to do a bit more walking. Then you can sleep as long as you want," she promised. There was no way Audrey could move his large body from the car without his help.

Preston opened his eyes momentarily, but the shine of the parking lot lights was too bright. He winced and closed his eyes, mumbling something as he put his head back onto the headrest. In an instant, he passed out again.

"Preston, I need you to walk." Her voice was more commanding this time as she grabbed him by the arm in an attempt to guide him up.

Preston, only half conscious, used every last bit of energy he had to hoist himself up from the seat. Audrey walked him to the door of her apartment, stumbling along with him as she struggled to keep him upright.

"You can sleep on the futon. I'll go get you some blankets," she said.

Audrey transformed the couch's frame into a bed and helped guide Preston down onto the futon mattress. She went to her closet and grabbed a couple of extra blankets. On the way back to Preston, she stopped in the kitchen to get a bottle of water to place by his head.

When she returned, Preston had already passed out again. Lucy had come out from the bedroom to investigate the situation. Audrey covered Preston with the blankets, prompting Lucy to jump up on the futon to sniff around. Lucy began to purr and knead at the soft blankets, stretching out alongside Preston's passed-out body. She looked up at Audrey, unapologetic at her choice of sleeping arrangements. Looking down at the duo, Audrey smiled and thought, *Cats know good people. I hope he is not allergic.*

As Audrey lay down on her bed, she thought of her sister. It had been almost a month since she'd seen her. Audrey missed her so much. Maybe she would come home for the holiday weekend, she hoped, as she dozed off to sleep.

———

Saturday, September 1, 2001
7:00 a.m.
The pounding in Hannah's head woke her up before the daylight came through the twelfth-story window of her apartment. She groaned as she came to, feeling the effects of too much sake the night before.

Wait, what was last night?

She tried to think clearly through her hungover state. As the fog in her brain slowly lifted, she remembered the ride up in the elevator. Her hazy memory recalled stumbling out when the doors opened, kissing Travis until they reached her apartment door. She remembered fumbling with her keys and finally flinging the door open, leading Travis to her bedroom while unbuttoning his dress shirt.

A shiver suddenly went through Hannah's entire body. She realized she was under the sheet, totally naked. The bed was cold. Suddenly her blood turned red-hot, realizing she was alone in the bed. He was *gone*. His clothes were *gone*.

He left! What a complete scumbag! I am a total idiot!

She wasn't sure if she wanted to cry or break something. Just as Hannah was about to scream out in pure rage, she heard something in the kitchen. A cabinet door opened and then shut, then the refrigerator door. She heard some crinkling of paper and then the faucet running.

What the hell?

One of her roommates must have changed plans and come back to the city, she reasoned, her blood still boiling.

Suddenly a person appeared in the doorway of her bedroom. There stood Travis, dressed in his work clothes from the day before, holding a plastic serving tray from the cabinet. On it, he had arranged a glass of water, two half-dried-out strawberries from the fridge, and the pretzel she had stuffed in her briefcase.

Hannah sat up in confusion, wrapping the sheet around herself to cover her bare chest.

"You need to do some grocery shopping. That is one sad refrigerator," Travis ragged. "This is the best I could do with what I was working with. Breakfast in bed, my lady." He bowed down to display the tray.

Hannah sat stupefied, mouth open and contorted. Just moments ago she thought she had made the biggest mistake of her life. She was cursing the very ground he was walking on, wherever he was. In those few moments she wondered if everything he had told her was a lie, part of a big scheme to get her into bed. A minute before he stood in her doorway with breakfast, she thought she had been duped by a horrible person, who may or may not have even been named Travis.

"I thought you'd left," Hannah blurted out.

The look on his face cut her like a knife. In the silence she could hear his hurt.

"I would never do that," he replied after a moment.

Hannah suddenly remembered about his dad and how he had left them. She felt horrible at what she'd implied.

"I just...when I woke up and you weren't here...I'm sorry. I didn't mean to...sometimes guys just do that and...I'm making it worse...I'm s-s-sorry," she stammered.

Travis came around the side of her bed and sat on the edge. He picked up a sweatshirt off the floor and handed it to her, turning his head so that he could give her privacy to cover up.

"Listen, I'm not just every other guy. I don't know how to explain it, but I feel like I was meant to meet you in the subway yesterday—like two worlds came crashing together, literally, for a reason. I know that probably sounds corny, but I feel it in my heart. I stayed last night because *you* asked me to and it felt right. I feel like I've known you my whole life, even though we only met twenty-four hours ago, pretty much to the minute," he said, holding up the watch on his wrist.

Hannah listened, settling back down, comforted by his reassurance. "I understand exactly what you are saying. I feel it too," she concurred.

"I will make you a promise. From now on, until whenever *you* decide, I promise nothing physical. I simply want to spend time with you and get to know every part of you. I will show you the city, and introduce you to new places. No funny business at all. Deal?" he asked, holding out his hand for a handshake.

"Deal." Hannah shook his hand formally to seal the deal. Even though she didn't regret the night before, she didn't want to rush things. She wanted this to be something so much more. She wanted to learn everything she could about Travis.

"Okay, we have a long weekend to work with. Let's start tonight. I'll swing by around six o'clock to get you. Wear good walking shoes," Travis said with a wink.

Taking a small bite of the stale, cold pretzel, Hannah silently apologized to Audrey. She would not be going home to Connecticut to visit. Instead, she would be spending the weekend with Travis in the city.

CHAPTER 8

September 1, 2001
12:00 p.m.

"Stop it," Audrey mumbled in a semi-asleep state, batting Lucy's paw away. Lucy was sitting on her chest, tapping her face with her paw to wake her up. She only did that when her breakfast was late.

What time is it?

Squinting at the clock, she was shocked to see the time. *Noon!* No wonder Lucy was impatient for her breakfast.

"Okay, okay, I'm coming," Audrey patted Lucy's soft head reassuringly and rolled out of bed. She was still in her sweatpants and T-shirt, too tired to change when she'd gotten home in the middle of the night.

Audrey suddenly recalled that Preston was on her futon. Shuffling out of her bedroom, she saw Preston sitting up, holding his head. He looked completely miserable.

"I haven't been this hungover, ever," he groaned. Turning his attention to his hand, he tried to make a fist and winced. "I think I broke my hand."

"There's a bottle of water by the side of the futon. You should drink it," Audrey said, sounding motherly.

She went to scoop Lucy's food out of the container and put it in her pink dish, and then grabbed two power bars from the cupboard.

Handing one to Preston, she sat down on the chaise lounge next to the futon.

"Thanks. I doubt I can hold anything down right now," Preston said, politely taking the protein bar, anyway.

"So, what in the world happened?" Audrey asked.

"Well, the night started out fine. We got something to eat at The Pub. We were about to head over to The Painted Lady, but then the guys started doing shots. Things went downhill from there." Preston hesitated.

Audrey could sense he was uncomfortable and didn't want to tell her the whole story. Preston was such a loyal friend that she knew Scott must have said something horrible about her, causing him to snap.

"What did Scott say about me? I can take whatever it is. I only care about you," Audrey reassured Preston.

He sighed, wincing again at the pain in his hand. "Remember when I went into the city for the weekend to visit my buddy for his birthday? I parked here and walked to the train station?" Preston asked.

"Uh, yeah," she answered, confused.

Audrey lived within walking distance to the train station. Parking at the train station was not only impossible, but expensive too. Whenever Audrey's parents went to the city to visit Hannah, they always parked at her apartment and walked to the train station. When Preston had told her he was going to the city for the weekend, she'd offered for him to do the same. She had no idea where he could be going with this.

"Well apparently, one of the guys in the department on midnights, who also happens to be friends with Scott, drove through your parking lot to see if anyone's car was here. Basically he was spying on you. He saw my truck here in the middle of the night," he explained.

Preston's truck was unmistakable. Similar to Preston's, you couldn't miss the commanding presence of its large frame. Additionally his truck was candy-apple red, perfectly waxed and shined. It was easy to spot.

Audrey suddenly realized exactly where this was going. She dropped her head in disgust.

Preston continued, "In front of all the guys, Scott asked me what it was like to…you know. I can't even repeat what he said, Audrey. I just snapped."

"Preston, I'm sorry. You didn't have to defend me. We both know that it's not true."

"That's the problem. *We* know it's not true, but it has run through the entire department," Preston said.

Audrey was deflated.

Are these guys seriously spying on me? Talking about me? Making up rumors about me?! How pathetic!

She never would have imagined that they would pry into her personal life before she was even out of the academy. Up until a few hours before, she naively thought she was fairly anonymous. Now she was realizing that she was the subject of every conversation between guys she hadn't even met yet.

"I can handle anything these guys throw my way," Audrey said. "You are a good friend, Preston. Thank you for defending my honor."

"My only regret is that I didn't get in a few more punches. The guys pulled me off of him before I could get in another pop." His face suddenly turned pale. "Someone in the bar called the cops. That can't be good for a recruit in the academy. I think I'm screwed, Audrey." Preston put his head in his hands.

"Let's see what happens Tuesday. For now, let's go get your truck and get you home," Audrey said, helping him up off the futon.

———

September 1, 2001
4:30 p.m.
Hannah had spent the day in bed, nursing her hangover. She drifted in and out of naps, making sure to take sips of water in between. The only time she got out of bed was to take two Tylenol. Each time she drifted off to sleep, she thought about the night before and the feelings she was starting to have for Travis.

She woke up to the sound of a loud fire engine siren, down below on the street. It jolted her awake. Hannah looked at the clock. It was 4:30 p.m. Travis said he would be coming by at six o'clock. Even though she felt much better after her day of rest, it would still take her a while to pull herself together.

First, I have to call Audrey.

Audrey was her very best friend. They told each other everything. The day before had been such a whirlwind that she hadn't had a chance to ask Audrey how her Shotgun Certification had gone. Hannah also couldn't wait to tell her about Travis.

She picked up her phone and dialed Audrey's apartment landline phone number. The phone picked up on the first ring.

"Hey, Hannah," Audrey answered, sounding exhausted.

"Hey, Sis, you sound tired. Is everything all right?" Hannah asked with concern.

"Long night, long week…long five months," Audrey replied.

Hannah knew how badly Audrey had wanted to become a cop. She also knew her sister was tiring of the long academy days. Getting her nose broken definitely did not help. She could tell there was something more though. She put aside her excitement about Travis for a moment.

"You're doing great, Audrey. I am so proud of you," Hannah said, trying to give her encouragement. "Are you sure everything is okay?"

"Nothing I can't handle. I'm just grateful for the long weekend. Are you coming home?" Audrey asked excitedly.

"Uh…about that…" Hannah couldn't contain her excitement any longer. She felt bad that she felt so elated, when her sister was going through a hard time, but she couldn't contain herself. "I met a guy," Hannah burst out. "His name is Travis. We just met yesterday; I ran into him in the subway. Actually he ran into me in the subway, like literally. He works in the North Tower, all the way up on the 104th floor, can you imagine? Anyway, I really like him. He's different than all the other city guys I've met. I can't explain it. Oh, and he is really cute," she added giddily.

It had been a long time since Audrey had heard her baby sister so excited. Even though Audrey had hoped Hannah would be coming home that weekend, her heart was full with the thought of her sister's newfound happiness.

"That's very exciting. I can't wait to meet him," Audrey said, truly happy for her.

"I have to start getting ready. He's coming by at six o'clock to get me," Hannah squeaked with excitement. Then she sincerely offered, "Are you sure you are all right? I can cancel and come home instead. Really, if you need me, I will."

"Are you kidding me? I can't wait to hear all of the exciting details of your weekend. I need to live vicariously through you. I can't do that if you are here watching *Law & Order* with me on my futon. Have a great time, Sis."

Hannah hung up the phone and ran to her closet. She stood in front of her open closet, wondering how she would pull off sexy paired with comfortable walking shoes. She pulled out black boot-cut pants and a black-and-silver tank top.

It was September 1 in New York City. The days were warm, but the nights were starting to cool down. She grabbed a black pashmina, just in case she got chilly. *Shoes*, she thought, tapping her chin as she stood perplexed in front of her closet. In a bin underneath her hanging clothes, she found a pair of black Converse sneakers. *These will have to do.*

Hannah had just enough time to shower, dry her long blonde hair, throw some curls in, and put on her makeup. She was just unplugging her curling iron, when the buzzer rang to her apartment.

It was six-o'clock on the dot. She pressed the talk button. "I will be right down!" she said into the intercom.

Grabbing a black Coach crossbody bag from her closet shelf, she took her wallet from her briefcase and shoved it in. Her keys were still in the same place on the kitchen table, where they had been tossed passionately the night before.

She stood for one final check in front of the full-length mirror, which was hanging on the back of the bedroom door. Trying to control the butterflies in her stomach, she smoothed over her outfit and practiced her smile.

Hannah stopped outside of her apartment door, making sure she'd locked each of the locks—the main door lock and *two* deadbolts. Even though her building had an intercom system and doorman, her mother had made the building manager install an additional deadbolt lock on her door. Hannah had thought it was completely unnecessary.

On the way down in the elevator, she took several deep breaths, trying to slow her rapidly beating heart. As soon as the elevator doors opened into the lobby, she saw Travis standing outside in front of the building, waiting for her. Every step she took toward him felt electric.

Hannah pushed through the revolving door, making eye contact with Travis halfway through. At the sight of her, he smiled a charming smile, his blue eyes twinkling in the early evening light. He looked handsome in a polished city boy way, his medium-length hair brushed casually over to the side. He was dressed in khaki pants, a gray short-sleeved Ralph Lauren polo shirt, and gray Vans skate shoes.

"You look beautiful," Travis said, reaching for Hannah's hand. He leaned forward, kissing the top of her hand.

Hannah was enchanted. "So what random adventure do you have in store for us tonight?" she asked.

"You'll see," he said, flagging down a taxi.

He opened the door for Hannah and climbed in after her.

"Take us to City Hall Park and Centre Street please," Travis said to the taxi driver through the window.

The driver nodded without turning around.

"I should know the city better by now," Hannah said, slightly embarrassed. "I should probably know what is at City Hall Park and Centre Street, but I don't venture out much."

"I will teach you everything you need to know about the city," Travis said, pulling a camera to his lap, which she hadn't noticed was hanging over his shoulder. "This is one of my favorite places to photograph. Wait until you see the views. We are going at the best time; the lighting will be perfect." Travis's passion for photography was shining through.

"You are a photographer too? Is there anything you don't do?" Hannah asked.

"I told you, I am a very interesting guy," Travis said with the same boastful grin as the morning they'd met.

"I try to experience everything I can. I never take a moment for granted." Travis turned to stare out the cab window, up at the buildings reaching into the sky. "The way I see it, if you live each day to the fullest, life can never be too short."

Hannah was silent for a moment, thinking about his words. So often she let little things ruin her day—spilled coffee, a late train, a rip in her pantyhose.

The taxi came to a hard stop, with an aggressive press of the brakes. Travis reached over to pay the driver as Hannah peered out the window wondering why they had stopped in front of the Brooklyn Bridge. Travis got out of the cab and reached for Hannah's hand, helping her out onto the bustling street.

She had never been close enough before to notice the beautiful architecture of the Brooklyn Bridge. The two stone towers tasked with holding up the suspension cables were of neo-Gothic design, each containing pointed arches, where thousands of vehicles passed through each day.

"So! Have you ever walked across the bridge?" Travis asked with a wide grin.

"Oh no...um...never," Hannah replied with apprehensive surprise.

Hannah's fear of heights was exacerbated especially over bridges. The design of the World Trade Center towers helped mitigate her fear of heights on the eighty-fourth floor. The tall narrow windows and the open layout inside somehow made her forget that she was so high up. The thought of a bridge spanning a large body of water below, held up by suspension cables and stone, was not something she'd ever been comfortable with. When she was little, Audrey had always held her hand in the back seat when their parents drove over bridges. She would let Hannah know when she could open her eyes, once they were on the other side.

The thought of crossing the bridge on foot both terrified and exhilarated Hannah. Even though she was nervous, there was something about Travis that made her want to try new things. She trusted him completely.

"Let's do it," Hannah said, exhaling the deep breath she had been holding.

"There is nothing to worry about. Wait until you see the views of the city from halfway over the bridge. No matter how many times I come here, there is always something amazing to photograph. I can't wait to share this with you," Travis said.

They began walking toward the bridge, entering onto the wood-planked walkway. Hannah took a few steps forward and suddenly stopped. She was unable to take another step forward.

"What's the matter?" Travis asked.

"I'm terrified!" Hannah confessed.

"There's nothing to worry about. If it makes you feel any better, P.T. Barnum took eighteen elephants across this bridge in 1884, just to prove how safe it is. So there's that," Travis proudly informed her.

Hannah laughed nervously.

"Trust me." Travis turned to look into her eyes. He reached for her hand, trying to reassure her. "You just have to worry about the crazy bicyclists, so make sure you don't wander into the bike lane. They will literally run you down." He pointed down at the white lines clearly marking the separation between pedestrian and bicycle lanes.

They walked hand in hand up the slight incline of the bridge's walkway. The warm evening breeze was starting to pick up and turn cooler as they entered over the water. Hannah was glad she'd brought her wrap with her.

Travis's strong hand enveloped Hannah's, giving her a feeling of safety and security. Her fears started to subside, and suddenly she was in total awe of the sights in front of her. The sweeping views of the city from above the East River were breathtaking. Every step they took seemed to give a different view. Hannah stopped momentarily to take in the beauty. Travis stepped back and took a picture of her reaction.

"Oh gosh!" she exclaimed with embarrassment. "I wasn't ready for that."

"Sorry, I just had to. The look on your face was perfect," Travis said apologetically. "Small moments like that are what people most often forget. That's why I love taking pictures. With pictures, memories live forever when our memories fail us. They last long past our physical presence here on Earth," he said.

"Okay, as long as I get my turn at taking your picture with that camera!" Hannah said, pretending to swipe for the camera.

"Fair enough," Travis agreed. "I am hardly in any pictures, always the one taking them. I suppose there should be some proof of my existence."

They continued walking slowly hand in hand, letting people filter by around them. The whole world seemed to fade into the background when she was with him, as if the city were all theirs. It felt like they were the only two people on the bridge.

Suddenly Travis stopped. He pulled Hannah in front of him and turned her to face Lower Manhattan. She gasped at the panoramic view of the skyline from the bridge. The towering skyscrapers looked so modern in contrast to the one-hundred-year-old bridge that they stood on. Unmistakable and strikingly beautiful, the Twin Towers stretched far into the sky, right in front of their eyes.

"Can you believe we work there?" Travis asked, awestruck. "We have to get a picture together, with our towers in the background."

Our towers…

There was such an incredible feeling of pride, working in those towers. They were powerful, strong, and indestructible—an unmistakable visual icon of Lower Manhattan.

"Excuse me," Travis called out to a stranger walking by, "would you please take our picture?"

The man stopped without missing a beat, carefully taking hold of the camera.

Travis positioned himself next to Hannah, with the towers in the background. He slung his arm over her shoulder and pulled her in close to him. Her long blonde hair blew upward in a gust of wind as the kind passerby snapped the picture.

"Thank you, sir," Travis said.

The unknown man smiled, handed back the camera, and turned to continue on his way.

As fast-paced as New York City was, Hannah always found people to be helpful and kind. There had been countless times she was lost or not sure which subway train to take. Perfect strangers stopped in the middle of their busy day to help her—to help each other. There was a flow to the city that its people had perfected. She quickly fell in love with New York City, especially its people.

They walked in silence most of the rest of the way, totally content with each other's company. Hannah got lost in her thoughts. She wondered how she could feel so strongly about someone so quickly. She hoped he felt the same about her too. Hannah wanted to spend every minute she could with him. There was still so much to learn about him, so much she wanted to know.

They came to the end of the bridge.

"Welcome to Brooklyn," Travis announced with outstretched arms. "Now let's get some famous Brooklyn pizza."

He led the way, turning left off the pedestrian walkway, weaving Hannah in and out of the flow of people entering to cross the bridge to the Manhattan side.

"This is called the DUMBO section of Brooklyn," he informed her.

"Oh! Named after the elephants that crossed the bridge?" Hannah asked innocently.

Travis unintentionally burst out in laughter.

"Hey!" Hannah exclaimed, chuckling at her own ignorance.

"DUMBO is short for Down Under the Manhattan Bridge Overpass," he whispered, shielding her from embarrassment.

"Oh yeah, that makes sense, I suppose," Hannah replied sarcastically.

"Eh…that's boring. I like yours better," he said. "Over there is Brooklyn Bridge Park." Travis pointed toward the banks of the East River. "Supposedly there is an old carousel being restored that will one day be moved here to the park. I heard it's a vintage carousel built in 1922 by the Philadelphia Toboggan Company, but it was damaged in a fire at an amusement park in Ohio. Word is, once it's renovated, it will be an operational carousel and moved here for all to ride."

"That sounds magical," Hannah said.

"When it opens, we will come back to ride it," Travis promised, putting his arm around her shoulder. "Come on, I know the best pizza-by-the-slice place right around the corner. We can grab a bench by the water and watch the boats go by. I love coming here at night."

The sun had set, and the night sky was slowly overtaking the daylight. A thin, pink layer of clouds was trapped between the two skies, and the half-moon was becoming visible.

"Is this where you take all of your lady friends?" Hannah teased Travis.

"Well, I can see why you would think that, being the strapping and handsome young man that I am," he replied with mock conceit. Travis then got quiet for a moment before saying, "The truth is…I don't really have time to date."

Hannah looked at him suspiciously. It was hard for her to believe that such a good-looking, charming guy, like him, didn't have loads of girlfriends.

"Really, it is true," Travis protested. "I guess I'm just not the typical twenty-five-year-old guy. I'm a son, brother, and hypothetically a father—in essence, the man of my family. Eli needs a lot of support. He has a lot of doctors' appointments and therapies. My mom can't do it all. I help as much as I can," Travis explained as they strolled along the Brooklyn streets.

"Speaking of Eli," Travis said, changing the subject, "Brooklyn Bridge Park is his favorite place. He loves to park his wheelchair and watch the boats go by. Don't go giving him any sympathy though. He's a wise guy. He loves to people watch, and you wouldn't believe the things he says sometimes! He likes to razz me pretty good too." Travis shook his head.

"I like him even more all of a sudden," Hannah said, smiling at the thought of Eli razzing Travis. "He sounds great."

"He is great; he's my hero actually. I know he looks up to me and all because I am his older brother, but I truly look up to him," Travis said. "He could get down about life if he wanted to but he never does. He never gives up. His sense of humor keeps us all going. Isn't that something? *He* keeps *us* going. He has the best laugh I have ever heard. It is infectious."

"I am sure your mom is pretty amazing too. I mean, she raised two incredible boys, and I'm sure that wasn't easy doing it on her own. She must be a very strong person," Hannah said.

"She is amazing. After my dad left, she put herself through law school. My grandparents helped take care of me and my brother while she earned her law degree. She passed the bar exam, and after finding an amazing school in the city for my brother, she applied to law firms nearby so that she would never be far from him."

"You are very lucky to have her," Hannah said.

They turned onto Atlantic Street, stopping in front of a small neighborhood pizzeria. Travis turned to her. "*Scamorza?*"

"Huh?" Hannah replied confused.

"It's like mozzarella, only better. It is their specialty," Travis explained.

"Sure, I mean, I tried sushi last night and liked it. You have earned my cuisine trust," Hannah replied.

"Two slices of *Scamorza* please," Travis ordered.

The paper plate was barely visible under the enormous slice of pizza. They walked back to the park to find a bench near the water.

"So, you know a lot about me. It's your turn. You mentioned your sister. What is she like?" Travis asked.

The question suddenly sent a wave of sadness to her heart. Hannah missed her sister so much, and here she was in total bliss, while Audrey was having a hard time back home.

"Her name is Audrey. We are twenty months apart. She's my big sister, but we might as well be twins. My parents called us 'Double Trouble' when we were little. She is in the police academy right now. Actually, she's almost done. She graduates in a few weeks," Hannah said.

"Uh-oh, a cop for a sister; I'd better watch out," Travis joked.

"Yup, you'd better watch your step. She is tough," Hannah replied.

Travis folded his pizza slice in half and took a bite.

"Did you just fold your pizza in half?" Hannah asked in astonishment.

"This is how New Yorkers eat their pizza. Clearly, I have a lot to teach you," he said, winking at Hannah and then taking another folded bite.

The sun had completely disappeared, and the lights of the Brooklyn Bridge shone brightly against the black sky. Hannah set her paper plate aside and snuggled up close to Travis on the bench. Travis felt her shiver and pulled her pashmina up over her shoulders. She rested her head on his shoulder as they sat in silence for a long time, needing nothing more than to be together.

"I'm working a courier shift tomorrow. Maybe I can stop over afterward. I'll bring you something to eat so that you don't starve to death in that apartment of yours," Travis teased.

"You don't have to bring anything; I just want to see you," she said dreamily, lost in the magic of the moment.

All was right in the world, sitting next to Travis Russell, under the lights of the Brooklyn Bridge.

CHAPTER 9

Monday, September 3, 2001
9:00 a.m.
Labor Day

Hannah rolled over in her bed, bumping into Travis lying at the edge of the mattress. After a Sunday evening eating Chinese food directly from containers at her small round kitchen table, she'd offered for him to stay the night. He promised to sleep fully clothed on the edge of her bed, with one foot on the floor, like the old days.

With the morning sun pouring in through her bedroom window, Hannah chuckled at the sight of him lying at the edge of her bed, fully clothed, with one leg dangling over the side. He was a true gentleman and true to his word.

She studied his face as he slept. Her eyes searched every feature: his perfectly shaped lips, strong jawline, and defined cheekbones. The dark eyelashes looked even longer, sweeping downward onto his cheeks, like a bird with open wings soaring high in the sky. She brushed her fingers gently through his thick brown hair, careful not to wake him. His natural golden highlights came alive in the morning sunlight. If he had been more of a vain man, he may have pursued a modeling career. Hannah wondered if he even knew how beautiful he was both inside and out.

Travis's eyes opened slowly, meeting her studying gaze. "Good morning, beautiful," he said, reaching out to touch her face.

Hannah's heart skipped. She wanted to tell him how she felt. Instead she simply smiled, wondering if her eyes would reveal the feelings she held inside.

Does he feel the same way?

She searched his eyes for signs.

Travis pulled her close, cradling her head to his chest. Hannah drifted back off to sleep, feeling the warmth of his body under her head.

The next thing Hannah felt was her body being gently nudged.

"Hey, sleepy head. It's eleven o'clock in the morning. I have a great idea for the day, but you have to get up." Travis stood beside her bed, trying to rouse her awake. "I'm going to run home, get changed, and get some things together. I will be back in an hour to get you."

Hannah didn't bother to ask what he had planned. She trusted that whatever it was would be romantic and wonderful—something new she had never done before or a memory she would never forget. She didn't even care what they did anymore. She just wanted to be with him.

"Okay, I will be ready," Hannah said sleepily

Travis kissed her forehead and hurried toward the door.

Hannah jumped out of bed, rushing to the shower.

Afterward, she carefully selected the perfect outfit from the closet. Hannah loved fashion and shopping. She was always up on the latest trends. She slid into her favorite denim skirt, securing it with a studded buckle belt. It would be a hot day in the city. She grabbed a white halter top from the hanger, pairing the look with white K-Swiss tennis sneakers.

Hannah stood in front of her full-length mirror, momentarily panicking at the sight of her unruly hair. She wouldn't have time to curl and style it. But she had the perfect solution in mind. Returning to her closet, she grabbed her white Von Dutch Trucker Hat, gathered her long blonde hair into a ponytail, and pulled it through the back of the hat.

"Cute," she said, approving her look. Hannah grabbed her crossbody shoulder bag and headed down to street level to wait for Travis.

She stepped out into the warm summer air. Bruno, the doorman, had taken up post outside, getting some fresh air and enjoying the sunshine.

"Good afternoon, Ms. Hannah," he greeted her. "Happy Labor Day. Are you enjoying your day off so far?"

Hannah's face radiated with excitement. "I sure am!"

Bruno had become a dear friend of hers. She often stopped and talked to him on shift, sometimes for hours. They talked about family, work, and the latest happenings in their lives.

"If you don't mind me saying, Ms. Hannah, you have been looking quite happy lately. There must be something, or *someone*, causing you to smile like that," he said with a wink.

Hannah was just about to start telling Bruno all about Travis, when he came walking up the sidewalk, swinging a picnic basket in one hand and a bouquet of flowers in the other. Hannah noticed that he also had a blanket draped over his shoulder.

Travis smiled as if it had been days since they had seen each other. The blanket began to slide off his shoulder as he tried to juggle everything in his hands. He reached out and handed Hannah the bouquet of flowers.

"These are for you. I found flowers this time," he said.

"The pretzel was pretty romantic too," she said, graciously accepting the flowers. "They are beautiful. Thank you." Hannah felt like she was floating on air.

Travis used his newly freed hand to grab the blanket that had slid down onto the sidewalk.

"Ah-hem," Bruno pretended to clear his throat, expectantly waiting for an introduction.

"Oh! I'm sorry! Bruno, this is Travis. Travis, this is Bruno," Hannah said, snapping out of her trance.

"Ah, so you're the one responsible for this big smile on her face," Bruno said. "I have never seen her so happy."

"She makes me happy too," Travis replied, winking at Hannah.

Bruno reached out for the flowers. "Allow me, Ms. Hannah. I'll take these in and put them in water for you. They will be behind the desk when you return."

"You are the best, Bruno. Thank you," Hannah said.

"You two have fun!" Bruno called out as they walked down the sidewalk arm in arm.

Travis and Hannah rode the subway uptown. When they got off at the Columbus Circle stop, Hannah realized where he was taking her.

"It's the perfect day for a picnic in Central Park. Don't you think?" Travis announced as he led her to the southwest entrance. Hannah was embarrassed to admit that she had never been to Central Park, a massive oasis of greenery and beauty in the middle of the bustling city.

"I have never been here," she admitted.

"I figured that," he replied with a smile.

They strolled lazily along the walkways until Travis found the perfect spot overlooking the lake. Hannah immediately recognized the iconic Bow Bridge from well-known movies, most recently, *Keeping the Faith*. Hannah had gone back to visit Audrey one cold, snowy weekend the winter before. They'd scoured the shelves at the local Blockbuster store, ahead of the storm, until they agreed on the romantic comedy based on the unlikely love triangle between a rabbi, priest, and their childhood friend Anna.

Dressed in their warmest pajamas with a bowl of freshly popped popcorn, they'd lain under a blanket on Audrey's futon, debating who Jenna Elfman's character, Anna, should choose: Father Brian Finn, played by Ed Norton, or Rabbi Jake Schram, played by Ben Stiller—both willing to risk it all to win her love.

Hannah once again felt the pang of missing her sister. She would make time next weekend to visit her, she promised herself.

"This is breathtaking," Hannah said, taking in all the scenery. Rowboats gently glided on the lake, passing slowly under the bridge. Couples in love stood atop the bridge, looking down at the glistening water below. Families were spread out on blankets, and energetic children ran free on the vast open lawn.

Travis set out the blanket for Hannah to sit down. He placed the picnic basket down and took a seat next to her. Hannah stretched out her legs and turned her face up to the sun. It was a beautiful day, with plenty of sunshine, disappearing for only a few seconds at a time behind small, white dotted clouds.

"Are you hungry?" Travis asked. "Scrap that question. I've seen your refrigerator. You are hungry," he replied to his own question.

Hannah snorted. She actually had been so swept up in the morning that she hadn't even thought of food. Suddenly she was ravenously starving.

Travis pulled out an assortment of thoughtfully selected picnic foods: aged cheeses, sliced meats, a French baguette, olives, grapes, and a chilled bottle of strawberry-flavored sparkling dessert wine. Travis had covered every detail, remembering also to bring small plates, napkins, and two flutes.

Hannah was impressed. "Wow, this is amazing."

"I stopped at Chelsea Market on my route yesterday. I have been planning this since Friday night. I was hoping that you would want to spend your day off with me," Travis said.

He popped open the sparkling wine and poured it into the flutes. They raised their glasses in a toast.

"To our day off together," Travis said.

"The first of many," Hannah responded, with a clink of her glass.

The strawberry wine was sweet and fizzy. It was the perfect accompaniment to a late summer picnic in the park. She sat back, watching the kids chase each other, screeching with joy. Hannah smiled, wondering what it would be like one day to be a mother.

Suddenly a beautiful butterfly, its black wings painted with an intricate pattern of bright turquoise, fluttered in front of Hannah's face. After dancing playfully around her for a moment, the butterfly landed directly on Hannah's hand. Hannah smiled with delight, trying not to move a muscle. She had never had a butterfly land on her like that.

Travis reached into the picnic basket and quickly pulled out his camera. "Someone from heaven is visiting you," Travis said, pulling the camera slowly up to his face. He caught the shot seconds before the butterfly took off.

"Is that what that means?" Hannah asked, wanting to believe it to be true.

"That's what I believe, at least. I think nature has a way of connecting us with those we have lost; you just have to believe," Travis said.

"Hmmm." Hannah pondered. She thought back to all the times she'd noticed a cardinal fly by. She had always tried to convince herself that it was her grandmother coming to visit, but she struggled to believe. Maybe Travis was right. Maybe all she had to do was open her mind and heart to the possibility.

Hannah turned her attention to the children playing a game of tag nearby. "Look at them, not a care in the world. I miss being a kid sometimes." She reflected back on her happy childhood.

"I don't know," Travis said.

Hannah, surprised by his response, turned to look at him with inquisitive eyes.

"I guess my childhood wasn't exactly ideal." Travis shrugged his shoulders. "When my dad left, I made a promise to my mom that we would be okay and that I would never leave her side. I suddenly became the man of the house at thirteen. I wouldn't change a thing about my life though. Well, except for one thing."

"What?" Hannah asked seriously.

"I would totally change my name! I mean, really, Mom? I wish she'd named me something simple like 'Matt' or 'John.' Travis sounds like a superhero; talk about pressure!" he joked.

Hannah laughed. Travis always knew how to lighten the mood.

"If I have a son one day, I'm going to name him 'James.' James has a strong, yet modest, ring to it," Travis said.

"James," Hannah repeated. "James Russell. I like it."

She picked up his hand and held it in her lap, resting her head on his shoulder.

Hannah knew it seemed crazy, since they had only known each other for a few days, but she felt like she was falling in love with Travis. Hannah had never felt that way about anyone before.

Tell him how you feel...

Hannah was just about to speak, when suddenly the moment was interrupted by the shrill sounds of a woman's frantic screams. Travis and Hannah were startled to their feet.

A woman about twenty feet away was standing at the edge of her blanket, flailing her arms in complete panic. "Somebody, please help my baby!" she screamed, dropping to her knees on the blanket.

Travis sprinted across the lawn, pushing through the crowd. On the blanket a small child lay rigid, arms and legs jerking, his eyes rolled back in his head.

Travis recognized what was happening immediately. Eli had suffered for years with seizures as a result of his cerebral palsy. Hannah stood there feeling helpless. She had no idea what was happening.

Suddenly a man from the crowd jumped in and grabbed the boy's arms, attempting to hold him still.

"No, let go!" Travis yelled with an authority in his voice Hannah hadn't heard before. "Do not hold him down! He needs space!"

The man didn't listen to Travis.

In one effortless motion, Travis grabbed the man by the back of the shirt, throwing him off the boy.

"Everybody, back up! Give him space!" Travis yelled to the crowd.

"Hannah, listen to me. I need you to clear everything from this blanket right away," he instructed her.

Hannah quickly jumped into action, pushing forks, plates, and toys off the blanket. The hysterical woman was standing over Travis, screaming and begging him to help.

"Are you Mom?" Travis calmly asked.

"Yes! Please help us! What is happening?" she screamed.

"He's having a seizure," Travis gently informed her. "He will be all right. You just have to stay calm. I need you to call 911 and let them know your son is having his first seizure."

A woman in the crowd handed the mother her cell phone and pulled her aside to help her call 911.

Travis carefully cradled the boy's head and gently turned him on his side. Crouching down next to him, he talked softly to the boy, "You're going to be all right. Everything is okay."

Travis was completely in control of the situation. Hannah stood frozen, wide-eyed and shaking.

Time felt like it was passing in slow motion. After what felt like an eternity, the boy slowly came to. His rigid muscles released, and his body was still. His mother dropped to her knees beside him, sobbing.

"Stay calm; talk to him softly," Travis reminded her.

Within moments an army of NYPD, FDNY, and EMS came barreling across the lawn, with equipment. They loaded the boy up onto the stretcher and escorted his mother along with him into the ambulance.

The crowd began to disperse, and Hannah let out a deep breath.

Travis turned to Hannah. "Are you okay?" he asked, rubbing her arm.

Before she could catch her breath to respond, an older gentleman from the crowd approached Travis.

"Excuse me," the man said, "I saw how you handled that. You are a true hero."

Travis blushed.

"Thank you, sir, but I am no hero. Those folks over there are the real heroes." Travis pointed to the FDNY, NYPD, and EMS.

The man reached out to shake Travis's hand. "Maybe you should join them one day."

"Oh, I'm not that brave," Travis replied modestly.

The man looked intently at Travis, still gripping his hand with a strong hold. "We never really know how brave we are until put to the test. Only then, what lies deep within us rises to the surface," he said cryptically, turning to walk away.

There was something about his words that sent a chill through Travis's body. Travis smiled an uneasy smile, unsure of what to say next. The man strolled away, resuming his leisurely day in the park, but his words lingered in Travis's head.

"Let's take a walk over the Bow Bridge," Travis said to Hannah, attempting to put the entire scene behind them.

Travis stopped by their blanket to grab his camera first. The elegantly shaped bridge had the appearance similar to a violinist's bow. Though appearing to be built of whitewashed stone, the structure was actually constructed of cast iron. As they stepped onto the hardwood walkway, Hannah admired the stunning architecture of the bridge. She studied the interlocking circles along the banisters as they walked to the crest. Travis snapped pictures along the way of anything that caught his eye.

"That's Fifth Avenue right there." He pointed with his chin, snapping several pictures with his camera. "Smile," Travis said, turning to point the camera at her.

Hannah wasn't ready for a photo. She quickly brushed her long ponytail over her shoulder, straightening her Von Dutch hat, and smiled.

"All right, it's my turn with that camera," Hannah said, grabbing it out of his hand.

She took a close-up of Travis, then another, giggling with each click.

"Hey!" he exclaimed, playfully grabbing for the camera.

Hannah quickly hid it behind her back. Travis tried to reach around her, but with each attempt she shuffled backward, out of his reach. Finally he caught Hannah in his strong arms, leaned her back, and kissed her romantically on top of the Bow Bridge. They couldn't have been any more in love.

CHAPTER 10

Tuesday, September 4, 2001
8:00 a.m.

Audrey sat in her academy seat, fidgeting anxiously. It was the day of the final run qualification. She was nervous about passing but plaguing her even more was the terrible feeling she had about what was going to happen to Preston.

She knew the news about what had happened Friday night had already circulated throughout the department, and she was sure it was the first item on the chief's desk that morning. To make matters worse, she had hoped the swelling in her face would have gone down over the long weekend, but she was still having trouble breathing through her nose. As long as Preston was there with her, she could get through the qualification.

"Please, don't let Preston get kicked out of the academy," she quietly begged under her breath.

The guys started to filter into the academy room, groggy and unmotivated after the long weekend. Preston walked through the door, with a nervous look on his face. He placed his duty bag on the floor by his feet and rolled the chair out to sit down.

"Hey," he feebly greeted Audrey, anxiously pulling statute books out of his bag.

Ethan and Jonathan shuffled in together, talking softly. She knew they were talking about the events of Friday night. Everyone was speculating about what would happen to Preston. The door suddenly flew open with force. Scott stormed in, wearing his navy-blue academy baseball hat, pulled down low.

What a coward, she thought. He can't even show his face.

Scott threw his bag down on the floor and sat down in his chair with a huff. He looked up from under his brim to give Preston a nasty look.

Audrey wondered what the other guys thought about what Scott had said. She knew that Preston had stuck up for her, but she didn't really know exactly where the rest of them stood. Would they ultimately side with one of the guys over her, simply because he was a guy? Did they stand idly by that night while Scott disparaged her? Her thoughts were suddenly interrupted. Jonathan broke the silence in the room.

"Hey, Scott, you're going to have to take off that hat for the Pledge of Allegiance anyway, so you might as well show your face now," Jonathan said, his usual lighthearted tone gone.

Scott ignored Jonathan and looked over at Preston.

"This isn't going away, you know," Scott threatened as he pointed across the room. "I know people."

Ethan jumped in without missing a beat. "You *know* people?" Ethan mocked, "Imaginary friends don't count. Face it.

You got tuned up and you deserved it." Ethan's face turned serious as he leaned forward across the desk. "And if you ever say anything like that again," he continued, "I'll be the one to kick your ass."

The door to the academy room suddenly opened again. Audrey's heart dropped when she saw Eileen, the chief's secretary, enter the room.

Eileen was a soft-spoken, nurturing woman in her early fifties, with short, bobbed blonde hair and hazel eyes. The mother of two college-aged boys, Eileen suffered terribly from empty nest syndrome. Audrey was always comforted by her motherly presence when she saw her. Unfortunately Eileen only made the trip down the hall from the chief's office when it was an urgent matter. Audrey knew exactly why she was there that morning.

"Recruit Briggs…um…the chief would like to see you," Eileen nervously said.

Her desk was located directly outside of the chief's door, so she was privy to all of the happenings in the department before anyone else was. Her body language clearly revealed it didn't look good for Preston.

Audrey felt responsible for the whole thing. Anyone who knew Preston knew he was kind and gentle. He was suddenly in a terrible situation because of her.

Preston made eye contact with Audrey as he stood up and walked toward the door. Audrey's heart sunk into her stomach.

Eileen walked Preston out of the classroom, disappearing into the hallway. Audrey's chest heaved with each stressed breath. Before she even had time to process what had just happened, the instructor entered the room to begin class. They were going to learn how to administer a Breathalyzer test that morning, but she couldn't think of anything other than Preston and what would happen to him.

"Get that hat off your head," the instructor barked at Scott.

Scott begrudgingly removed his hat, revealing a big black ring around his left eye.

Audrey stared directly at him. She knew he could feel her eyes on him, but he was too cowardly to look up at her.

They stood for the Pledge of Allegiance as they did each day and transitioned right into Breathalyzer 101.

Five minutes into the instruction, the door to the room opened again. Preston walked in, his face flushed. He walked over to his seat and gathered his statute books from the desk. Audrey watched in shock as Preston packed all of his belongings into his bag.

This cannot be happening.

Preston ducked low, trying not to interrupt the lesson, but everyone's focus was on him. He zipped up his duty bag. Taking a step toward the door, he leaned down to Audrey and whispered, "I would do it again." Just like that, Preston disappeared out through the door, escorted down the hallway by an officer in uniform.

Audrey felt like she was going to cry. She quickly composed herself, realizing Scott would love nothing more than to see break down. Audrey kept a stone look on her face, while her emotions churned inside. She was not listening to a word about the Breathalyzer machine.

She had to pull herself together. The final run was next. Over the course of the academy, there were four qualifying runs. After five months of rigorous training, all recruits were expected to be in top physical shape. There would be no second chance. Anyone who failed the final run failed out of the academy on the spot.

Audrey was not a strong runner. She finished last every time. Preston had always stood on the sidelines, cheering her on, but now she didn't have him. She could hardly breathe through her broken, swollen nose, and there was still terrible pounding in her head. Both of her eyes were still black and blue.

Failure is not an option, she reminded herself.

Audrey noticed the guys putting their DUI books away and suddenly realized class had ended. It was time to get changed into PT gear. All the guys went in one direction to their locker room, and she walked down the hall to hers, alone.

She was tiring of the academy, and it was starting to show. No longer did she have patience for the boring classroom academics. Being a cop couldn't be learned in a book. She was ready to get out on the street.

Audrey was always the first recruit ready for PT. There was no one to talk to in the locker room, nothing to distract her from her task of getting changed. She was always the first outside.

Audrey pushed on the heavy exterior door leading her out into the sticky air. Her face immediately began to throb from the humidity. She walked across the field, toward the fenced-in running track, already feeling lightheaded.

Audrey didn't expect anyone to be at the track yet. As she got closer, she noticed a tall, slim—yet broad-shouldered—young officer in uniform. He was holding a clipboard in one hand, while resting the other arm on his gun belt. A stopwatch hung around his neck. Clearly he was there to administer the final run qualification. When he noticed Audrey approach, he straightened up, as if he had been expecting her specifically.

"Hey, Mike O'Shea," he said, extending his arm for a handshake. "Recruit Moretti, right?"

The fact that he knew exactly who she was irritated her immediately. It exacerbated her already bad mood. Trying to respond politely, she replied, "Yes, Audrey Moretti."

O'Shea assessed her swollen face. "Listen, I'm sure they will make an exception and let you qualify next week instead if you—"

Audrey cut him off. "I'm all set," she said curtly.

She didn't mean to be rude, but she knew that was simply not an option. It would be perceived, especially by guys like Scott and Sergeant Gaston, as special treatment. She would be demeaned "weak" and labeled "incapable." She had to earn everything twice as hard as the guys. She had to prove herself twice as much.

"Okay, I respect that," O'Shea said, smiling at her. "You are going to make a great cop."

His slightly crooked smile revealed a small dimple in his left cheek. Audrey for the first time noticed how handsome he was. She turned her head away, suddenly remembering how horrific her face looked.

"I'd better go stretch," Audrey said, taking a few steps to the side.

She leaned over to stretch her hamstrings, turning her head slyly to sneak a glimpse. O'Shea was tall and muscular, with wide strong shoulders. She guessed he was around twenty-eight years old. His hair was shaved on the sides, and just long enough on top to reveal wavy, thick blond hair. She couldn't help but notice his arms flexing as he held the clipboard up to read. Being early September, they hadn't changed over to long-sleeved uniforms yet. His short-sleeved uniform shirt revealed on his left forearm a brightly colored tattoo of the American Flag.

Audrey tried to get herself to focus. Suddenly she was not sure if the butterflies in her stomach were about the run or O'Shea.

Jonathan and Ethan had made their way to the track and joined in stretching with her. Scott stood alone, along the fence.

Ethan looked over his shoulder at Scott and shook his head. "Can you believe that guy?" he said purposely loud enough for Scott to hear. Ethan then turned his attention toward Audrey. "Are you good, Audrey?"

It was obvious that she was still in pain.

"I'm going to have to be. What's my other option?" she asked rhetorically.

"Good luck, Audrey," Jonathan said, giving her a high five. "You've got this."

"Thanks, guys," she said.

The class lined up at the starting line and listened for O'Shea's instructions.

"All right, everyone, you know the deal by now. This is your final mile and a half run. That is six laps around the track. You all know your qualifying times, so pace yourselves accordingly. I'll be recording each of your finish times. Good luck to you all." He glanced quickly at Audrey.

O'Shea gave them a moment to organize themselves side by side on the starting line. Audrey wished she could ignore the throbbing in her face and the pounding in her head from her broken nose. Most of all, she wished Preston was lined up right next to her on that starting line, the way he always had been.

"Get ready, recruits!" O'Shea announced, holding the stopwatch in position.

"Go!" he yelled, pressing the button on the top of the stopwatch to begin the timer.

Audrey had made the mistake many times of starting out too fast, causing her to lose steam in the final laps. She also knew she couldn't start off too slow, or she would run out of time. It was a delicate balance between pass and fail.

The class started together as a group, but with each step she watched the guys pull ahead of her. Soon she knew they would come around the track again, lapping her from behind.

Qualifying times were determined by a metric, combining age and gender. Audrey was never more painfully aware that she was the only female in the class than during the run qualifications. Her head started pounding shortly into the first lap. The swelling of the membranes inside of her broken nose did not allow much air to pass through. She tried to breathe through her mouth instead, but that quickly made her chest burn. She was not getting enough oxygen into her lungs. Unable to regulate her breathing, she began to slow down. Audrey became aware that she was in trouble. Ethan and Jonathan were coming up from behind her.

"Keep going, Audrey," they encouraged her as they passed her on the track, patting her back.

Soon all of the guys had finished and were standing on the sidelines, breathing heavily. She glanced at her running watch. She was falling way behind.

Halfway through her fourth lap, she started to feel dizzy. The feeling was familiar. It was the same way she'd felt the day her nose got broken in the baton ring. She had refused to go down that day; she had refused to quit.

Audrey had to find that fire again, but without Preston there, she just wanted to give up. Her mind started to wander, imagining graduation day without Preston. He deserved to be there. How could she finish the academy and he not?

The negative thoughts in her head started to take over her will to succeed. Her body and brain began shutting down. All Audrey could feel was the pressure in her face, as air tried to pass through her swollen nose, and the lightness in her head from the lack of oxygen.

She was just about to give up, when she heard the clanking of keys and the sound of heavy footsteps coming up from behind her. Audrey suddenly realized that O'Shea was running beside her, with his heavy boots and thirty-pound gun belt still on.

"Keep going, Audrey. You are almost there," O'Shea said calmly. Holding the stopwatch up to check the time, he added, "One more lap, but we need to pick up the pace, okay?"

Audrey had no air in her lungs to speak. She nodded, understanding exactly what he was telling her. She was so close to finishing, but she was also so close to failing. She had to dig deep and find whatever strength she had left to run faster.

Then O'Shea said something that ignited the last bit of energy and grit she had left inside. "Don't give Gaston what he wants."

How did he know about Sergeant Gaston? What else had Sergeant Gaston said about her?

O'Shea's words shot down to her soul in an instant, as if he had ignited a stick of dynamite inside of her. Fire came up from within, and suddenly her legs were pumping faster than they ever had before. Her body propelled forward as though her feet weren't even touching the ground. O'Shea kept up right beside her, helping her keep pace. All she could hear was the pounding of his heavy black boots hitting the track and the jingling of the tools on his gun belt. Audrey was so focused that she did not even realize she had crossed the finish line.

"That's it!" O'Shea exclaimed as he hit the stopwatch timer. "You passed by five seconds."

Audrey stumbled over to the side, by the fence, and sat down just in time before she passed out. She tried to blink away the stars that were spinning around in front of her eyes. Someone brought over a bottle of water. She was too consumed with her condition to notice who, but she assumed it was either Jonathan or Ethan. If Preston were there, he would have been sitting right next to her.

After a few minutes, O'Shea walked over and squatted down next to her. "You did it. Great job!"

Audrey was still trying to catch her breath. "Thank you for doing that," she replied through gasps of air.

"Do you need a few minutes before we go in?" O'Shea asked.

"No, I'm okay."

O'Shea stood up and reached his hand out to help her up. Her heart skipped a beat, noticing his light green eyes up close. *Why is he being so nice to me?*

Suddenly a terrible thought crossed Audrey's mind. Her heart suddenly sank with the thought of the rumor going around about her. She turned abruptly, leaving O'Shea standing awkwardly by himself. He jogged after her to catch up.

"Hey, wait up," he called ahead to her, confused.

Audrey picked up the pace, making a beeline to the building. "Thanks again." She waved over her shoulder, never looking back at him as she ducked into the building.

Once inside the solitude of the woman's locker room, she collapsed on the long rickety wooden bench. She was mentally and physically exhausted. For the first time she wondered if becoming a police officer was worth it. Once it was all she had ever wanted, but she found herself enduring things she'd never imagined. It didn't just affect her. Preston was possibly kicked out of the academy for good—because of *her*. That's what hurt the most.

Audrey refused to cry, but she felt like she was going to burst. *Get up*, she scolded herself. She forced herself to her feet, feeling the blood immediately rush to her nose. When she caught a glimpse of her battered face in the wall mirror, she boiled over. Turning toward the lockers, Audrey let out a deep roar of pure frustration. Losing control, she kicked a locker as hard as she could, producing a large dent in the door.

Suddenly a toilet flushed from the stalls, startling Audrey. She thought she was alone in the locker room.

A female officer in her late fifties appeared from the stalls, zipping up the fly of her khaki pants. Her ultra-short red hair was styled upward on top. She was dressed in the class B uniform, which consisted of a navy blue polo shirt—with the department patch sewn on the chest—khaki pants, and black lace-up shoes. Audrey had not noticed the holstered gun on the corner chair when she'd entered the locker room.

You need to be more observant, Audrey.

The female officer nonchalantly weaved the holster through her belt and fastened her belt buckle. She was completely unfazed by Audrey's outburst.

Audrey stood in awkward silence for a moment until the officer finally spoke. "I'm Detective Hansen. You can call me Sharon," she spoke from across the locker room while tucking the polo shirt into her belt.

Audrey didn't have a chance to introduce herself before Sharon continued talking.

"I wish I could tell you it gets easier, kid. I have been on the job for twenty-five years. If you think it is bad now, imagine being a female cop here back then. You wouldn't believe the stories I could tell you."

"I believe it," Audrey replied. "I'm sorry about that; I just—" she said, beginning to apologize for kicking the locker.

Detective Hansen interrupted Audrey's apology. "You've reached your breaking point? Want to give up? Completely had it? Don't do it. You have just as much right to be here as they do."

"Yeah, but…it's just that there is this rumor going around that isn't true," Audrey began to explain.

"Let me guess. The rumor is that you are sleeping with one of the guys. Honey, these guys have had me sleeping with every guy in this department...and I'm gay," Sharon said, shaking her head. "Hey, I heard about what happened with Riccio." Sharon changed the subject. "I heard you didn't go down though. You're going to be just fine, kid."

Sharon sat down in the chair and brushed off her black shoes.

"I was the first female officer in this department. I came on the job in 1976. You would think by the year 2001, there would be way more female cops here than there are. Yet you are the only female in your academy class. This department has 125 men and only four females. Do you know what that means?" Sharon finally looked up at Audrey.

Audrey began to speak, but she quickly realized that Sharon was not actually asking her a question.

"You will have to be tougher, stronger, and braver than all of them put together to get the respect you deserve," Sharon answered.

Audrey sat silent, absorbing what Sharon was saying.

Suddenly Sharon stood up from the chair. "Take a shower, get changed, and take a few minutes to get your mind right. I'm teaching your next class, so don't worry about being a few minutes late.

"Thanks," Audrey said as Sharon walked out of the locker room.

Audrey sat on the lonely bench for a few minutes, digesting everything Sharon had said.

Preston!

She reached into her duty bag on top of the bench and grabbed her cell phone, hoping to see a voicemail from Preston. There were no missed calls and no voicemails. She dialed his number. It went directly to voicemail.

"Preston, hey, it's me. Please call me, and let me know what is going on. I can't do this without you. I just beat up a locker. I'm a mess. Call me back as soon as you can." Audrey flipped the phone shut.

Audrey got cleaned up as fast as she could and took a deep breath as she walked down the hall to the academy classroom. She arrived just in time for class. Sharon was just beginning crime scene investigation instruction. Sharon's voice was different. It was stern and hard, much different than the way she spoke to Audrey in the locker room. Her commanding presence had the guys sitting upright, with full attention. Sharon gave Audrey a nod of acknowledgement when she entered the room. Audrey even noticed a very brief, slight smile appear on her face before quickly resuming her instruction.

Audrey thought back to their conversation in the locker room. "You can call me Sharon," she had said to Audrey. Audrey wondered if she had just made her first female friend on the job.

The next hour raced by as Audrey feverishly took notes on everything Sharon taught. Physical evidence and collection fascinated Audrey. She hoped to one day become a detective, just like Sharon.

As soon as the class ended, Audrey's thoughts immediately raced back to Preston.

She quickly packed up her books and placed them into her duty bag. She stood up quickly and flung her duty bag over her shoulder.

"Thank you, Shar—Detective Hansen," Audrey said, catching herself.

"See you tomorrow, kid," Sharon replied with a smile.

Audrey spent the rest of the day sneaking into the bathroom during breaks to call Preston. Each time it went directly to voicemail.

Four o'clock finally came. She had only made it through one day without Preston, and it felt like an eternity.

Audrey shuffled alongside the guys on their way to the parking lot. Her duty bag was getting heavier and heavier by the day. By the last weeks of the academy, it was so stuffed full of binders and statute books that her aching muscles screamed as the strap pulled heavily down on her shoulder. It had been a long afternoon inside, with no windows. She winced at the sight of sunlight. As soon as she hit the fresh air, she came to almost a complete stop. Standing in the parking lot was O'Shea. She realized he was waiting for her. Audrey's temper started to flare.

What is he doing here? The audacity of this guy!

"Hey!" he said, lighting up when he saw her. "I just wanted to check on you and see how you were feeling from this morning?"

Audrey had no energy left to respond tactfully. "Listen, you are wasting your time. I am not going to sleep with you." She held up her hand for him to stop.

O'Shea stopped suddenly, as if he had walked into a brick wall. "Um...w-w-wow," he stuttered in shock. "That was not my intention at all. I apologize if I made you uncomfortable."

Audrey could see the hurt and embarrassment in his eyes. He turned and walked back toward the police department.

She stood frozen for a moment, horrified by her own response. She hadn't meant to be hurtful. She was just in a bad place—defensive, angry, and depleted. Seeing the hurt look in his eyes made her feel even worse, but it was too late to take it back.

The day felt like an epic failure.

The moment she got into the car, her cell phone rang.

"Preston! I've been worried sick about you!" she exclaimed into the phone.

"Hey, Audrey, I'm sorry I haven't answered. I just couldn't bring myself to talk to anyone. I have been walking around in circles, trying to figure out what I'm going to do if I get kicked out."

"Preston, you aren't going to get kicked out—" Audrey started to say.

"It is officially with internal affairs," Preston said, interrupting her. "I'm suspended until the outcome of the investigation."

"It's an internal investigation?" Audrey exclaimed. Her mind raced.

"I can talk to the investigator and clear up this whole mess. I'll just explain everything. You will be back in no time," Audrey said.

"It doesn't look good for a recruit to have an internal investigation, Audrey. The chief was not happy."

"We are going to get you back, Preston. Don't worry. I am not graduating this academy without you," she said emphatically.

Preston sighed. "It's not looking good, but I guess we'll see."

"Hey, have you heard of a guy named O'Shea, by any chance?" Audrey blurted out.

She immediately felt self-centered for asking the question in the middle of Preston's crisis, but he seemed relieved to change the subject.

"Yeah, I actually know him pretty well. We were in the same National Guard unit for a couple of years. Great guy," he answered.

Audrey's heart sank.

"Is he a slick, womanizing kind of guy?" she asked, feeling awkward about the question.

"O'Shea? Nah, he's a real stand-up kind of guy, actually. Why?" Preston asked.

Audrey wanted to shrink under the driver's seat of her car and disappear.

"Ugh…" She sighed. "I think I messed up big-time. I'll tell you another time. Right now let's just concentrate on getting you back to the academy. I'll talk to you tomorrow, Preston."

Flipping the phone closed to hang up, she rested her forehead on the steering wheel and closed her eyes.

Tomorrow has to be a better day…

CHAPTER 11

Tuesday, September 4, 2001
7:45 a.m.

Travis skipped along the busy sidewalks toward Hannah's apartment. He was taking a different route to the subway that morning, walking a few blocks over to meet Hannah first.

Travis felt on top of the world. The connection he had with Hannah felt natural, as though they had known each other for years. He could not believe it had only been a few days since they first met in the subway.

Travis rounded the corner and spotted Hannah standing under the awning of her building, waiting for him. Her long blonde curls cascaded over her black blazer. Hannah's face lit up when she saw him coming.

"Good morning, lovely lady," Travis greeted her. He kissed her hand, showering her with his irresistible charm.

"Good morning. I wish we could go back to work on a Tuesday every week," she said. She was still swept up by the whirlwind, romantic long weekend they'd just had.

"Well, I have a surprise for you," Travis informed her as they walked together to the subway station.

"Of course you do," Hannah replied.

Travis was full of surprises, and it made her feel alive. In all of the time she had lived in Manhattan, she hadn't experienced before the magic of the city. She was suddenly trying new things and going on adventures she'd never thought possible. He took her out of her comfort zone into a world of awe and amazement.

"I want to take you to the top of the world!" Travis announced dramatically, with his arms stretched up into the air.

Hannah looked at him apprehensively. "That sounds high. Heights and I don't mix."

"We don't even have to go far to get there. It's actually right above your head each day," Travis said.

"If you are referring to the observation deck on top of the South Tower, no way!" she responded.

Travis had anticipated her reaction and was prepared with his rebuttal. "Just hear me out. Imagine the most breathtaking views of New York City. On a clear day like today, you can see up to fifty miles."

They came to the steps of their subway station.

"Nope," Hannah said definitively. "The eighty-fourth floor of the tower is as high as I go, and even that terrifies me most days."

Travis looked at her incredulously as they entered the subway station, and walked swiftly toward the platform. "I cannot believe you've worked in the South Tower for two years and never ventured up there."

Suddenly, Travis stopped Hannah in the middle of the flow of traffic. People impatiently went around them.

"This is where it all started," Travis said, standing in the exact spot where they collided days before.

"I remember like it was yesterday," Hannah said sarcastically. "Let's go before we miss our train again."

Hannah knew she was only momentarily let off the hook about going to the observation deck. The train appeared from the dark tunnel in the distance, the bright lights inside the train illuminated against the dark windowless subway station. The train came clunking and screeching to a stop in front of them. They stepped up onto the train from the platform. There were no available seats, but that didn't bother Hannah one bit. With Travis's arms wrapped around her as the train lurched around corners and sped toward their stop below the World Trade Center, she was reminded of how safe she felt with him. She recalled how all of the fear had disappeared as she crossed the Brooklyn Bridge with him by her side. Had she let her fear take over, she would have missed an incredible experience.

Hannah turned to face Travis. "I hear there's a Nathan's Hot Dogs up on the observation floor," she said with a sly smile.

"I'll meet you at our fountain at five o'clock," Travis said.

Our fountain. Hannah loved the sound of that.

They filtered out of the subway station into the World Trade Center Mall, passing the storefronts along the way. There was a buzz in the air, an energy that could not be described with words. Thousands of people were on their way to work in the towers. Some stopped to shop in the high-end stores with their extra time; others short on time made a beeline to the revolving doors leading to the elevators. Everyone who had the honor of walking through those corridors knew that working at the World Trade Center was special.

Travis stopped in front of the coffee kiosk Hannah passed each day.

"I'm going to grab a coffee here; do you want anything?" he politely offered.

Hannah looked down at her watch. It was 8:25 a.m. She only had five minutes to get to the office.

"Thank you, but I don't have time. I can't be late," she said hurriedly.

"Okay. I'll meet you at the fountain later." Travis kissed her sweetly on the cheek.

Hannah was enjoying the old-fashioned courtship. His gentle kiss on her cheek made her heart flutter.

"Oh and hey," he called to her as she started to walk away, "don't forget to look up. Maybe you will see me." He flashed his bright smile.

Hannah winked back at him, taking in one more glance before turning toward the large glass turnstile doors that separated the mall from the lobby of the South Tower. She picked up her pace, crossing the lobby to the South Tower elevators. Suddenly, she heard her name being called frantically.

"Hannah!" The sound echoed off the large stainless steel elevator doors and marble walls of the lobby.

She turned to see Miles running toward her, waving his hand in the air to catch her attention.

He pushed through the crowd that stood waiting for the express elevator to descend from the seventy-eighth floor.

"She said yes. She said yes!" Miles exclaimed.

Hannah's face lit up. "Miles! I am so happy for you! Congratulations. I told you she would say yes!"

Miles paused for a moment to catch his breath. "You should have seen her face. She didn't expect it at all. It was perfect! We could see clear across Manhattan in every direction. She was so in awe of the view that she hadn't noticed me pull out the ring. When she looked back at me to point out the Empire State Building, I was on my knee with the ring out in front of her!"

Hannah was totally entranced, imagining Miles and Stephanie's romantic moment up on the observation deck, overlooking all of Manhattan. There was no more magical place to fall in love than New York City. She was suddenly looking forward to Travis taking her to the top of the world later that day.

Miles continued talking as they entered the express elevator to the sky lobby. "We decided we don't want a long engagement. I hope you don't have any plans for New Year's Eve yet," Miles said, his eyes twinkling with excitement.

Hannah's face lit up with surprise. "I'm invited?"

"Of course you are invited! You're one of my best friends. Stephanie remembers you from the Christmas party last year. She really likes you. I remember how nervous she was to meet everyone, and you made her feel so welcome."

"I really like her too. You two were made for each other, Miles."

The elevator propelled seventy-eight floors upward in seconds.

Hannah imagined herself on Travis's arm, walking into a fancy wedding venue on New Year's Eve. She couldn't wait to celebrate the union between Miles and Stephanie. She would dance slowly with Travis on the dance floor and talk about how that would one day be them. Hannah was so excited to ask Travis to be her date, and she decided there would be no better place to do so than the top of the South Tower later that afternoon.

Shuffling out of the elevator into the seventy-eighth-floor Sky Lobby, Hannah turned to Miles. "Hey, how did you know that Stephanie was the one?"

Miles thought for a moment, leading the way to their express elevator. "I can't really explain it. It was a feeling inside that I just knew. I felt like I had known her my whole life. When we were together, everything else faded away, kind of like we were the only two in all of New York City," Miles explained.

Miles had just described the exact way Hannah felt about Travis.

"She was the first thought in my mind in the morning, and the last when I went to sleep. You just know, I guess," Miles continued.

"When did you tell her how you felt?"

"We were on our third date, and I just couldn't hold it in. I thought to myself, why wait? You never know if you will ever have the chance to say it again. I could have walked out of the restaurant that night and got hit by a city bus, and she would have never known that I was in love with her. That would have been tragic." Miles shook his head at the thought.

Hannah stared off for a moment, thinking about what Miles had just said. That thought had never crossed her mind.

After all, they were so young. They had plenty of time to tell each other how they felt. She hadn't considered the unexpected. She couldn't imagine the regret of the unspoken. What if she never got to tell him how she felt?

"That night, I looked up from our chocolate molten lava cake. I stared directly into her eyes and blurted out that I was in love with her," Miles said, staring off dreamily, recalling the moment.

Miles was still lost in his thoughts as they stepped into the local elevator. He reached through the crowd to press the button for the eighty-fourth floor.

"What did she say when you told her?" Hannah asked with anticipation.

"She said she was in love with me too. Look at us now. We are getting married!" Miles said, his face radiating happiness.

The elevator stopped at each floor, letting people off on the way up. They finally reached their floor. Miles and Hannah shuffled past the remaining people on the elevator. The elevators, restrooms, and three stairwells were all centrally located in the core of each floor.

Marilyn caught sight of Hannah and Miles approaching. She buzzed open the large glass door and jumped to her feet in anticipation. "Well?" she asked Miles, holding up her crossed fingers.

"She said yes!" he proudly announced.

Marilyn squealed in excitement. "Congratulations! I can't wait for you two to start having babies!"

Hannah rolled her eyes playfully.

"You will get it one day, my dear Hannah, trust me. Speaking of babies, I have some exciting news too," Marilyn announced. "I am having another grandbaby!"

"Oh how wonderful, Marilyn!" Hannah said.

"All of this good news lately, and so much love in the air!" Marilyn looked cautiously around the room for signs of Berkley lurking. "Now back to reality." She shooed Hannah and Miles along their way.

Hannah placed her briefcase down on the floor in her cubicle. She booted up her computer and then walked briskly to the conference room to start prepping for the nine o'clock meeting. She loved when the conference room was empty and quiet. She could hear her own thoughts for those few short moments in her day. Looking out at the North Tower, she wondered if Travis had made it up to the 104th floor yet with his fresh cup of coffee.

Hannah stepped closer to the windows cautiously, gazing up to the top of the North Tower. For a moment, she entertained the idea that she might see him. Even though she knew that was impossible, it comforted her just knowing she could look over and that he was somewhere up there.

CHAPTER 12

Tuesday, September 2, 2001
5:00 p.m.

Hannah paced back and forth in front of the fountain in the plaza. She leaned back and craned her neck to find where the towers ended and the sky began. She suddenly had second thoughts about going up to the observation deck. From where she stood down below, it looked as if the tower reached into the heavens.

"I can't do this. No way am I doing this," Hannah frantically said to herself.

"Too late. I already bought the tickets." Travis's voice startled Hannah. He came up from behind her and placed his hands on her shoulders. "I promise you will love it." His soft blue eyes reassured her.

Travis took her hand and led her into the South Tower, and then up to the mezzanine level, to the ticketing area for the observation deck. Already having their tickets in hand, they proceeded directly to the roped lines. A young man in his early twenties, wearing a blue polo uniform shirt and dress pants, cheerfully greeted them.

"How many today?" the employee asked.

"Just the two of us," Travis responded, handing him their tickets.

The man checked the tickets and then clicked the counter in his hand, adding two to his tally.

"Enjoy," he said, gesturing them to proceed.

They had taken just a few steps forward, when a woman, wearing the same blue polo shirt and dress pants as the ticket clerk, approached them with a camera in her hand. Behind her was a photo station. She was luring tourists over for a souvenir photo of their day at the World Trade Center.

"Would you like your picture taken?" she asked.

"No, thank you," Hannah responded politely.

"Actually, sure, that would be great. Thank you." Travis smiled at Hannah, aware that she was not as enthused about the picture as he was. He grabbed her hand, pulling her toward the photographer's staging area.

"I look awful! Look at me, I'm a mess," Hannah protested.

"You look beautiful," he reassured her.

The photographer positioned Travis and Hannah in front of the lighting umbrella and snapped several shots. "Now hold your arms up, like you are touching the sky," she instructed.

Hannah and Travis complied, feeling as silly as they looked. They reached their arms up over their heads and posed for the camera. The photographer then handed Travis a ticket with a number and explained where to purchase their souvenir photo. Hannah wasn't listening; she was too nervous.

They continued walking ahead, winding through red velvet ropes until they reached the metal detectors. Hannah felt relieved at the sight of security. They were checking bags and scanning bodies. She felt safe, reassured by the security measures in place.

Enjoy your trip to the top of the world," the security officer said cheerily, motioning for them to proceed down the hall.

As they walked down the corridor toward the elevators, Hannah studied the large-framed posters of the current Broadway performances that were displayed on the walls: *Rent*; *42nd Street*; *The Phantom of the Opera*; *Beauty and the Beast*; *Chicago…*

Travis noticed Hannah studying the framed signs. "Which ones have you seen?"

"Oh," Hannah said, sounding a little embarrassed, "I have never been to a Broadway show."

"You have never been to a Broadway show?" Travis asked.

Hannah shook her head, still studying the framed posters on the wall.

Travis likewise shook his head, but in his case, out of disbelief. "Well then, I will just have to take you to see them all."

At the end of the corridor, a woman wearing the blue polo shirt uniform was stationed next to the last silver stanchion in front of the elevators. "How many?" she asked.

"Two," Hannah answered nervously. She had butterflies in her stomach.

The woman clicked the small silver counter in her hand and directed them to join the group that was waiting in front of the elevator doors. "The elevator will be here in just a moment. Please step aside to allow passengers to unload before getting on."

Hannah could tell by her robotic tone that she made that announcement dozens of times that day. As promised, the elevator arrived within moments. The doors chimed as they opened, revealing dozens of smiling faces. No one looked scared or upset. It put Hannah's mind at ease. She grabbed Travis's hand as they shuffled into the elevator with the group.

There was some small talk among the strangers in the elevator and a few nervous laughs as they rose higher and higher into the sky. Hannah felt her ears pop from the rapid change in altitude as the elevator made its way to the 107th floor interior observation area. Suddenly, Hannah started to feel a wave of panic rise inside. She imagined the speeding elevator failing to stop at the top, launching them off of the building into the air. She couldn't stop her mind from imagining what a free fall from that height would be like. Her anxiety was about to explode into an embarrassing scene when the elevator came to a halt on the 107th floor. Her knees wobbled as she stepped off the elevator. Straight ahead a banner read WELCOME TO OUR WORLD.

When they rounded the corner to the interior observation area, Hannah saw hundreds of people lining the windows, looking down at the tops of bridges and skyscrapers below. Benches lined the windows, allowing spectators to relax while taking in the incredible views. Kiosks were positioned every few feet, providing visitors an educational overview from that vantage point. There was even a gift shop, and to Hannah's delight, Nathan's Hot Dogs, disguised as a subway car.

They walked closer to the windows, Hannah's knees wobbling with each step. Travis pointed out the window. "There's the Verrazano Bridge."

Hannah reluctantly moved closer to the window, peeking down at the view below. The bridge looked as small as a child's toy from that high. In fact, the entire city looked like a toy model from that height. Hannah noticed the boats zipping by on the water below, leaving tiny white trails of churned water behind. The people walking along the riverfront below looked as small as ants.

They stopped along the windows, each view different from the last. Travis pointed out landmarks along the way: the Statue of Liberty, the Chrysler Building, the Empire State Building. Straight down below, he pointed out Battery Park.

"Are you ready for the top?" Travis asked.

"I think so," Hannah said hesitantly.

They slowly walked toward the escalators that would bring them to the outdoor observation deck, three floors above. Hannah stalled, stopping in front of a penny press machine. "Do you have any change?" she asked.

Travis reached into his pocket and pulled out the change he'd received from his coffee that morning. Sifting through it, he pulled out one shiny penny and two quarters.

Hannah placed the coins in the silver tray and slid it forward into the machine. She looked through the different images and selected the Twin Towers with the cityscape in the background.

"You can do the honors," Hannah offered.

Travis grabbed the handle and cranked the lever, threading the penny through the gears until it clinked into the coin receiver. Hannah held it up. Stamped into the flattened penny was an imprint of the Twin Towers, rising high above the cityscape. Inscribed at the top, it read THE WORLD TRADE CENTER, 2001.

Hannah handed the penny to Travis. "You keep it," she said.

"I will cherish this forever," he said playfully, holding the penny to his heart.

Hannah mustered her courage and stepped onto the escalator. On the ride up, she noticed that the walls were painted a joyful blue, even the ceilings were blue. They rode three levels up to the 110th floor. At the top, a glass revolving door brought spectators out to the outdoor platform on the roof.

Hannah let Travis go first. She took a deep breath and entered into the vestibule after him. Taking a few cautious steps out onto the blue walkway, she gasped at the sight. With nothing more than air between her and the views of the city, she felt as if she were flying. She felt like a bird soaring high in the sky, looking down at the wonders below. No walls or windows in front of her, just the wind blowing through her hair and the city laid out in front of her.

It was a clear day, giving way to crystal views as far as she could see. Hannah's curiosity took over her fear as she stepped closer to the railing. She could not believe her eyes. A helicopter was flying *below*. She stepped back to give herself a moment.

"Travis, helicopters are flying *below* us!" Hannah said, catching her breath.

Travis redirected her to the other side of the platform. "Come look over here." He led her to the opposite side. They were suddenly looking across at the top of the North Tower. The antenna spire on top of the building shot another 362 feet into the air. "That's my floor right there," Travis said, pointing down six floors below the top of the building.

"Doesn't it make you nervous to be all the way up here everyday?" Hannah asked.

"Nah, I love it. It makes me feel alive being up in the sky, looking out over the greatest city in the world."

"We are quite lucky to work here," Hannah agreed.

Travis turned to Hannah and wrapped his arms around her. They both started to speak at the same time.

"Sorry, you go first." Hannah laughed.

"No, you go; mine can wait," Travis replied.

Hannah could hardly contain her excitement. "My friend Miles just got engaged, and he is getting married on New Year's Eve. I know it is a few months away still, but I was wondering if…if…" She stammered for a moment, suddenly feeling shy. It was all new to her. She had never been interested enough in a guy to ask him on a date.

Travis raised his eyebrows. "If…?" Travis asked.

Hannah shifted nervously. "Would you be my date?" She quickly blurted out.

"I would love nothing more than to be your date," he said.

Hannah let out a sign of relief.

"Now I have something to ask you," Travis said. "Would you like to come over this weekend to meet Eli and my mom?"

Hannah was taken by surprise. Inviting her to meet Eli and his mother was a big deal. He was completely letting her into his world.

Hannah felt a flutter of nerves in her stomach. What if they didn't like her? What if she didn't know what to say to Eli? She was terrified of saying the wrong thing. She knew how much Travis adored Eli and how much he respected his mother. She had to make a good impression on both of them.

"I would absolutely love to meet Eli and your mother," Hannah answered, "but…"

"But?" Travis asked worriedly.

"I'm so nervous! What if they don't like me?" Hannah confessed.

"They will love you, just like I…" Travis suddenly stopped. He cleared his throat before saying, "They will love you."

Did he almost just say what I think he was going to say? Hannah wondered.

It seemed crazy that they could feel so strongly about each other after only a few days. Hannah spotted the Empire State Building off in the distance. She wondered if Miles had stood in that same exact spot when he had proposed to Stephanie. Remembering what Miles had said earlier that day in the elevator, Hannah felt the sudden need to tell Travis how she felt.

She took a deep breath in. "Travis, I—"

"Excuse me!" A short, portly woman with a heavy Southern accent suddenly interrupted. "Would you please take our picture? It's our first time in New York City!"

Travis turned around to see who she was talking to and quickly realized she was talking to him.

"Sally, come here!" she yelled out to another woman who was waddling across the observation deck, with shopping bags slung over each of her arms. "This handsome young man is going to take our picture! Hurry up! He's waiting!" she yelled obnoxiously across the deck.

Hannah could not believe the timing. She was just about to tell Travis how she felt. Maybe it was a sign that it wasn't the right time. Maybe it *was* too soon.

"I swear, I spend my life waiting for my sister," the woman said under her breath. "Hurry up!" she yelled again. Suddenly, the woman noticed Hannah. "Well, look at you two young love birds. I hope I didn't interrupt." She turned to study Travis. "Ohhh! You are one handsome young man." She reached out with her short, plump fingers and grabbed Travis's face.

His eyes widened with surprise. He looked at Hannah out of the corner of his eye for help.

Hannah tried to hold in her laughter at the sight of Travis's face in the woman's clutch. The sister finally waddled up to them, letting Travis off the hook. The first woman released Travis's cheeks from her grip.

"Allow me," Hannah said, reaching for the camera. "Say, New York City." She snapped several pictures of the two sisters. Hannah then handed the camera back to the woman.

"You are a lucky young lady," the woman said to Hannah. She winked at Travis as she and her sister toddled off.

Once the sisters disappeared around the corner, Hannah reached out to grab Travis's face. "You are one handsome young man," she repeated.

"I can't believe she grabbed my face," Travis said, blushing slightly. "Anyway, let's try that again. What were you going to say before all of that?"

Hannah lost her courage. She scrambled to think of something else to say. "Oh. Um…I was just going to say that…I… am getting hungry. How about we grab one of those Nathan's Hot Dogs?"

Travis was oblivious to Hannah's diversion. "Two famous dogs coming right up!" Travis said, wrapping his arm around Hannah. They made their way back through the revolving door, down three flights of escalators, and to the hot dog stand.

As they stood in line, Travis looked over at Hannah. "What's better than this?" he asked, resting his arm over her shoulder.

"It doesn't get better than this," Hannah replied, feeling literally on top of the world.

CHAPTER 13

Friday, September 7, 2001
2:00 p.m.

D ozens of gallons of milk were lined up on the asphalt next to the hose, which was mounted on the side of the academy building. Several thick mats were arranged in a large square out in the grassy field.

The recruits awkwardly swung their empty gun belts around their waists and fumbled with the buckle until it was securely latched. The leather was stiff and shiny—a telltale sign of a "new guy" on the job.

The class had perked up the day before with an important announcement from Commander Conrad. He was the head of the academy, and when he spoke, the class listened. "Bring your duty belts tomorrow, and be sure to have your issued pepper spray holster on," he had instructed.

Audrey's duty belt had hung in her closet for five entire months, collecting dust. She was tired of classroom academics and was itching to do more practical work. She snapped several keepers around her waist, firmly securing her duty belt to the belt looped through her khaki academy uniform pants.

Commander Conrad came out of the building, walking swiftly toward the class gathered on the asphalt. Sergeant Gaston followed behind him, carrying a small box in his hands.

"Line up and stand at attention!" Sergeant Gaston barked.

Forming a horizontal line with their bodies, the recruits stood at attention with backs straight, chins up, and chests out. Each recruit stood perfectly still, their arms positioned at their sides with thumbs lined up along their uniform pants.

Gaston started at one end of the line, standing face to face with each recruit. One by one, he told them, "At ease." Then he handed each recruit a can of pepper spray.

Audrey could have sworn she saw the commander roll his eyes at Sergeant Gaston.

Commander Conrad then stepped in front of the class. "Today is Pepper Spray Certification," he said to the group, a stern look on his face.

The class shifted nervously as they waited for instructions. It was another hot September day, and the sun was beating down hard on their faces. Trickles of sweat ran down from their foreheads.

Commander Conrad passed each recruit over with his eyes. He was tough but fair. Audrey had gained a deep respect for him over the many months of the academy. She had learned a great deal from his lengthy experience in the police department as well as his decorated military background. He never took advantage of his authority. Instead he earned the respect and trust of the recruits with his admirable experience and respectable demeanor.

Commander Conrad spoke slowly and clearly. "Pepper spray is exactly what it sounds like. The substance is concentrated capsicum, which is just a fancy name for chili peppers. Anything it touches will burn like hell. I don't care how tough you are, you will be brought to tears. You may be wondering what all of those gallons of milk are for. Milk helps to neutralize the burn of the capsicum. You will use it to decontaminate your eyes and skin. Today your pepper spray will be fired—at you."

The recruits shifted nervously.

"Who can tell me what the purpose of this training exercise is?" Commander Conrad asked.

Scott answered immediately. "Sir, the purpose of this training exercise is to observe how to properly deploy the pepper spray at a combatant." He sounded confident.

"No," Commander Conrad replied curtly.

Scott's face flushed with embarrassment.

"If you deploy your pepper spray in the line of duty," Commander Conrad explained, "*you* will be exposed to it. If you are outside, the wind will blow it back at you. If you are inside, it will fill the room you are in, and you will breathe it in. Lastly if you lose control of your canister, someone could use your own pepper spray against you," Commander Conrad explained. "You need to be familiar with the effects. It will burn your eyes and throat. Mucus will flow from your nose. You will have difficulty breathing, and it will feel like you are suffocating. But it will not kill you." His face then became serious, and the tone in his voice deepened before he continued. "But you need to learn how to fight through it. Your life *will* depend on it."

He paused a moment to let his words sink in, then said, "Sergeant Gaston will now give you instructions on how we will proceed."

Sergeant Gaston stepped up, puffing his chest out. "Listen up, *recruits,*" he sneered. He loved to emphasize the word "recruits" to remind the class they were lowly beings. "*I* will be spraying each one of you," he continued, darting his eyes directly at Audrey.

Audrey's heart sank. There was a satisfaction in his voice when he emphasized "I," and she was sure he had clearly looked directly at her.

Sergeant Gaston continued with the instructions. "After I spray you, you must fight until you pin me to the ground for three full seconds."

Audrey knew he would try everything to make sure she couldn't pin him down. But Audrey knew the depths of her mental strength better than he did. She had proved herself beyond what she had ever thought she could endure. Her face had finally healed, and she could breathe again. She had worked herself into the best physical strength of her life in those five academy months. Most of all, she had a fire inside of her that would not let anyone stand in her way. She was ready.

"As Commander Conrad said, the gallons of milk lined up over there are to neutralize the capsicum. We are not out here to have milk and cookies," Sergeant Gaston said condescendingly to the group.

Sergeant Gaston called up Ray first. They were positioned facing each other on the mat. Ray un-holstered his pepper spray canister and handed it to Sergeant Gaston. Gaston pulled the canister up, aimed it at Ray's eyes, and depressed the red button on top. A steady stream of brownish-orange spray shot through the air, landing directly on Ray's face.

Ray blinked furiously, and let out a roar of discomfort from the burning in his eyes. Sergeant Gaston lunged at Ray, grabbed him by the shoulders, and wrestled him to the ground. They were coughing, choking, and struggling to breathe, until Ray finally pinned Sergeant Gaston to the ground.

"One! Two! Three!" Commander Conrad slapped his hand on the mat with each count.

One by one Gaston called each recruit, leaving Audrey for last. It was a mental tactic she was already prepared for. He was so predictable.

Finally it was Audrey's turn. She walked onto the mat, keeping a blank canvas on her face. She wanted and *needed* the element of surprise.

Audrey stood opposite to Sergeant Gaston. She un-holstered her pepper spray and handed it to him. Before she could even get herself situated, he held up the canister, depressing the red button without warning. In slow motion, she saw the steady stream of spray come directly at her eyes. She instinctively blinked when the oily substance hit her face, but it had seeped immediately into her skin and eyes. The burn was instant, intensifying every second. She blinked wildly, trying to clear her vision, but quickly realized that only made it burn worse. She kept her eyes closed and fought blindly instead.

Audrey was suddenly pushed backward off her feet with incredible force, landing flat on her back. Gaston was on top of her, trying to pin her down. The wind had been knocked out of her, and she felt like she couldn't breathe. Gaston was trying to grab her arms so that she couldn't fight, but she was stronger and more evasive than he'd expected. She managed to push him off, but she felt him return almost immediately.

Audrey couldn't see. She was coughing and choking, gasping for air from the burning in her lungs. The wetness from her nose flowed down onto her top lip. She couldn't breathe. It felt like she was going to die. *"It will not kill you. You must learn to fight through it,"* she heard the commander's earlier words in her head.

Using all of her strength, she threw Gaston to the side, rolling on top of him. She tried to pin him down, but he quickly threw her off, landing back on top of her. Her lungs were burning, both from the pepper spray and raw exertion.

Gaston was able to grab her arms, pinning them hard to the mat. No matter how much she tried, she was unable to free herself. Her energy level was starting to dwindle.

Audrey's legs were her strongest asset. Many years of yoga had made her body strong and flexible. She knew she would need that advantage to overpower him. She pulled her knees up underneath Gaston, placing her feet flat on his chest. With all of her might, she shoved him off of her with such force that he went flying backward. Before he'd even landed, she had scrambled up onto her feet. Squinting through burning eyes, she found him lying on the mat and dove on top of him. She had knocked the wind out of him. Straddling his breathless body, she pinned him down.

"One! Two! Three!" Commander Conrad called out again, slapping his hand on the mat with each count. This time, the whole class joined in.

Audrey had successfully pinned Gaston to the ground. Everyone except for Scott was cheering, enjoying the sight of Gaston lying flat on the ground, trying to catch his breath.

Ethan and Ray helped guide Audrey over to the decontamination station.

"I could have watched that over and over again," Ethan said with a satisfied smile. He picked up a jug of milk. "Lean over and try to open your eyes," he instructed Audrey.

Her eyes burned like fire. As soon as Ethan poured the milk into her eyes, she felt immediate relief. There had been no greater satisfaction in her life than pinning Gaston to the ground. She wished Preston had been there to see it.

Audrey blinked until her vision cleared, just in time to see Gaston hoisting himself up from the mat. Unable to stand upright, he had one hand on his knee, supporting his body. He refused to look over at Audrey standing at the decontamination station. She knew that would surely not be his last attempt to thwart her, but for the moment she reveled in her victory.

What a great way to start the weekend, Audrey thought.

CHAPTER 14

Friday, September 7, 2001
11:45 p.m.

The building swayed right, then left. With a sudden snap, Hannah was thrown to the ground. She could see the water of the East River underneath her feet as she slid sideways across the eighty-fourth floor, toward the windows. *The building is going to snap in half!* She frantically tried to grab desks and furniture as she slid by. She was just about to crash through the windows, plummeting thousands of feet to the sidewalk below, when she felt someone grab her arm.

"Hannah," someone gently said in her ear, "it's all right."

For a moment she was saved, but seconds later she slipped from the grasp. Hannah's body crashed thought the window, free falling into thin air. She had spiraled halfway down to the ground below. She suddenly felt arms wrap around her and catch her body.

"Hannah, wake up, you're having a bad dream," Travis said gently in her ear. His arms were holding her tight.

With one deep breath, she came to, realizing that she and Travis had fallen asleep together on the couch in her apartment.

"It was so real," Hannah mumbled, brushing loose strands of hair from her face. She was covered in sweat.

"Do you want to talk about it?" Travis asked.

Hannah was confused for a moment, still trying to come out of the nightmare.

"I was at work," she said, trying to make sense of the dream. "Then something happened to the building, and it started to topple. I slid across the floor and crashed through the window."

Hannah shuddered, thinking about the free fall to the ground. She could *feel* it in her dream. It was not the typical dream she usually had about the towers. She often dreamt that the elevators broke loose from their cables. Halfway up to the Sky Lobby, there would be a sudden snap, and she would plummet dozens of floors in seconds, waking up just before she crashed to the bottom. This dream was so different; it was too real.

"It was just a dream. You are safe," Travis said, comforting her. "Let's get some more sleep. We have a big day tomorrow,"

Hannah suddenly remembered that she would be getting up in the morning to meet Travis's mom and Eli. She closed her eyes and tried to get the dream out of her mind. Hannah focused on the warmth of Travis's body next to her, and his arms holding her tight. She drifted back off to sleep, thinking about how perfect her life was becoming with Travis by her side.

Saturday, September 8, 2001
9:00 a.m.

Hannah stopped suddenly on the sidewalk, halfway to Travis's apartment. She tried to subdue the nervous butterflies.

"What if they don't like me?" Hannah asked Travis.

"Relax," Travis said. "Have you seen yourself by the way?"

Hannah was wearing a pinstripe Yankees jersey and a matching Yankees hat. It was not at all what she'd planned to wear to meet his mother and Eli for the first time, but Travis had a surprise for her earlier that morning. As Hannah had stood in front of her closet, searching for the perfect outfit to make a good impression, Travis had pulled two Yankees vs. Red Sox playoff tickets from his pocket. "Dress for the game," he'd said. "We will go right from my place."

Hannah had never been to a Yankees playoff game. She could hardly contain her excitement, but as they walked toward Travis's apartment, she felt like her knees were going to give out. She was so nervous to meet his family.

There was a buzz in the air, a palpable energy that radiated throughout the city. The greatest rivaling teams in baseball were fighting for the championship and their chance at the World Series, right there at home in Yankee Stadium.

A man passing by on the sidewalk in the opposite direction called out to Hannah. "Go, Yanks! We need a win today!"

Hannah smiled, giving him the thumbs-up as he passed by.

She then turned to Travis. "Are you sure about this?" she asked, referring again to her outfit.

"Listen to me. There are no bigger Yankees fans in the world than my mom and Eli. You couldn't make a better impression, trust me," he assured her.

Suddenly a new thought sent Hannah into a panic. "What do I call your mom?" She nervously wrung her hands.

"Something nice," Travis replied, laughing at his own joke.

Hannah did not appreciate the humor at that moment. "I'm serious. Do I call her by her first name? No. That would be rude," she answered herself. "Do I call her Ms. Russell? Is that her last name? I never asked if you kept your father's name or if Russell is her last name? Oh my goodness, I am so unprepared."

"It's Russell. Eli and I took her last name. She is the one who raised us, along with the help of my grandparents. So we are all Russells, but I assure you, she will not let you be that formal. Relax," Travis reassured her again.

"Okay, I need to stop and get flowers for her," Hannah said. She already had Eli covered. Hannah had made a special trip to Circuit City on a mission to hunt down the latest *Harry Potter and the Sorcerer's Stone* Game Boy Advance game. Hannah had picked Travis's brain about Eli and what kinds of things he liked. Harry Potter was at the top of the list. She had also recalled Travis telling her that Eli loved his occupational therapy sessions because he got to play video games to practice hand-eye coordination. Hannah had the video game tucked in her crossbody bag and couldn't wait to give it to him.

"I happen to know a place that sells beautiful flowers right around the corner." Travis winked. Hannah assumed that was where he got her flowers the weekend before. She picked out a colorful bouquet of yellow, pink, orange, and purple zinnias. They were cheerful and bright, wrapped in bright pink paper.

"You picked one of her favorite flowers," Travis said. "See, you're already hitting it off."

It was a short walk the rest of the way to Travis's building. The large glass entry doors were equipped with an automatic handicap accessible button. Travis walked past the mailboxes, into the lobby, and then took a left down the hallway.

"We're on the first floor. My mom worried about being on a higher floor if there is a fire or emergency. Eli is not happy about it. He wants to ride the elevator, and you know, push the buttons and all that fun stuff. So we take him up to the rooftop garden a lot, just so that he stops giving us such a hard time," Travis said.

"Ohhh... a rooftop garden," Hannah said. "That sounds lovely."

Travis passed several doorways and then stopped in front of apartment twelve. "Here we are."

Travis had just put the keys into the door, when suddenly the door slowly began to open. Eli was halfway down the entryway hall in his wheelchair, pressing the automatic door button on the wall. Travis motioned for Hannah to go in first. Eli pushed a button on his armrest, moving his wheelchair forward toward Hannah.

Hannah waved shyly. "Hi, you must be Eli." She extended her hand to shake Eli's.

"And *you* must be Hannah," he said, kissing the top of her hand.

Hannah was caught by surprise. Of course she should have known he would be as charming as his brother. She turned to Travis. "I see you have taught him some things."

"Actually, I learned that one from him," Travis said, winking at Eli.

The apartment smelled of fresh baked muffins and fresh citrus. A woman came from around the corner, wiping her hands on a kitchen towel. She was in her midfifties, with straight, shoulder-length dark brown hair and the same sparkling blue eyes as Travis had. His mom was beautiful and confident. Hannah felt immediately intimidated by her presence. She untied her apron and tossed it over the back of a chair in the living room.

It was the critical moment—making a good first impression on the mother of the guy she was in love with. Hannah smiled, feeling her nerves twist inside of her stomach.

"Hello, Hannah," his mom said, with outstretched arms. She embraced Hannah with a warm hug. "It's wonderful to meet you. I've heard so much about you, *and* a Yankees Fan!" she said, raising her eyebrows in approval.

"It's so nice to meet you—" Hannah began.

"Please, call me Rosemary."

Hannah relaxed, feeling wrapped up in the warmth of Travis's family. She could feel the immense amount of love in their home.

"Yankees fans are always welcome here," Rosemary said, helping to break the ice.

"These are for you." Hannah handed the bouquet of flowers to Rosemary.

"Oh, Hannah, they are beautiful! Thank you. Zinnias are my favorite."

"She picked them out herself. I didn't even tell her," Travis said, with a pleased smile.

Hannah reached into her crossbody bag and pulled out the video game. "I hear you like Harry Potter," she said, turning to Eli.

His face lit up and a smile spread across his face. "Thank you! Thank you! Thank you!" Eli exclaimed. He looked over at his mom with bright blue eyes, pleading to play the game.

"*After* breakfast," Rosemary answered.

Eli took Hannah's hand and guided her into the apartment alongside his wheelchair. "Come see my room," he said. Eli pulled her down the hall and turned into the first bedroom. It was every thirteen-year-old boy's dream bedroom, completely decked out in a Harry Potter theme. Stepping into Eli's room was like walking straight into the Hogwarts School. Maroon-and-gold curtains hung on each side of his bed.

A sign that read GRYFFINDOR hung in the middle over his headboard. The walls had been painted to look like a stone interior. Gorgeous murals of wizards, witches, owls, gargoyles, and magic wands were painted along the stone walls.

"Travis did all of this," Eli said proudly.

Hannah turned with her mouth open to see Travis standing in the doorway. "*You* did this?" Hannah could barely speak.

Travis shrugged modestly.

"So you are an artist too." Hannah shook her head in disbelief.

A framed photograph on top of the dresser caught her eye. It was a picture of Eli and Travis. Eli was looking up at his older brother, lovingly. She could tell how much he adored Travis.

"I love your room, Eli. I wish my room were this cool," Hannah said.

"You can come hang out anytime," Eli replied.

"I think I'll take you up on that offer," Hannah said.

"Come here," Eli said, specifically to Hannah. "I have something to show you".

Eli directed his wheelchair out of his bedroom and into the hallway. He stopped Hannah in front of a cluster of framed pictures on the console table.

"This is Travis when he was five," Eli said, picking up a small-framed picture. "Check out those plaid pants," he teased.

"Do you see what I mean?" Travis said. "He really gives it to me!" Travis balled up his fist and rubbed it playfully on top of Eli's head. "You're lucky I love you."

Eli's laugh was just as contagious as Travis had said. Hannah felt so much joy inside of her heart. She had quickly fallen in love with Eli and Rosemary too. The aroma of coffee and breakfast being prepared in the kitchen wafted through the air.

"I'm going to see if your mom needs help with breakfast," Hannah said.

As Hannah walked to the kitchen, she looked around the room. The walls were filled with framed pictures of Eli, Travis, and Rosemary from over the years. There was no trace of their father anywhere on the walls.

"Can I help with anything?" Hannah offered Rosemary, who was mixing pancake batter next to the sink.

"Sure," Rosemary said. "How about you butter the toast?"

Hannah picked up a butter knife and sliced it through the soft butter.

"He really likes you," Rosemary whispered behind her spatula.

Hannah blushed.

"He has never brought anyone here to meet us. I think he *really* likes you," Rosemary repeated.

Hannah recalled how she had almost told Travis how she felt when they were on top of the South Tower the other day. She was mad at herself for chickening out.

"I feel the same way," Hannah said.

Hannah thought she saw a tear in the corner of Rosemary's eye.

Travis sat down on the couch next to Eli. "So, what do you think?" Travis whispered.

"She's the one," Eli replied confidently.

CHAPTER 15

Saturday, September 8, 2001
12:30 p.m.

Audrey sat at a high top table at the Blue Line Pub, a favorite spot frequented by local cops and firefighters. Located in the artsy downtown, within walking distance of her apartment, it was her regular spot. She had convinced Preston to get out of his house and meet up to watch the Yankees vs. Red Sox playoff game. All of the televisions in the bar were tuned to the game.

Audrey ran her finger around the rim of her pint glass. She peered out the window at the people walking by on the sidewalks of the quaint downtown. Preston came walking through the door, looking completely disheveled. His hair was unkempt, and he had let his facial hair grow. Audrey hadn't seen him since he was escorted out of the building the week before. Preston pulled out the barstool and sat across from Audrey.

"Oh my," Audrey said, "you are... not looking so good."

Preston brushed his fingers through his messy hair. He looked as though he hadn't slept in a week. "I gave my statement yesterday. They are now interviewing some of the guys who were there that night."

Audrey let out a burst of breath in disbelief. She couldn't believe how far it was going. "I want to give a statement," Audrey said frantically, "I'll explain that you were defending me. I can clear this whole—"

Preston cut her off. "I don't want you to worry about this. It's not your fault."

Audrey sighed in frustration. He had to know her better than that. She was going to have her voice heard one way or another. She just had to figure out how.

"So fill me in. What have I missed?" Preston asked.

"You are never going to believe this," Audrey said, leaning forward over the pub table. She made it halfway through the gripping account of how she had pinned Gaston during Pepper Spray Certification and was about to tell him how she'd kicked him through the air, when something on the television caught her eye.

Bernie Williams was up at bat, but that was not what drew her attention. Directly behind home plate, in the stands, she could have sworn she saw her sister. Audrey had been thinking so much of Hannah that she figured she was just seeing things.

"So I got my legs up underneath Gaston, and I launched him through the air. He landed like a ton of bricks on his back—"

Suddenly the room erupted in cheers, interrupting her story. Everyone in the bar was on their feet screaming, "Go!"

Audrey turned her attention to the TV again. Red Sox catcher Joe Oliver was scrambling to retrieve a wild pitch, and Bernie Williams was rounding first base.

Preston and Audrey jumped to their feet. "Go!" they screamed, joining in with the rest of the bar.

Bernie Williams slid into second base, and the umpire emphatically motioned "SAFE" with his arms. Audrey slapped Preston's hand triumphantly, high in the air.

"I've got to see that again," Preston said. There was color in his face for the first time since he'd walked through the door.

The camera cut away from Bernie Williams catching his breath at second base to a slow motion replay. In the background, the blonde woman sitting behind home plate caught Audrey's eye again. Audrey squinted, wondering again if her eyes were playing tricks on her.

"Oh my God! I think I see...my sister?"

"What?" Preston asked. "Is she at the game today?"

"I don't know. I've hardly heard from her in two weeks. I think she is in *love*."

A moment later, Tino Martinez hit a two-run home run, scoring Bernie from second base.

"Yes!" Preston screamed. You could feel the walls of the bar vibrating as the crowd cheered wildly.

Audrey jumped to her feet from her barstool. Clear as day, in the background, she saw her sister. The way her blonde ponytail swung when she jumped up from her seat, and her unmistakable bright white smile confirmed what Audrey had thought.

"It *is* her!" Audrey exclaimed. She rummaged through her purse to grab her cell phone and quickly dialed Hannah's phone number.

David Justice was up at bat and was positioning himself in batting stance. Audrey caught another glimpse of her sister behind home plate. She was rummaging through her handbag. Suddenly, the phone call was answered.

"Audrey!" Hannah said loudly into the phone, plugging her opposite ear to block out the noise of the roaring crowd at Yankee Stadium. "I'm at the Yankees Game!" she exclaimed.

"I know." Audrey laughed. "I'm watching you. So this is how I find out what my sister has been up to!"

"I'm sorry. I promise, promise, promise I will be home next weekend. I have so much to tell you!" Hannah yelled into the phone.

"Oh, I see you again," Audrey said as her sister appeared in the camera angle once more.

Hannah waved excitedly. "Travis, wave to my sister," she said off to the side, nudging his arm.

The handsome young man next to Hannah leaned in and waved. Audrey could hear him in the background say, "Hi, Audrey!"

"You tell that handsome man next to you that I said hello. Enjoy the rest of the game. Go, Yanks!" Audrey said.

"Love you, Sis," Hannah said before flipping the phone shut.

Audrey turned to Preston. "Yup, my sister is in love."

Preston grumbled something as he took a sip of his beer. The last thing Preston wanted to hear about was a magical romance. He couldn't even bring himself to shave in the morning. "So, what's the story with O'Shea? You said you would tell me later," Preston asked, still keeping an eye on the game.

Audrey hadn't been able to get O'Shea out of her mind since the day she'd snapped at him.

"Ugh. I think I messed up, Preston. I was angry, you know, with the whole rumor going around. I thought he was trying to hit on me, but I think he may have just been trying to help. He timed the final run, and I swear I was about to give up, when he started running the rest of my laps with me. Then he was in the parking lot at the end of the day to check on me, and I lost it on him. I just assumed he was trying to hook up," she said.

"Um, or…maybe he is just a nice guy," Preston said. "Look, all I know is that he had a long-term girlfriend when we were in the unit together. He seemed more like the settle-down kind of guy. He was pretty devastated when they broke up actually."

Audrey felt her heart deflate. "I was really rude to him." She lowered her head into her hands. "He looked so hurt."

"Just talk to him. He's a good guy. I am sure he will understand," Preston said.

"I will. The next time I see him I'll apologize," Audrey pledged. "I just feel like everything is going wrong. I never thought this academy thing would be so hard."

"Tell me about it," Preston chimed in. "I haven't told my family that I'm suspended. They still think I'm going into the academy everyday."

Audrey sighed. She took the last swig of her beer and then motioned to the waitress for another round. The time spent with Preston was exactly what she needed to mentally reset. She needed to get him back to the academy somehow.

The game ended with a final score of 9-2 for a huge Yankees' win.

Her sister was happy and in love, the Yankees would continue in the playoffs, and Audrey would march into the academy that week and fix everything. She would talk to internal
investigations to clear Preston's name. Then she would find
O'Shea and make things right.

"Maybe things are starting to look up, Preston," Audrey
said.

"Could things get any worse?" he grumbled.

"Things can always get worse," Audrey replied.

CHAPTER 16

Monday, September 10, 2001
2:30 p.m.

Hannah peered out the tall, narrow windows of the eighty-fourth-floor conference room and sighed. Puffs of dark clouds whipped by as the wind whistled on the other side of the glass. Miles appeared next to her with a cup of coffee in his hand. "Looks like quite a storm coming in," he said.

A big pellet of rain spattered the window in front of them.

"It doesn't look good for tonight's show." Hannah pulled out a conference room chair to sit down.

She had been looking forward to the dance performance that night. It was part of the Evening Stars On Stage concert series at the World Trade Center. Every summer a temporary stage was erected in front of the North Tower in the plaza. People came from all over, during their lunch hour and in the evenings, to listen to live music outdoors and be entertained by various performances.

It was one of Hannah's favorite parts about working at the World Trade Center. The concert series was a true gift to the people of New York City, and she felt privileged to work right where it all happened. On a very quiet day in the office, she could sometimes hear the music from eighty-four stories below.

The performance that night was part of an eleven-day celebration of dance produced by the Lower Manhattan Cultural Council. Hannah had coordinated a small group from the office to go together. She invited Miles, Don, and Marilyn. She was looking forward to introducing Travis to everyone. Miles invited Stephanie to join them too. It was going to be such a wonderful night, but it would be completely ruined by the weather.

Miles could see the disappointment on Hannah's face. "There's always tomorrow," he said encouragingly, patting Hannah's shoulder.

Hannah picked up the handset of the phone in the conference room and dialed Travis's cell phone number. He answered on the first ring. There was a lot of background noise, and she could tell he was outside the building.

"I was just about to call you," Travis answered loudly over the whooshing wind in the background.

"Where are you?" Hannah asked.

"I'm down in the plaza. The skies are about to open up. They just canceled the dress rehearsal for the performance and sent the dancers home. It doesn't look good for the show tonight."

"I know," Hannah said with disappointment in her voice. "I am literally watching the storm clouds fly by the window right now." She tried to wrap her mind around the fact that she was as high as the clouds. Suddenly the terrible dream she'd had a few nights earlier flashed through her mind. She shuddered, recalling the feeling of crashing through the windows and free falling toward the ground. She quickly forced it out of her mind.

"Apparently there is a hurricane off the coast. It is going to be a stormy night," Travis said.

Hannah sighed.

"Hey, we will just go tomorrow night instead. Plus I have a backup plan," Travis said.

Hannah loved how Travis always knew just what to do. He was positive and full of life.

"I am heading back to the office now before I get soaked," Travis said. "Remember...look up—"

"I know...maybe I'll see you," Hannah completed his sentence.

———

Monday, September 10, 2001
6:30 p.m.
Hannah hurried into Travis's apartment building to escape the torrential downpour outside. She shook off her umbrella as she entered the lobby. Still in her work clothes, she had rushed straight to Travis's apartment.

It was unusual for Hannah to work late, but the biggest break in her career was about to happen the next morning. Berkley had awarded her the honor of being one of the lead presenters in a high profile meeting. The conference room would be filled with top hedge fund managers and consultants from all over the country. It was an opportunity that could propel Hannah's career forward, if she did well.

Berkley was a nervous wreck. He reminded everyone involved in the meeting to come in an hour early by sprawling out a hastily written message in all caps on the whiteboard in the conference room: TUESDAY, SEPTEMBER 11— M^{EET}ING BEGINS 9:00 A.M., SHARP. ARRIVE AT 8:00 A.M. IF YOU WANT TO KEEP YOUR JOB!

Hannah knew it wasn't an empty threat from Berkley. She decided to polish her presentation and prep the conference room before she left that night.

Hannah wiped her wet sneakers on the entryway mat in the lobby of Travis's apartment building. Travis suddenly appeared from around the corner.

"You might as well bring that with you." He pointed to her umbrella.

With the heavy rain outside, she assumed his backup plan would be indoors. "Why would I need my umbrella?"

"Just follow me." Travis led her toward the elevator.

"Um…your apartment is that way," Hannah said, confused.

"When are you going to learn to trust me? Cover your eyes, and don't open them until I tell you."

Hannah covered her eyes with her hands, and let Travis lead her. She heard him push the elevator buttons, and then the doors closed. She guessed they had gone up about fifteen floors, when they came to a stop and the doors opened again.

"Keep them closed," Travis reminded her, "and no peeking."

She stumbled along blindly as Travis held her by the arm. Suddenly she felt a rush of fresh air and raindrops.

"Ah! I'm getting wet!" Hannah exclaimed.

"Only for a second," Travis assured her.

A moment later she no longer felt the pelting of cold raindrops, but she could tell they were still outside.

Travis took both of her arms and positioned her. "Okay, now open," he said proudly.

Hannah opened her eyes and gasped. They were on the rooftop, surrounded by dozens of flickering candles, lit under the covered pergola they stood beneath. The rooftop garden was lush with beautiful flowers and green plants. Raindrops danced on top of the canopy, rolling steadily off the sides, like a trickling waterfall. Hannah looked around in awe. City lights had begun to come alive against the gray backdrop of the stormy sky. String lights hung haphazardly across the outdoor garden.

Travis stood by Hannah's side, allowing her to take in the romantic setting. "Have a seat," he said, taking her hand.

Hannah settled into the comfy outdoor couch under the pergola. On the side table, she noticed a portable compact disk player and a stack of varying CDs.

"You pick," Travis said.

Hannah looked over her options: Van Morrison's *Moondance*, Billy Joel's *The Bridge*, *James Taylor's Greatest Hits*…

She popped the Van Morrison disk out of the case and placed it in the top of the CD player.

"When you said you had a backup plan, I thought maybe you had front-row seats to the Michael Jackson concert tonight," Hannah teased.

"The King of Pop's thirtieth anniversary celebration? I don't have that kind of pull!" he replied.

"This is better, anyway." Hannah nuzzled up next to him, feeling the damp tropical breeze from the storm blow through her hair.

Travis pulled a warm blanket up over their legs. They sat in silence for a few minutes, listening to the rain as they unwound from the day. The storm had picked up, causing the candles to flicker in the wind. Though the rain was getting heavier, they were warm and dry, sheltered under the pergola.

"Hey, I was thinking," Hannah said, "I promised my sister I would come home to visit this weekend. Would you like to come with me?"

"I thought you would never ask." Travis smiled. "I would love to. You miss her, don't you?"

"I miss her a lot," Hannah replied, feeling sad for a moment. "I can't wait for you to meet each other."

"Well, now it is my turn to be nervous," he said.

"Don't be nervous. She will love you." Hannah paused. She felt a sudden overwhelming need to tell him how she felt—like she would never get the chance again. Her heart started beating fast, and the palms of her hands suddenly got warm. She turned toward Travis and looked into his beautiful blue eyes. "I love you."

Travis's cheeks turned rosy. He took Hannah's face in his hands. "I have loved you from the moment we met, and I will never stop."

The melody of Hannah's favorite Van Morrison song played softly in the background. Travis pulled her face toward his and gently kissed her lips. Life could not have been more perfect than that moment, kissing the man she loved in a rooftop garden during a late summer rain storm.

Travis's cell phone rang on the table, startling them both from the romantic moment.

"The pizza is here!" Travis announced.

Hannah smiled. "Is there anything you don't think of?"

"I knew you'd be hungry. I'll run down and get it. Be right back." He kissed her forehead as he stood up from the couch.

As Travis disappeared through the door leading from the rooftop into the building, Hannah grabbed her cell phone from her briefcase and dialed Audrey's number. She was prepared to leave a voicemail, but Audrey answered on the last ring.

"Audrey! I only have a minute," Hannah blurted out. "I'm coming home this weekend. Travis is coming too. I can't wait for you to meet him. I just told him I love him, and I have so much to tell you. Audrey, I can't believe how happy I am."

"I am so happy for you, Sis. I can't wait to meet him too," Audrey said.

Hannah detected a hint of distress in Audrey's voice. "Are you okay?"

Audrey sighed. "Yeah, I just have a couple of things I have to handle tomorrow; that's all. I'll fill you in this weekend."

"Okay. Love you, Audrey."

"I love you too, Hannah. See you in a few days."

Hannah hung up the phone, feeling over the moon. It felt so good knowing she would see her sister in just a few days. She was so excited to bring Travis home to meet her family too.

Travis returned holding a large pizza box. Paper plates and napkins were stacked on top of the box. He ran from the door to the shelter of the pergola.

Travis cracked open a can of 7UP and served Hannah a slice of pizza. Her hands shook from the damp chill in the air, as she reached for the plate.

They sat under the pergola, feet up on the ottoman, each with a slice of pizza in hand. Hannah looked out at the twinkling lights in the distance as the rain pelted down on the city. The sky had changed from gray to almost black, as the gloomy day turned to nighttime.

Travis switched out the CD when the last Van Morrison song had finished. The sounds of Billy Joel floated in the air as Travis settled back into the couch next to Hannah. The music brought Hannah back to a memory long ago, causing her to smile.

"When Audrey and I were little, we used to dance to Billy Joel songs on the record player. We sang at the top of our lungs, playing the electric air guitar," Hannah recalled with a giggle.

Travis was amused. "Can I mention that to your sister this weekend?"

"Not if you want to live."

Travis suddenly jumped to his feet, placing his pizza down on the side table. "This song"—he paused a moment to let Hannah hear the instrumental beginning—"is my favorite Billy Joel song."

Hannah only vaguely recognized it. Travis reached his hand out, pulling Hannah to her feet to dance. When the words began, Travis sang along to the melancholy tune. They danced slowly as he sang softly in her ear, with the sound of the rain tapping above.

Hannah buried her head in his chest as she listened to the song's words. She never wanted time to change. She wished that everything could stay the way it was in that moment, forever. Travis took her hand and twirled her under his arm. She spun around, like she was floating on air.

"What makes this one your favorite song?" Hannah asked, as they slowly swayed back and forth.

"Listen to the message," he said. "Time is fleeting. Nothing stays the same forever. We have to cherish what is right in front of us today. It's the way I try to live my life."

Hannah recalled their conversation in the taxi the night of the Brooklyn Bridge and it suddenly clicked.

"If you live each day to its fullest, life can never be too short," she repeated his words from that night.

"You do listen to me!" he teased.

A strong breeze blew through the pergola, like a wind tunnel, carrying a mist of cool rain with it.

Hannah shivered.

"Let's get under the blanket and get you warm," Travis said.

Changing out the CD one last time, Travis then lay down across the couch. He held his arms out, inviting Hannah to join him. She stretched out next to his body, feeling warm and comforted. The candles flickered in the breeze, and the tapping rain above made her sleepy.

With her head on his chest, listening to his heartbeat, she drifted away to the sweet sounds of James Taylor. Hannah made a silent wish before she dozed off.

Please, let this stay this way forever…

PART TWO

The storm existed well before the arrival of the dark clouds, the winds, and the rain. It had been churning, brewing, and strengthening its will of destruction from far, far away. It arrived fast and fierce in the city, passing through with an ominous display of darkness. The departure of the storm unveiled a most brilliant blue sky. A vibrant blue unlike any sky that had been seen before, showing us that after every storm, clouds will eventually clear, the sun will one day shine again, and no entity—no matter how dark and sinister—will ever win against love.

CHAPTER 17

Tuesday, September 11, 2001
6:45 a.m.

Hannah's eyes slowly opened, squinting at the bright blue morning sky stretched out over the city. The storm had passed sometime during the night, and the sky was a shade of blue Hannah had never seen before. With her head still on Travis's chest, she realized they had slept on the rooftop all night.

Hannah jumped up in a panic. She had no idea what time it was, but by the volume of traffic of the streets below, it was sometime during rush hour. Hannah was still in her work clothes from the day before. She had to get home to her apartment, shower, get dressed, and be in the office early for her presentation. Berkley wanted her there at eight o'clock, sharp, an hour before the executives arrived at the eighty-fourth floor of the South Tower.

Hannah checked the time on her cell phone. *6:45 a.m.!*

J .S .   F A R M E R

"Travis," Hannah said urgently as she shook him awake. "We slept out here all night. I have to go."

Travis opened his eyes and looked around in confusion. "What time is it?" he asked groggily, rubbing his eyes.

"It's 6:45 in the morning!"

As she tied her sneakers, she looked out over the city and the incredibly blue sky above. "Look at that sky! I have never seen that color blue before."

Travis squinted, adjusting his eyes to the bright morning light. "Cerulean," he said.

"What?"

"Cerulean; it's a shade of blue," Travis replied, "exactly the color of the sky right now."

Hannah took one last second to take it all in—the cool morning air, the view of the city, the cloudless cerulean blue sky, and the excitement of their new love.

"I have to be in early," Hannah said regretfully.

Since the day they met, they made the trip to work together every morning.

"That's okay. I'm going to be a little late today anyway. I can tell I'll be dragging," Travis replied.

"Hey! Let's have lunch together, outside in the plaza. This day is too beautiful to be inside," Hannah suggested.

"I'll meet you in front of the fountain at noon." Travis wrapped his arms around Hannah and gave her a lingering kiss goodbye.

"I love you," he said, staring lovingly into her eyes.

———

Tuesday, September 11, 2001
7:35 a.m.

Hannah stood up from the edge of her bed and stuck a pair of black pumps in her crossbody bag. She had chosen a black power suit, with a white blouse underneath, for the presentation. Short on time, she needed sneakers on her feet to move through the crowds quicker. The moment she got to her cubicle, she would slip into her heels to complete her outfit. Before rushing out of her apartment, she grabbed a bottle of water from the barren fridge and stuck it in her briefcase.

Hannah walked briskly along the sidewalk, toward the subway station. The radiant blue sky commanded her attention once again. She stood in awe for a moment before descending down the steps into the dark subway.

Hannah was still caught up from the whirlwind evening the night before. Sleeping all night on the rooftop was purely unintentional and entirely magical. She was grateful to the bright blue sky for rousing her from her comfortable sleep. Had she overslept, she would have destroyed her entire career in one morning.

Without Travis, the train seemed to travel along the tracks exceptionally slow that morning. Hannah exited the train at the World Trade Center stop, below the North Tower. She picked up the pace as she walked through the mall, turning left at the coffee kiosk. Even though Travis would be running late that morning, she knew he would still stop there before making his way to the 104th floor. Hannah knew his routine; she had studied him. Martha, the owner of the kiosk, would know exactly his order before he even had to say it. After paying with two singles, he would take the handful of change back and stick it in his right pants pocket.

The rest of the way to the office was a blur. Thoughts flurried through Hannah's mind as she rode up in the elevators. One moment she was practicing her presentation in her head, the next moment her thoughts raced back to the night before, dancing with Travis in the rain. She had never been happier. The sun was shining, her career was taking off, and she had fallen in love in the city.

Hannah stepped off the elevator on the eighty-fourth floor to see Berkley waiting on the other side of the glass doors. She looked down at her watch. It was 7:59, exactly. He pushed open the door when he saw her.

"Let's go. Coffee needs to be started, and I want a run-through of your portion of the presentation!" Berkley barked.

"Yes, sir. I'll just put my things down and be right in," Hannah said in her most competent voice. It was such a huge day for her career.

Hannah kicked off her sneakers and slipped the black heels onto her feet. She was usually never in the office that early. Most of the employees at her firm started their workday around 8:30 a.m. The office was quiet except for the sound of Berkley in the conference room, berating some poor soul on the speakerphone.

That morning was the first day of school for several districts in the city. Many employees would be rushing into the office late after getting their children situated on their first day. It was also Election Day for the primary. People would be stopping to vote on their way to work.

Hannah unlatched her laptop from the docking station and walked speedily to the conference room. Berkley was hunched over the speakerphone, with his back turned to the door. "Hannah!" he impatiently summoned her.

"I'm right here, sir. I'm ready," she said, swiftly plugging her laptop into the projector.

Berkley waved his hand hastily, signaling for her to hurry up and run through the presentation.

Hannah took a deep breath and confidently read through each slide, pretending she was speaking to a room full of executives. Berkley spent the full twenty minutes of her presentation scrolling through his BlackBerry and skimming emails, only sporadically looking up at Hannah.

When Hannah was done with her presentation, Berkley barked, "It's good. It's fine. Be back at 8:45. I want everyone in this room and ready before they get here. Marilyn will let me know before she brings them down."

Hannah nodded. "Yes, sir."

She quickly scanned the room to make sure everything was perfect. Before leaving the conference room, she turned on the coffee maker and straightened the coffee mugs on the counter.

On her way back to her cubicle, she ran into Don, who was just arriving at the office. "Good luck today, Hannah! It's a big day, kid." He patted her on the back.

"Thanks, Don." She held up crossed fingers.

Miles was at his cubicle when she got back to her desk.

"Good morning, Miles," Hannah said cheerily, still on cloud nine.

"Hi, Hannah. You are awfully cheerful today," Miles greeted her. "Hey, did you see that sky out there today? I think the weather is good for the concert tonight. Are the plans still on?" he asked, pushing his glasses snugly to his face, with his index finger.

"You bet!" Hannah replied.

She then sat down at her desktop computer and quickly shuffled through dozens of emails. She still had a few minutes to kill, so she decided to check out the AOL news headlines: *High Primary Voter Turnout Expected…Skies Clear After Big Storm…Michael Jordan Rejoins NBA…*

Boring news, Hannah thought to herself.

She checked the time on her computer. It was 8:44 a.m. She figured Travis was settling into his workstation right about then, with his fresh cup of coffee. She opened a new email and typed a quick note to him before heading into the conference room for the rest of the morning.

Thank you for an amazing night…

Send.

As Hannah stood from her computer, the photo of her and Audrey at the Jersey Shore made her pause. She picked up the picture frame and studied the photo, unnerved by the sudden pit in her stomach. She didn't have time to assess what she was feeling. It was time for her to report to the conference room. She kissed the tips of her fingers and pressed them to Audrey's smiling face in the picture.

"I'll see you soon, Sis," she whispered. Hannah couldn't shake the bad feeling as she walked toward the conference room.

————

Travis walked along the storefronts in the World Trade Center Mall, whistling a joyful tune. He came to a stop in front of the coffee stand.

"Good morning, Martha," Travis greeted the woman behind the counter. His presence at the coffee stand every morning had become routine, right down to the minute.

"You're late," Martha said, looking down at her watch, taking note of the time.

Travis hadn't had time to put his watch on that morning. In his haste to get out the door, he shoved his watch into his pocket and flew out of his apartment building. Travis stood at the coffee kiosk, having no idea what time it was. "What time is it, anyway?" he asked, reaching into his pocket to retrieve his watch.

As he wiggled the watch out of his pocket, he heard a clink on the floor. Searching the floor to see what had fallen from his pocket, he spotted the shiny flattened penny from the observation deck. He quickly bent down to retrieve it. He held up the shiny penny that read WORLD TRADE CENTER, 2001 and showed it to Martha.

"It's my good luck charm. I keep it in my pocket everyday," he said.

Martha smiled, concentrating on pouring his usual dark roast coffee into a medium-sized coffee cup, securing it with a white lid. "It's almost 8:45, dear. You'd better run." Martha handed him his coffee.

Travis gave her two dollar bills from his pocket. She had already collected his change from the drawer and simultaneously handed him twenty-one cents back.

"Thanks, Martha, I'll see you tomorrow." He shoved the change into his right pocket.

"Okay, dear, see you tomorrow," she replied as Travis turned to continue on toward the glass turnstile doors leading into the North Tower lobby.

On the other side of the turnstile, Travis noticed Carl, an attorney from his office, heading toward him in his motorized wheelchair. Carl was a heavyset man in his early sixties, with reddish brown hair and copper freckles dotting his face. He had suffered a traumatic brain injury from a skiing accident in his twenties. Though he survived the incident, he never did regain the use of his legs. Carl worked with Travis in the disability law department and had the reputation of being a ferocious and unmatchable attorney.

Carl came closer, maneuvering his wheelchair against the traffic heading toward the elevators. Travis could see he was flustered, his copper freckles almost disappearing against the backdrop of his flushed face.

"Hey, Carl, you're going in the wrong direction. Is everything okay?" Travis asked with concern.

"I don't know where my head is at today," he replied. "I put my briefcase down when I got my coffee, and like a dunce, I must have left it there. My ID badge, wallet, and everything is in there." Panic started to rise in his voice.

"No worries. I just came from there; I'll just run back and grab it," Travis quickly reassured him. "Wait here. We'll be on the next elevator up, with your briefcase."

Travis's whole world had consisted of taking care of Eli, thus Carl represented the hope Travis had for him. It was hard for Travis to imagine Eli all grown up one day and on his own, but Carl was the proof that Eli could live a happy and independent life, with a successful career.

Travis turned back into the turnstile, heading out into the mall. Remembering the time, he upped his pace to a slow jog.

A long line had formed at the coffee kiosk. Martha had her back turned, busy filling coffee orders. The coffee rush was usually much earlier, and Travis noted that many people were running late that morning.

Travis's eyes scanned the floor around the kiosk, not wanting to disturb Martha. There, between impatiently shifting legs, was a black briefcase. Travis grabbed it and started jogging back toward the glass doors. Pushing through the turnstile, Travis triumphantly held up Carl's briefcase.

"Thank you, Travis. I owe you one," Carl said, gratefully taking hold of his briefcase and placing it on his lap.

"Nah, it's nothing," Travis replied.

Travis walked alongside Carl's wheelchair toward the elevator.

"Hey, did you see that sky out there today?" Carl asked Travis.

"Incredible," Travis replied. "Cerulean."

Carl looked at Travis in surprise. "I didn't know anyone else knew the color cerulean."

"One of the many reasons we are friends, Carl," Travis said with a wink.

The express elevator arrived seconds after they arrived in front of the large silver doors. Travis held the doors open, allowing Carl to maneuver his wheelchair in. The rest of the group loaded into the elevator, including a woman so pregnant that she looked like she would give birth at any moment.

The doors closed, and the elevator began to pull toward the sky. Travis reached into his pocket to find the flattened souvenir penny. As he held it between his fingers, he felt like the luckiest guy in the world.

CHAPTER 18

Tuesday, September 11, 2001
8:46 a.m.

Hannah walked into the conference room, joining an anxious Berkley and a half-dozen other presenters, who were nervously standing around. She drifted over to the windows briefly and let her eyes follow the North Tower all the way to the top. Looking up to the 104th floor, she entertained the thought of Travis peering down at her, giving her an encouraging thumbs-up.

The phone in the middle of the conference room table rang. Berkley answered on the first ring. "Okay, yeah, yeah, yeah," he said hurriedly into the phone. He then aggressively slammed the receiver down and turned to everyone in the room.

"All right, people, they're almost all here," he bellowed. "Marilyn will be escorting them down in a few minutes. I expect perfection from each of you. Anyone who screws this up won't have a job tomorrow."

Hannah breathed in slowly, trying to calm her nerves, but something felt terribly wrong. Suddenly, out of the corner of her eye, an object appearing outside the windows in the distance caught her attention—something terribly out of place, something very wrong. The walls started to shake, and the coffee cups on the counter began to rattle. To her horror, she realized a large airplane was flying low, way too low, barreling straight toward the North Tower. The high-pitched scream of an airplane engine got louder by the second.

"No," she gasped, her voice barely audible. She reached out as if she could somehow stop it. "No!" she screamed as the plane crashed high into the adjacent North Tower. A large fireball burst out from the opposite side of the North Tower, where the plane had struck. It ricocheted off the South Tower, traveling down the side of the building in front of the conference room. Hannah saw a blast of bright light and felt heat on her face as she instinctively ducked down. For a moment, she thought she was having another one of her nightmares.

I am going to wake up, and Travis will be right next to me...

But the screams in the room were too real. The potent smell of jet fuel and smoke immediately seeped in through the windows. When she opened her eyes seconds later, the chaos outside the windows in front of her was incomprehensible. Thick black smoke billowed out through a giant gaping hole in the south facade of the North Tower. Office papers and debris rained down just outside the windows of her conference room. Hannah looked around the room. Some had dove under the conference room table. Others were still standing in the same place, in too much shock to move.

Marilyn came running into the conference room frantically. "What just—" she stopped suddenly, seeing the devastation outside the window.

Hannah couldn't move. She stood, staring out the window in total shock. Marilyn rushed to Hannah's side. Hannah looked at Marilyn, searching for reassurance in her eyes, but only shock and horror were mirrored back.

"A plane, it was an airplane," Hannah said breathlessly in disbelief.

Just then, large objects began to fall in front of the windows. Objects that she recognized somewhere in her conscious mind, but made no sense in the setting. First an office chair, then a desk, plummeted from the narrow windows next to the gaping hole in the facade. They flew at lightning speed toward the ground below. Shards of glass rained down. Clouds of thick black smoke billowed out from the newly broken windows.

What is happening? Hannah's mind raced.

Suddenly Hannah sucked in a deep horrified breath. "Oh my God!" she exclaimed at what she saw next.

Marilyn saw the same horrific sight at the same moment. People were standing on the ledges of the upper floors of the North Tower, hanging out from the windows. Thick black smoke poured out from behind them. They were *trapped*!

Marilyn pulled Hannah's head away and buried it in her chest.

"Don't look, honey. Please don't look," Marilyn pleaded.

———

Berkley stood in front of the conference room of stunned employees, his back to the devastation outside the windows.

"Everyone, stay calm; we are okay here. I think this was just, uh…" he stammered, trying to compose himself, "a terrible accident. We shouldn't be in any danger here in the South Tower."

Hannah started to hyperventilate. "I have to call him. *He is up there*," she said, grabbing Marilyn's arm. She then turned and ran out of the conference room, toward her cubicle, with Marilyn following close behind.

Miles was on the phone with Stephanie. He covered the mouthpiece. "The news is saying it was a small Cessna. Must have been pilot error or something," he said, sounding unsure.

"That was no small Cessna, Miles. The news is wrong," Hannah said confidently, digging for her cell phone in her briefcase.

She flipped open her phone, praying there would be a call from Travis. Maybe he hadn't made it in yet. Maybe he was still chatting with Martha at the coffee kiosk. Her heart dropped. There were no calls from Travis, and the screen on her cell phone said NO SERVICE.

Hannah frantically picked up her desk phone and dialed Travis's cell phone number. Her hands were shaking. "Come on, come on…" she said as she waited for the phone to connect.

Beep… "All circuits are busy right now. Please try again later," a robotic voice message played on the other end of the phone.

Hannah turned to Marilyn and Miles. "We have to get out of here," she said urgently, "something is very wrong."

She looked down at the picture of her and Audrey, recalling the pit in her stomach right before heading to the conference.

Marilyn shifted nervously. "Berkley said we aren't in any danger here. I think we should stay. You know how much he hates those emergency drills. Imagine how mad he will be if we left."

Hannah turned to Miles. "Miles?" Hannah pleaded.

"I don't know, Hannah," he replied uneasily, "the news is saying it was a small plane. It seems like a random accident."

Hannah sighed, frustrated that no one felt the same sense of urgency. "Please come with me," she pleaded again. "I have a very bad feeling."

Just then Berkley came out of the conference room to make an announcement.

"I have just been given word to stay in place. This appears to be an isolated incident. They are evacuating the North Tower as we speak. Once everything calms down, we will start the meeting."

Marilyn turned to Hannah. "Well, there you have it."

"But—" Hannah tried to protest.

"Listen, dear," Marilyn interrupted, "I know you are worried about Travis, but why don't you just wait to hear from him. I am sure he will give a ring as soon as he can. They are evacuating them right now."

Hannah sensed that Marilyn didn't want her to leave because if she did, she'd surely be fired. Hannah knew it too, but everything in her body told her to get out of the building. Suddenly Hannah heard her mother's voice say, *Always trust your gut.*

She looked down again at the picture of Audrey on her desk. Hannah flung off her heels and put on her sneakers, frantically tying the shoelaces really tight, and then grabbed her briefcase. She knew what her decision would mean for her job, but she suddenly didn't care.

"Please," Hannah desperately begged Marilyn and Miles, trying one last time to change their minds.

"I promise if I start to feel unsafe in any way, I'll evacuate," Miles promised.

Marilyn looked regretfully at Hannah. "I have a lobby full of executives to escort to the conference room in a few minutes. I need this job. I've got grandbabies to spoil."

Hannah felt helpless. "I wish you would change your minds," she said before quickly hugging Marilyn and Miles. She then zipped quietly around the corner, toward Don's cubicle. Don was shutting down his computer and slowly loading files into his briefcase.

"Are you leaving?" she whispered just below the cubicle wall so that Berkley wouldn't see her.

"I was thinking about it. I'll take any excuse to leave the office," Don said nonchalantly.

"Okay, let's go," she whispered hurriedly.

Don looked at her in surprise. "Wait. *You* are leaving? What about your big presentation? Berkley is going to lose his mind."

"I don't care about the meeting. Something isn't right." Every second that went by, Hannah felt a growing sense of danger. "Don, we have to leave now," she said sternly.

"Go ahead and get a head start. I'll catch up," he said.

"No, Don, now!" Hannah snapped.

"Okay," he said, startled by Hannah's tone. "Let's go."

Don finished shoving the last papers into his briefcase and rose quickly from his office chair.

They walked briskly past cubicles and groups of confused employees standing around. Some people were on the phone with loved ones, and others were frantically trying to pull up news reports on their computers.

The television in the foyer was broadcasting live with the words BREAKING NEWS sprawled across the screen. Grainy, shaky images from news cameras on the ground were struggling to zoom in on the devastation right outside of Hannah's office windows. Hannah kept her head down as she walked. The foyer was full of executives waiting for the meeting to start.

"I took a red eye from Los Angeles for this meeting," she heard one of the executives say in an arrogant tone. "My time is valuable. I expect to still have this meeting today."

Hannah knew that Berkley would never cancel the meeting. Her absence would be the end of her days at Berkley and Stanton, but a powerful intuition was guiding her. In no uncertain terms, she had to get out of the building.

Don pushed open the heavy glass doors and walked straight to the elevators.

"No elevator, Don. We are taking the stairs, just like they teach during the emergency drills."

"Are you crazy? Do you know how long that will take us?" Don asked.

Hannah pushed open the stairwell door. A few people had slowly started to filter into the stairwells, looking unsure about leaving.

"No elevator, Don," Hannah repeated, standing her ground.

"You're killing me, kid," Don said, begrudgingly following Hannah into the stairwell.

———

Audrey sat in her academy seat, more aware then ever of the empty spot next to her. It had been over a week since Preston had been suspended from the academy. She fidgeted under the table, nervously planning her two goals for the day: talk to the chief on Preston's behalf, and make things right with O'Shea.

Audrey attempted to drown out the instructor's dull, monotonous lesson on report writing by visualizing how she would approach the chief that morning. During morning break, she planned to walk down the hall to see Eileen, who would be sitting at her desk outside of the chief's office. Then Audrey would explain about how Preston was only defending her against the degrading innuendos.

Eileen would be sympathetic and supportive, convincing the chief to see Audrey right away. He would welcome her and allow her to clear up the whole situation. She would explain that Preston was defending her honor and even suggest that he should be commended for his loyalty and upstanding values. The chief would realize that Preston's integrity should be the standard for all law enforcement and would thank her for coming in to clarify the whole misunderstanding.

Audrey's next mission would be to find O'Shea to apologize. She envisioned waiting for him in the parking lot at the end of the day. Maybe she would ask him to join her at one of the picnic tables on the side lawn under the unusually blue sky that day. She would apologize for treating him with such callousness. He would forgive her and tell her not to worry about it. Then, everything would be perfect.

Audrey just needed to get through the rest of the soul-crushing, two-hour report writing class first. She had just begun to doodle on her sample police report, when the door to the academy room flew open. Eileen stood in the doorway, with a worried and confused look across her face.

"Uh…a plane just hit the World Trade Center," she said, sounding just as confused as the look on her face.

Audrey's eyes widened as she tried to process the words she heard. "The World Trade Center?" Audrey blurted out. "Which tower? Is anyone hurt?" Audrey asked frantically.

"I don't have any more information. I am sorry, Audrey. Do you know someone there?" Eileen gently asked.

Audrey stood up from her seat so fast that she knocked her chair backward. She grabbed her cell phone from her duty bag. "My sister. She works in the South Tower," Audrey said desperately. "Please excuse me," she then said to the instructor as she walked quickly out of the room to the hallway bathroom. Her fingers shook as she dialed Hannah's cell phone number.

Audrey prayed Hannah would answer, but there was only silence at the other end as her phone tried unsuccessfully to connect. Audrey hung up and dialed again. More silence. The calls were not going through. The panic started to rise in Audrey's throat. She felt like she couldn't breathe. She flung open the bathroom door and returned to the classroom, where everyone sat silently. They were all waiting for more information. The instructors had gathered in the corner of the room, nervously discussing the few details they knew.

"I need to use the landline, sir, please," Audrey said, trying to keep her composure.

He nodded, picking up the hand receiver and giving it to her. She tried Hannah's number again. After a long silence, a recording played. "We cannot complete your call at this time. Please hang up and try your call again later." Audrey slammed the phone down onto the receiver.

Just then, Eileen appeared again in the doorway. She cleared her throat before speaking. "The chief is watching the situation closely," Eileen said, trying to sound reassuring. The color suddenly drained from her face. Audrey could tell she had more information. Eileen looked nervously around the room. "This appears to be…a terrorist attack. We're getting word that the airplane was hijacked and purposely flown into the tower," Eileen glanced at Audrey apprehensively before proceeding, "and they believe there may be more planes coming."

Audrey's chest tightened. *Terrorist attack, hijacked, there may be more planes coming…*

"The chief has given permission to dismiss the class to the break room, but the building is going into lockdown shortly. No one in, no one out," Eileen said, her concerned eyes falling again upon Audrey. "The news is on the television in the break room."

Audrey fought back tears. She bolted from the room and barreled down the steps to the break room in the basement. Several officers were already watching the large television mounted on a rolling cart. The rest of her classmates filtered in silently behind her.

The image on the television made Audrey gasp out loud. The top of one of the towers was burning—flames shooting out from a large hole high up in the building, black smoke billowing out and upward against the serene blue sky.

Audrey's eyes scanned the images on the television, trying to discern which tower was on fire. The shaky camera image pulled back from its zoom just enough to reveal the tall spire antenna on top of the building, shrouded by heavy black smoke.

"The North Tower," she said out loud, but it was little consolation. Seeing Hannah's tower in the backdrop of the devastation, there was no doubt that Hannah was in grave danger.

Get out of there, Hannah, Audrey silently pleaded, hoping she could somehow hear her. *Mom!* She suddenly thought.

She dialed her parents' home number on her cell phone. Her mother answered sleepily after several rings. In her parents' retired years, they enjoyed sleeping in. Audrey never called that early.

"Hi, honey; it's early," her mother answered sleepily, "is everything okay?"

"Have you heard from Hannah?" Audrey asked urgently.

"No. Audrey, what is going on?" Her mother's voice now sounded concerned.

"Turn on the television," Audrey answered.

"Uh…okay…what channel?" her mother asked, confused.

"Any channel…every channel," Audrey responded.

"What? What do you mean every channel?" A moment later, she heard her mother gasp. Her father in the background exclaimed something inaudible.

"An airplane crashed into the World Trade Center," Audrey said.

Her mother gasped again. "Is that Hannah's—?" her mother began to ask.

Audrey answered immediately, "No, that's the North Tower."

Her mother breathed a sigh of relief, but Audrey knew more.

"Mom, listen to me. I have some information here." Audrey paused before saying the rest. "This is likely a terrorist attack. We are being told there may be more planes coming," Audrey barely choked out the words.

There was silence on the other end of the phone. "Oh my God," her mother finally whispered into the phone, understanding what Audrey was telling her.

"I'll get more information. If you don't hear back from me, please take care of Lucy," Audrey instructed. She knew she needed to get to the city, but *how*?

Audrey hung up the phone and tuned back to the images on the television. The time showed 9:01 a.m. on the bottom of the screen. Reporters were doing their best with the little information they knew. An eyewitness came on the air, talking to the reporters over the phone.

"I recognized it as a 737 passenger airplane," the witness stated with certainty.

Were there passengers on that airplane? Audrey felt sick with the thought.

Audrey could not take her eyes off the enormous burning black hole in the North Tower. She remembered Hannah mentioning that Travis worked on the 104th floor of the North Tower. The top floors were completely engulfed in thick black smoke.

The news camera that was zoomed in live on the burning tower, suddenly panned out, and something on the television came into view in the distance. Audrey squinted, trying to make sense of what she was seeing.

It couldn't be...

To Audrey's horror, she realized the object in the distance was a low flying airplane headed straight for the towers. "Oh my God," Audrey said, pulling her hands to her mouth. The airplane suddenly banked, taking a sharp turn directly toward the South Tower. In an instant, the plane crashed into the upper-middle floors of the South Tower, bursting immediately into a ball of fire.

Audrey's knees gave out from under her. Jonathan and Ray caught her before she fell to the ground. They escorted her over to a chair, where she sat down in shock. Panic ensued on the television as reporters tried to make sense of what had just happened.

Audrey heard one reporter say, "It looks like a second plane just crashed into the eightieth...maybe eighty-fifth floor of the South Tower.

Audrey looked up in disbelief. "My sister is there," she said, burying her head under Ray's arm.

CHAPTER 19

The stairwell was narrow, leaving only enough room for two people at a time on each step. As more and more people entered the stairwell, Hannah started to get a feeling of claustrophobia. There was a slight sense of urgency in the stairwell, but for the most part people remained orderly, even cracking nervous jokes along the way.

Don and Hannah had made it down only a few flights of stairs, when Don began to breathe heavily.

"Hannah, I can't make it down all of these stairs," he said.

"Take your time," Hannah said, even though her instinct was to speed up. To give him incentive to keep going, she added, "You can have a cigarette when we get to the bottom."

They had just reached the seventy-eighth floor, when a woman's voice came over the loudspeaker. The woman instructed everyone to remain in the building and return to their offices for safety.

Don turned to Hannah. "I'm going back up."

"No, Don, please! It's not safe," Hannah pleaded.

"You heard the announcement. This building is safe. If I were you, I would get back up there too, before Berkley realizes you're gone," Don said as he turned to the door leading into the Sky Lobby on the seventy-eighth floor.

"I don't give a crap what the announcement said." Hannah sounded almost hysterical.

She could not believe her eyes as she watched most of the people in the stairwell exit into the Sky Lobby toward the elevators. They were going back up to their offices!

"I'll see you tomorrow, kid…*if* you still have a job," he said. Then Don disappeared into the Sky Lobby to catch the next elevator up.

There was nothing Hannah could do; she had to keep going.

Only a few people continued down the stairs with her. The rest had exited the stairwell after the announcement and were crammed in the Sky Lobby.

With the stairwell less crowded, Hannah suddenly had the opportunity to pick up her pace. She flipped open her phone, hoping to see a signal, only to see the same screen message as earlier. She gripped her briefcase tighter and started running down the stairs.

She made it down twenty more flights of stairs, then stopped at the sixty-eighth floor to catch her breath. Suddenly her body was thrown forward by such a powerful force that she thought a bomb had gone off in the stairwell. The floor under her feet shifted forcefully, causing her to tumble down the flight of stairs in front of her. She came to a rest up against the wall, her head smacking hard up against the concrete. At first she thought the room was spinning from the blow to her head, but it was the building swaying right, then left.

The building is going to fall over! It was just like her nightmare a few nights before.

The tower lurched and twisted several times before finally coming to a stop.

Hannah pulled herself up from the landing, a sharp stabbing pain radiated in her head when she stood. Chunks of Sheetrock had come loose from the walls, and her black suit was covered with chalklike powder.

What just happened? Was there an explosion in the South Tower?

Hannah's mind spun wildly. Whatever it was, it was no longer an isolated incident.

Suddenly the stairwell began filling with smoke. Seconds later, people started pouring into the stairwells. Some were screaming and panicking; others were quiet and focused.

"Whatever happened to the North Tower just happened here," one woman said, her voice shaking.

"I think it was a bomb," another person speculated.

There was a sudden palpable rise in panic as people scrambled to make sense of what was happening.

"Maybe it was a gas explosion?" someone else guessed as the crowd descended urgently down the steps.

Hannah realized the people in the stairwell didn't know that it was an airplane that had hit the North Tower. She didn't dare say anything. That type of information would only cause panic, and they had to keep calm and orderly to get out.

The floor under Hannah's feet felt unstable. The walls seemed to creek and moan, the sound of steel and concrete grinding together. The stairwell became congested, as people fled from their floors into the narrow escape route. Hannah was suddenly slowed by the sea of people in front of her. She took each step slowly and methodically, shoulder to shoulder with someone she didn't know. The air was getting heavy. Smoke wafted down from the floors above, making it harder to breathe with every step. People began coughing and choking on the limited air they all shared in the cramped stairwell.

Hannah tried to tune out the nervous hum of conversation surrounding her. She concentrated on putting one foot in front of the other, but with each step, her sneakers were getting heavier and more cumbersome. Her feet were getting wet, but why?

A steady stream of water was suddenly flowing down the stairs, like a waterfall. The water was slick and had a straw-colored tint to it. It was hard to keep traction on the stairs. Hannah assumed the water was from the sprinkler system, but what was making it slippery? Within moments, the smell of fuel became unmistakable. Hannah then knew without a doubt that a plane had crashed into the South Tower too.

It was getting hotter in the cramped stairwell. Wet clothing hung on bodies. Many people had taken off their waterlogged shoes, making the descent wearing only socks, or even in their bare feet. Faces were frozen with fear and confusion. Some were calm and focused; others were weeping. Anything that could be easily removed from the day's attire—suit jackets, women's scarves, men's handkerchiefs, tissues from pockets—was used to cover their mouths so they could breathe.

Hannah was also having trouble breathing. Tears began to fill her eyes as dismal thoughts ran through her head. *Where was Travis? Were Marilyn and Miles trapped? Dead? Did Don make it back up to the eighty-fourth floor?*

Hannah started to lose her calm. *What if more planes were coming? What if the stairwell floods, trapping them all inside?*

Hannah couldn't go any faster. She suddenly realized how grim the situation had become. They were all trapped inside a narrow, smoke-filled stairwell—inside a burning, buckling building.

Hannah was just about to lose it, when she felt a hand on her arm. A soft, shaky voice suddenly spoke. "I know we don't know each other, but…will you hold my hand?" a woman next to her asked.

Hannah had been so consumed that she hadn't paid attention to the person who had been shoulder to shoulder with her during their slow descent. The woman, not much older than Hannah, was striking, even in the worst of conditions. The beautiful dark brown skin on her face glistened with sweat, but her forehead was smeared with soot. She was tall and thin, with sculpted high cheekbones and catlike eyes that reminded Hannah of a lynx. Her long eyelashes hung low, and gray dust coated her perfectly applied mascara.

"I'm scared," she said, clinging to Hannah's arm, her eyes filled with terror.

Hannah noticed that she limped with every step. She looked down and saw a steady stream of blood pouring from a large open wound on the woman's leg. She didn't seem to be aware that her leg had been gashed open.

Hannah thought of Audrey and their plans that coming weekend. She clung to the belief that she and Travis would be on a train to Connecticut that weekend to visit her family. This woman, someone she had never met, also had a family to survive for. She needed Hannah's help.

Hannah reached down for the woman's hand and gripped it strongly. "I'm scared too, but we are going to get out of here."

Hannah could tell the woman was in bad shape. She knew she had to keep her talking. "What is your name?"

"Abina," she spoke softly.

"I'm Hannah. I wish we were meeting under better circumstances," Hannah said.

Abina let out a breath, her best attempt at a laugh.

They walked hand in hand down the steps, Hannah taking the weight off Abina's bad leg with each step down.

"I don't know how many more steps I can take. I feel weak. I can't breathe. I can't feel my leg," Abina said, looking woozy.

Suddenly the scratchy sound of a radio broadcast echoed off the walls in the stairwell. A man had a portable radio and had turned the volume up for everyone to hear. The announcer on the radio's voice was incredulous.

"At 8:46 a.m., Eastern Standard Time, an airplane crashed into the North Tower of the World Trade Center in Manhattan. Minutes ago a *second* airplane slammed into the South Tower of the World Trade Center,"

The stairwell erupted with gasps, the people becoming unstable as panic rose.

"Shhh!" the man holding the radio scolded.

The reporter continued, "Officials are reporting this is now believed to be a planned terrorist attack. As we speak, there are several aircraft not responding to air traffic control. Folks, our nation is under attack. I repeat, our country is under attack."

With that, panic fully let loose in the previously calm and orderly stairwell.

"*Shit*," Hannah said out loud.

People began to push forward, screaming at the people ahead to move faster. The situation was unraveling in front of her eyes. Hannah suddenly feared being crushed or trampled. The radio broadcast was drowned out from the noise in the stairwell.

A woman frantically began screaming. "We are all going to die! We have to get out of here!" she wailed.

The woman suddenly started pushing people out of the way, shoving her way down the stairs. A man followed behind her, pushing his way past the people in front of him. They disappeared down the flight of stairs below and out of sight. Hannah had to do something. They still had forty floors below them to safety. If more people started pushing and they didn't all stay calm, they surely would die in that stairwell.

Suddenly Hannah saw commotion ahead and people below parting the way. There was someone coming…*up*! Hannah could not believe her eyes. Firefighters wearing thick uniforms and carrying heavy equipment were climbing up through the hot stairwell, *into* the burning building.

Desperate to quell the panic and commotion on the flights above, Hannah immediately took charge.

"Everyone, listen up!" she shouted with authority in her voice. Still holding Abina's hand, she yelled up to the stairs above, "Firefighters are here! Help is here! Move to the side and let them up. Please stay calm!"

Suddenly a sense of relief came over the stairwell.

As the firefighters got closer to Hannah, she could see the sweat rolling down their beet-red faces, and hear their heavy breath with each step up. Hannah then came face to face with a fireman. As she helped Abina limp to the side to allow the fireman to pass, Hannah's eyes met his. He was young, barely in his early twenties, with his whole life ahead of him.

"Everything is going to be okay," he said reassuringly. "We're going to get you out of here."

The look in his eyes instantly became etched into Hannah's memory. His young face almost resembled a baby's, and his light brown eyes looked terrified and unsure. But without question, he continued to climb the stairs past Hannah and Abina and into the pure hell above. Hannah watched as the young fireman rounded the corner up the next flight of stairs, disappearing out of sight.

———

Audrey's body seemed to operate automatically, while her brain spun viciously, trying to make sense of what she just saw on the television screen. People in the break room were talking to her, but it was just background noise against the thoughts in her head. Before she knew it, she was in the hallway, leaping up the stairs two at a time. She felt like she was going to get sick, and she fought the tears that wanted to come. She had to keep a clear mind.

Audrey rounded the corner at the top of the stairwell and onto the main level of the police department. Four police officers holding long guns marched down the hall in formation, wearing helmets and heavy bulletproof vests. "Make way!" the front officer barked at Audrey, who had inadvertently stepped into their path. She quickly moved to the side of the hallway and stood at attention until they passed. She then lingered a moment to see if she could overhear any information.

"You take the east entrance, and you take the west entrance," the front officer instructed, pointing at two of the officers. "Jimmy, you take up post at the basement door by the range. I'll be out front. We need to seal off all access points to the building. Nobody in, nobody out."

The lockdown was starting!

Audrey panicked.

She couldn't stay locked down in the building. She had to get to Hannah!

Audrey stormed down the hallway toward the chief's office. To Audrey's surprise, Eileen was not at her desk outside of the chief's office. Under normal circumstances, anyone wishing to see the chief would have to go through Eileen, but that morning was anything but normal. Audrey noticed the chief's door was slightly ajar. Without thinking, Audrey burst through the door, coming to a sudden stop a few steps in.

She immediately regretted her hasty decision. Eight officers were being briefed by the chief. She stood awkwardly as she scanned the room. O'Shea was seated in one of the chairs, staring back at Audrey, his eyebrows raised. Sergeant Gaston was next to him, glaring at her.

"What's the meaning of this?" the chief exclaimed in a booming voice. "Eileen!"

"I'm…um…Eileen isn't there, sir. I'm sorry. The door was open and I … I didn't expect—I mean, I didn't know you were in a meeting,"

"Do you have any idea what is going on out there? Of course I'm in a meeting! Now exit my office, recruit. We will deal with your disregard for chain of command at a later time," he scolded her as he stood up from behind his mahogany desk to escort her out.

"No! Please, let me explain—" Audrey began.

"You have three seconds to leave my office before I personally write you up for insubordination," the chief warned. "Now get out!" He was at the door in seconds, holding it open for her to leave.

Audrey couldn't just walk out the door.

"My sister is in the South Tower," Audrey spoke, her voice cracking with desperation and emotion.

The chief's expression suddenly changed. He paused a moment, appearing to be deep in thought. It felt like an eternity before he spoke again.

"We are mobilizing a team to go into the city," he said, his tone softer. "That's what this meeting is about. These are the officers that will be going. We will do whatever we can to help your sister. Before they leave, I will have Eileen gather information about her. If you have any pictures you can provide the team, please get those to them before they leave."

Gaston shifted impatiently in his seat as if she were wasting his time. O'Shea sat listening attentively.

"I want to go," Audrey burst out.

Gaston shot up from his seat. "Absolutely not," he protested.

"Have a seat, Sergeant!" the chief barked at Gaston. He then turned back to Audrey, looking regretful. He lowered his head. "I can't in good conscience let you go. You are still a recruit here. All of the officers in this room are highly trained emergency response team members. They have been trained for this."

Tears welled up in Audrey's eyes. "With all due respect, sir, whatever is happening out there, whatever I just saw happen on that television, no one is trained for," she replied emotionally.

Gaston jumped in again. "This is ridiculous. She doesn't even have a gun on her belt yet. She will be a liability."

"I am going," she said with conviction, "with or without this department."

O'Shea spoke up. "Sir, I will take personal responsibility for her safety. Please," he said soberly, "her sister is there."

After a moment of silence, the chief spoke again. "You leave from here with the clothes on your back. Estimated time of departure is 1000 hours. You will load the emergency response team van with these guys. You are heading into a war zone, and I cannot guarantee your safety. We still don't know what we are dealing with yet."

"Yes, sir. I understand," Audrey said eagerly.

Gaston threw his arms up in the air. "You have got to be kidding!"

The chief turned back toward his desk. "Not another word out of you, Gaston," he growled. "Audrey, pull up a seat. You are a part of this meeting now."

CHAPTER 20

Traffic in the stairwell had slowed to a crawl. Smoke continued to infiltrate the stairwell from somewhere above. The stairwell had become somewhat quiet except for the sounds of gasping and hacking.

People were getting tired. Hannah found herself tripping over items left behind—shoes, briefcases, jackets. The clutter on the ground made it even more difficult to keep her footing. The gushing water from above had become a darker brown and even more slippery. It was all she could do to keep from falling every few steps.

Every few minutes, different sets of firefighters and police officers climbed past them, up into the burning tower.

Hannah was still holding Abina's hand. She noticed the blood gushing from Abina's leg was getting heavier. Deep down, Hannah knew that it was also Abina's blood that she was slipping on.

The somber quiet in the stairwell was shattered by shouts from the flights above. Hannah heard people gasping in horror, causing panic to spread through the stairwell again. Appearing from around the corner above, two firemen carried a badly burned woman down the steps. Hannah tried to turn her head, but it was too late. She saw the horrific sight of the woman's badly burned face, the charred tattered clothes hanging off her body, and her bloody, mangled leg.

"Move to the side! Move! Move!" one of the firemen screamed. The look in his eyes was wild with astonishment and horror.

What else did they see up there?

Hannah backed up against the wall as far as she could to let them go by. There was not much room for the two large firemen to squeeze by with the injured woman. As Hannah watched them disappear around to the flight below, she prayed for the first time in a very long time.

Hannah and Abina did not speak a word about the injured woman. It was too horrific to acknowledge. If they allowed their minds to actually absorb what they'd just witnessed, they might crumble.

Hannah focused on taking one step at a time. Suddenly Abina exclaimed, "Oh my, Hannah, you are bleeding!"

"What?" Hannah asked, startled and confused. She didn't feel any pain other than the bump on her head. She didn't remember getting cut. How could she be bleeding? Abina was looking in horror at her upper arm. Hannah looked and saw that blood had soaked through the sleeve of her white blouse. She instinctively grabbed her arm to feel for pain. *Nothing.* Starting to panic, she rolled up her sleeve, finding no injury whatsoever.

"What...?" Hannah started to say, trying to understand how she could be bleeding. Suddenly she got a sick feeling in her stomach when she realized where it had come from.

It wasn't her blood.

Hannah felt dizzy. "It is not my blood," she said to Abina. "The woman they just carried down..."

Abina's face fell, and her eyes went dimmer. They continued down several flights of stairs in total silence.

Hannah was nauseous from the thought of the blood on her shirt, the rancid smell in the stairwell, and the increasing stuffiness in the air. She was tired, scared, and losing hope. She could not give up. She had to find Travis. She had to see her sister and family again.

Suddenly she felt Abina stumble, her knees giving out midstep. Hannah helped steady her.

"Hannah, I'm feeling really weak. I don't think I can go on," Abina said feebly.

Hannah knew Abina had lost a lot of blood from her wound. Her striking dark brown eyes were deeply setting behind her heavy eyelids. She knew she had to do something to keep her conscious.

"We have to keep going, Abina." Hannah grasped her hand tightly. "Tell me about yourself."

Abina took a slow breath, trying to gather the strength to talk. "I'm from Ghana. I came to America three years ago." She paused to catch her breath. "My family back home is so proud of me...you know, living in the United States, working at the World Trade Center." Abina began to weep. "I'm never going to see my family again."

Losing hope was their biggest danger. Hope was all they had in that stairwell.

"Look at me," Hannah said intently. "We are going to see our families again; I promise."

Hannah stared into her dark brown eyes until Abina nodded slightly. Hannah had just made a promise she was not sure she could keep.

As they rounded the corner to the fifteenth floor, the pace picked up a little.

"We're almost out of here," Hannah reassured Abina.

Each flight down felt promising. Hannah held Abina's hand tightly with one hand; her other still fiercely gripped her briefcase. For the first time since being in the stairwell, Hannah felt confident they would soon be free.

They had just reached the eighth floor, when instantly everything came to a complete stop. There was some type of bottleneck happening below. Hannah's anxiety overwhelmed her. They were so close, yet still so far. Her legs were tired, and she was getting dizzy from lack of oxygen. She had been in the stairwell for almost an hour.

Abina stopped. She looked woozy and unsteady. "I'm going to pass out," she said just before her legs gave out. Hannah reached out to catch her as she fell forward onto a man and woman who were on the step in front of them.

"She's really injured; we need to get her help right away," the man said.

Hannah knew he was right. They needed to get her help immediately, or she was going to die right there in the stairwell. Hannah hooked her arm under Abina's armpit. The man propped up Abina's limp body, and the woman helped balance her. People willingly moved to the side, allowing them to carry Abina down through the crowded stairwell. Hannah felt horribly guilty for passing everyone, but Abina was dying.

Though Abina was tall and slim and could not have weighed more than 130 pounds, her limp, unconscious body felt like they were carrying a ton down the stairs. Hannah's lungs burned and her legs ached, but she had to keep going. Each flight felt like an eternity, until finally, she saw the light of the mezzanine level from the stairwell door below. They stumbled down the last flight of stairs, out into the lobby. Hannah was horrified by the sight. The once beautiful and bustling lobby was a scene of destruction and chaos.

They carried Abina out through the shattered glass doors and out into the plaza. Nothing could have prepared Hannah for the scene of death and destruction as she exited the Tower. Hannah wondered for a moment if a nuclear bomb had been detonated while she was in the stairwell of the South Tower.

After they left the cover of the building and were out in the open air, they were quickly forced to dodge falling debris from above. Black smoke was billowing from the tops of both buildings. Shattered glass crunched under their feet as they carried Abina across the plaza.

Hannah thought she was hallucinating. The sky was full of floating white objects, meandering their way down slowly from the sky, like a peaceful winter snowstorm. Hannah could not make sense of what she was seeing. She couldn't fathom that those white objects were reams of white office paper, blowing out from the shattered windows above.

"Straight ahead!" Hannah yelled when she spotted several ambulances and police cars parked on the street. "Let's get her to the ambulance!"

As they approached the ambulance, emergency medical personnel rushed over, taking hold of Abina and loading her onto a stretcher.

"Is she going to be okay?" Hannah nervously asked the EMT.

The EMT placed his two fingers on Abina's wrist. "She is badly hurt, and her pulse is weak," he replied before hurriedly loading her into the ambulance.

Within seconds, the ambulance pulled away and Abina was out of sight. As suddenly as Abina had entered Hannah's life, she had left it just as abruptly.

The two strangers who had helped carry Abina out of the building watched the ambulance scream off, with its lights and sirens blaring. They stood for a moment to catch their breath, turning to look in horror at the carnage behind them. Tears streamed down the woman's dirty cheeks.

Hannah suddenly began walking toward the wreckage they had just escaped. She had to find Travis.

"Hey! What are you doing?" the man yelled at Hannah. "You're going to get killed!"

She had no time to explain. She continued walking.

The scene was incomprehensible. It looked like a war zone. Debris flew through the air, pieces of building rained down, shattered glass crunched under her feet, and objects were way out of place. Desks, chairs, and airplane parts were scattered about. Thick black smoke from the buildings billowed high into the sky, reaching far and wide.

The blue sky was gone.

People sprinted around her as she went in the wrong direction. She knew where she had to go—*the fountain.*

If Travis was still alive, if he could get free, he would surely meet her there. The fountain, once sparkling blue, had turned murky, filled with papers, dust, and objects. It was not the same beautiful fountain she had met Travis at countless times, as their love blossomed. She frantically looked around, hoping to see Travis's head popping up from the crowd, like the first time they had met at the fountain.

All of a sudden, something landed a short distance from where she was standing with a violent *BOOM*! It hit the ground with such force that Hannah thought a bomb had just gone off next to her. She could barely make out the object that had hit the ground. Hannah looked up to see where the object came from, only to see a similar large object hurling toward the ground from high up in the North Tower.

Oh my God! People are falling from the tower!

Hannah tried to turn in time not to see it, feeling the impact hit the ground. She closed her eyes. It was too much for her to process. She stumbled backward, tripping on something large and soft on the ground behind her. She knew immediately what she'd tripped over. In her haste to find Travis, she hadn't noticed the many bodies strewn about the plaza.

Hannah started to hyperventilate. She could not control her breathing. She could not stand up. She could not open her eyes. Then she felt someone grab her arm and pull her up to her feet. For a brief second, she thought Travis had found her.

"Get up! You have to get out of here! The building is going to collapse!" A police officer was screaming at her, pulling her to her feet. She could barely keep her footing, stumbling as the officer pulled her away.

Hannah looked back over her shoulder. The top of the South Tower started to tip slightly and then began to crumble from the top.

"Run!" the police offer screamed.

Hannah tucked her briefcase under her arm and took off into a full sprint, running alongside the officer, toward the street. Suddenly a piece of steel from the collapsing tower hurled through the air, striking the officer's head from behind. He was killed instantly, just inches from Hannah.

There was no time to think, she had to keep running.

Hannah was steps from a police car parked on the street, when, without warning, a force from behind completely engulfed her. Like being overtaken by a powerful ocean wave, she was swept off her feet and tossed about, not sure which way was up. The force took her right out of her shoes and wrapped around her, like a heavy blanket. She felt her body hit the hood of the police car and roll off onto the other side, landing on top of her briefcase on the pavement.

The violent black cloud flew overhead like a tornado, debris piling on top like an avalanche. Hannah could not take a breath.

Everything went dark. Her chest was not moving.

I think I'm dead...

CHAPTER 21

Audrey stood in the dingy supply closet, deep in the basement of the police department. The gas mask and helmet that had been taken from the dusty shelf and shoved into Audrey's hands were both way too big for her.

"It's all I've got, kid, sorry," the salty, old veteran who manned the supply closet in the basement said. Audrey guessed that he had earned his cushy position by serving at least fifty years in the department.

"Thanks." Audrey dusted off the musty mask and helmet.

It's better than nothing, she hoped.

Audrey reported to the side door to meet up with the team. She stood awkwardly among the group as they waited for the ERT van to pull up.

O'Shea was the only person missing besides Gaston, who was still seething that she'd been allowed to go. She figured he was pulling around with the van, but where was O'Shea?

A moment later, O'Shea appeared from the hallway, joining them by the door. He handed Audrey a radio. "Here, you will need this. We'll be on channel seven when we get there. You can keep it on our main channel for now."

Audrey took the radio and shoved it into one of the many empty holders on her nylon academy duty belt. "Thanks," she said meekly, turning the tiny knob to the "on" position.

There was an armed officer on each side of the door. While the team waited to be cleared to exit the building, she listened to the constant flurry of activity over the police radios. Then a voice she recognized came over the radio, sounding urgent.

"Alpha 1 to Delta 65," the chief called over the radio to the desk sergeant. There was something in his voice that made her uneasy.

"Send all available units to the train station immediately. We are expecting mass amounts of trauma patients to be arriving via Metro North trains from the city. I repeat, send all available units to the train station immediately," he repeated urgently.

O'Shea glanced at Audrey, looking concerned and confused. "This doesn't sound good. Plus the chief never gets on the radio."

They were forty miles from New York City. If trauma patients were being sent up the rail line, there had to be tens of thousands injured. Audrey had a sinking feeling that she'd missed something while she was down in the basement. She glanced down at her watch. It was 1000 hours on the dot.

There was an awkward pause on the radio, and then the sergeant responded. "Delta 65 to Alpha 1, what is this in response to?" the desk sergeant inquired.

"The South Tower has collapsed," the chief answered immediately.

Audrey felt like she'd been hit by a freight train. She could not believe what she was hearing. She steadied herself up against the wall. Her chest was constricted, and she couldn't breathe.

O'Shea stood stunned next to her, unsure of what to say. The situation kept getting worse, and it now seemed hopeless.

Audrey refused to believe Hannah was dead. She had to believe that she'd gotten out of the building. Her thoughts spun around in her head, like a tornado. What if Hannah was one of the injured being loaded onto a train, while she went in the opposite direction to the city in search of her? Worse, what if she was in the tower when it had collapsed? Audrey's thoughts were interrupted when the side door suddenly flew open.

"Go! Go! Go!" the officer on guard barked.

Police departments were on high alert for fear they could be the next targets. They had to move fast. The officers ran to the ERT van as it pulled up along the curb. Audrey jumped up into the van, landing in a seat next to O'Shea.

"Let's go! Let's go! Get in!" Gaston screamed. As soon as they were all in the van, he gunned the gas pedal. The tires screeched as he pulled out of the parking lot.

Audrey looked straight ahead, dazed. It was surreal. The constant flurry of activity over the police radio was overwhelming. She could not hear herself think.

Gaston gripped the steering wheel tightly as the ERT van barreled down the road. He glanced up at the rearview mirror, taking his eyes off the road ahead. His evil eyes were framed inside the mirror as he glared at Audrey.

"Since we have someone with us who should *not* be here, let's make some things clear," Gaston said. "You all listen to me and only me."

O'Shea rolled his eyes.

"Second," he continued, "we don't know what we are going into. With what just happened at the Pentagon, we don't know what the next target may be. The only thing we know is that America is under attack. If I say we abort mission for any reason, we leave immediately."

Wait…the Pentagon?

Audrey turned to O'Shea. "What happened at the Pentagon?" she asked, confused.

O'Shea looked at Audrey, his green eyes looking sorrowful. It was obvious he had bad news to share. "Another airplane crashed into the Pentagon about twenty minutes ago."

Audrey's eyes darted back and forth, her mind frantically trying to put all of the pieces together. She'd missed a lot while she was in the basement getting her gear.

"We *are* under attack," she said under her breath.

"No expected survivors from the plane. A lot of people killed and injured on the ground," O'Shea informed her.

Audrey stared ahead, stunned by the news. With every passing minute, the situation unfolded worse than she could have imagined. Are there more planes in the sky? What was next? She could not shake the feeling that there was far more to come.

Audrey's attention was suddenly diverted by bright flashing police lights up ahead. As their van approached the I-95 South ramp, she noticed two police cars with flashing lights completely blocking the ramp. One of the officers approached the van on the driver's side.

Gaston lowered the driver's window and turned down the radio.

"Hey, you guys heading down there?" one of the officers asked.

"Yeah, we have no idea what we are heading into. As of right now, it's a rescue mission; my bet is it changes to a recovery mission only," Gaston replied callously.

"I hear it's bad. I have a buddy down there. He said there is no way anyone survived the South Tower collapse," the officer said.

Audrey winced and drew in a sharp breath. It felt like she had been hit in the stomach with a baseball bat.

The officer continued obliviously, "There were supposed to be thousands of injured being sent up on trains, but I'm hearing there aren't any patients to send."

Audrey's eyes filled with tears. It just couldn't be.

"All right, Gaston, let's get out of here!" O'Shea yelled from the back, attempting to keep the officer from saying more.

The officer ducked his head into the van. "You guys, oh… and gal, be safe down there. The news is saying there may be more targets. There are supposedly more planes up there not responding to air traffic control. Just keep your heads up. You know what I'm saying." He then waved them through.

Gaston stepped hard on the gas pedal again, sending the tires into a spin as the ERT van entered the highway.

Audrey was struck by the eeriness of the empty roadway. Theirs was the only vehicle on the highway. In huge letters, sprawled across the lit traffic sign, were the words:

I-95 SOUTH CLOSED
TO ALL TRAFFIC
NO ENTRY TO NYC

She had never imagined she would see such a sign. Every entrance ramp to the highway was barricaded off by flashing police lights. Only emergency personnel were allowed access.

Gaston turned the radio back up and was barreling down the empty highway. Suddenly Audrey heard the all too familiar urgent confusion in the broadcaster's voice again.

"We are getting word that another plane has crashed. There are reports coming in of heavy black smoke coming from a field in Pennsylvania. Officials believe this might be United Airlines Flight 93, one of the planes that has not been responding to air traffic control. We're awaiting more information, but all we know at this point is that there appears to be a plane crash in Shanksville, Pennsylvania."

Audrey focused on the rail line that ran parallel to the highway. As kids, Hannah and Audrey would pretend they were racing the trains while riding in the back of their parents' car. The train won every time.

Audrey craned her neck as they approached the first train station. No flurry of activity, no paramedics rushing to the aid of the injured departing filled trains, no trains at all. There were only empty ambulances and police cars, sitting—waiting. She hoped that the closer they got to Manhattan, she would see the train stations loaded with patients in need of medical care, survivors. But with each train station they passed, she saw the same empty scene.

"There is no way anyone survived the collapse," she recalled the cop at the barricade saying.

They reached the New York state line in record time. Gaston turned the volume all the way up, startling Audrey out of her thoughts.

The announcer on the radio did his best to remain calm, but his voice could not hide his despair. "Ladies and gentlemen, the North Tower has now collapsed." There was a brief silence as he gathered his composure. "It is 10:28 a.m., September 11, 2001, and the North Tower has collapsed. The Twin Towers are gone." There was silence on the radio for a moment, until the announcer spoke again, "Lord, help us."

They waited for more information, but the airwaves were silent. After a moment, the announcer returned. "I'm very sorry, listeners," his voice cracking, "I need a moment. I'll be going off air for a bit," he said apologetically.

Gaston pushed buttons urgently, changing the station from one to the next. There was no music playing, no lighthearted morning shows, traffic reports, or weather forecasts. Every station was reporting the same hopeless information.

Audrey sank further into the van seat, putting her head in hands. She closed her eyes and tried to imagine the scene they would encounter when they arrived. She knew she would not be prepared for what they were about to see, and Hannah was somewhere in the middle of the destruction, dead or alive.

O'Shea put his hand on Audrey's shoulder, her head still buried in her hands.

Indescribable anger quickly built inside of Audrey. The country she loved with all of her heart was under attack.

CHAPTER 22

Hannah was slowly roused conscious by the incessant beeping around her. In her semiconscious state, she thought her alarm clock was going off, and it was time to get up for work. She went to lift her arm to hit the snooze button on the alarm clock, but her arm wouldn't budge. Suddenly she was jolted fully awake by the crushing pain in one of her legs. Hannah tried to open her eyes, but they were caked shut with something she could not identify. She realized she was struggling to breathe. Something was packed in her mouth and nose, blocking her airway. She used her tongue to push the obstruction out of her mouth. Chunks of chalky paste crumbled and fell down her chin. She was suddenly able to draw in a shallow breath.

What is in my mouth? Where am I?

It was pitch-black, and she was confined, pinned down by a heavy crushing weight on top of her.

What is all that beeping? How did I get here?

Her memory then flashed back. She was running. The South Tower had begun to crumble. A police officer was running with her away from the falling building. She winced remembering him being hit from behind by flying shrapnel. Her last recollection was being engulfed by a cloud of dust and being lifted off her feet by an unearthly force.

Hannah realized it was the dust and ash from the tower collapse that was packed into her eyes, ears, nose, and mouth. She came to a sudden, sinking realization that she was buried alive under the debris of the collapsed tower. She began to panic.

How am I going to get out of here? No one knows I am under here.

"Help," Hannah tried to yell, but the weight of the debris on top of her chest caused her to barely make a sound. She tried to move her lower body, but a sharp, hot, intense pain shot straight up through her right leg. Something hard and heavy was pinning down her leg, not allowing it to budge. The pain was so intense that it felt as if it went straight into her bones. She tried to move her right arm again, but it was packed down tightly too. An air pocket of space to her left allowed her to move her left arm. Feeling around with her fingers, she felt the dusty handle to her briefcase. She remembered tucking it under her left arm as she ran from the collapsing tower.

Hannah began to realize how dire her situation was. She was buried alive, underneath a pile of rubble, dust, and debris. It was pitch-black, and there was only the sound of constant beeping.

Did the world end? Am I the only one left?

Hannah's breathing started to escalate with her panic. She knew she should not use up the limited oxygen she had down there. She had to stay calm, like she had in the stairwell.

The pain in her leg was getting worse, throbbing and sharp at the same time. Even though it was a warm late summer day, she felt cold, and her body started to shiver. She was sleepy and disoriented. She felt her body going into shock.

Stay awake, Hannah.

Despite her mind's best efforts, her body and mind shut down as she drifted away.

———

"Hannah…Hannah…"

Hannah's eyes slowly opened to reveal darkness. Her whole body was pain free. She had just heard something—a man with a gentle voice calling her name.

"Yes, who's there?" Hannah called out, confused.

"Are you okay, Hannah?" the voice asked.

"No, I don't think I am. My leg is hurt really badly," Hannah replied. "Are you okay? Where are you? Who are you?"

"Hannah—"

"Yes. Do I know you?" Hannah's mind raced.

"Your sister is coming for you. You have to hang on."

"What? How do you know my sister?" Hannah asked, trying to make sense of what she was hearing.

"We are going to be okay," the voice said.

"I'm so glad you are here with me. I thought I was alone under here," Hannah said.

"You are not alone," the voice replied.

"What is your name?" Hannah asked.

Silence.

"Hello?" Hannah called out. "Hello? Hello?" She tried one last time, but her calls were only met with silence.

"Please stay with me," Hannah pleaded. "We're going to get help. We're going to get out of here."

There was no response. In fact, there was total silence. Hannah suddenly realized that the beeping from earlier had stopped, and it had gone eerily quiet.

She had no idea how much time had passed. There was not a single speck of light, nothing but pitch darkness. She was in a semiconscious state, questioning her own sanity. Who was that person just talking to her? How did he know Audrey?

Suddenly Hannah had the worst thought. She was going to die down there and couldn't bear the thought of the pain it would cause her sister, her parents, Travis. She began to cry, but no tears came out. Hannah realized her mouth was chalky, and her eyes were completely dry. She was becoming dehydrated and feared it would take longer to be found than she could survive without food and water. She was alone, deep in the darkness, with nothing but her own despair. Her mind was giving up, and consciousness began to slip away again.

"I'm here with you," she heard the voice say as she faded out.

———

The streets of Manhattan were unrecognizable. The once vibrant blue sky was shrouded by a thick, dark cloud of smoke and dust. The streets were coated with inches of thick gray ash. People wandered aimlessly along the empty streets, disoriented with shock. Their dust-coated faces were streaked with sweat, and their tears were frozen with sorrow. Only the whites of their eyes stood out against the backdrop of their ash-covered faces. Business suits, dresses, and blouses were torn, tattered, and blanketed in gray.

The streets leading to Ground Zero were barricaded by NYPD. Gaston stopped the van at the first barricade, rolling down the window to speak with the officer standing guard. He looked disheveled and distraught.

"Thanks for coming, guys," the officer said, sounding exacerbated. "We need all the help we can get." He pulled his dusty microphone up to his mouth, calling ahead to the next barricade.

Audrey noticed the deep red lines of his bloodshot eyes, and his mustache was coated with ash.

"I've got mutual aid down here. I'm sending them in," the officer said.

As Gaston pulled the van forward, the tires kicked up the ash from the pavement and sent it in through the open window. The thick dust was unlike anything Audrey had ever breathed in, filling her lungs with a plaster-like coating and making her immediately choke.

The scene outside the windows of the van was heart-wrenching. Audrey's attention became fixated on a male officer standing by the curb. His shoulders slumped, head hung low as he cried on the shoulder of the officer next to him.

The van moved slowly along the deserted street, revealing more heartbreaking scenes. A firefighter helped a woman in a torn, dust-covered business suit limp along the sidewalk. Her hair was matted down with dried blood. Several feet away, a business owner was pouring bottled water into the dust-caked eyes of a passerby who had wandered by in shock.

Storefront windows were blown out. Inches of thick ash mixed with papers and debris covered the roads and sidewalks. Street signs were completely coated and unreadable. Audrey had hoped to see ambulances and EMTs tending to survivors, doctors and nurses flurrying around makeshift triage centers saving lives. But that was not what she was seeing at all.

At the next barricade, the officers cleared the way for the van. Audrey instinctively looked for the towers stretching up into the sky, unable to believe they truly were gone. Instead, there was a mountain of rubble, twisted steel, and smoldering ash, where the towers once stood. She could feel death all around her.

Bringing the van to a stop at the edge of the pile, Gaston aggressively shifted the van into park.

"Grab your gear!" he barked. "We stay together, and remember, I'm in charge! If I say we leave, we leave."

Audrey grabbed the old, clunky helmet and gas mask she'd been issued from the dusty shelf, fully knowing the equipment was so outdated it would do nothing to protect her. The most important thing she had in her possession were the three pictures of Hannah she'd grabbed from her locker before she had left.

Stepping out of the van, her shiny, polished black boots met the ash, which instantly coated them in gray. The ground felt soft from the inches of ash under her feet. There was total chaos in front of her. Firefighters, police officers, and EMS personnel scurried—wide-eyed and confused, battered and exhausted. Some had already climbed up on top of the pile— heaving steel, concrete, and debris aside to search for survivors.

Other rescuers had collapsed on the curb, covered in ash from helmet to boots. Their heads were hung low; some were crying. It was a scene Audrey could not take in. The strongest, bravest, most resilient people on earth, pushed to their furthest mental and physical limits. She knew they had lost brothers and sisters, relatives and friends under that mountain of destruction.

Audrey pulled the photos of Hannah out of her pocket. She looked around, scanning for someone she could show them to. A burly, middle-aged police officer stood a few feet away with his back turned, staring ahead at the destruction. She took several steps toward him, trying to read the dust-covered patches on his sleeves. Barely visible under the ash were the words PORT AUTHORITY POLICE DEPARTMENT.

"Excuse me, sir," Audrey said to the officer.

When he turned his head, Audrey gasped. There was a five-inch long gash on the side of his face, bright red blood oozing down his gray dust-covered skin. His eyes went right through her.

"Sir, you are hurt. You need help," she said, reaching for his arm.

He looked away from Audrey, focusing back on the mountain of rubble. "My entire squad..." he started to say. He was silent for a moment and then continued, "We were going in...to the North Tower, together." His eyes were distant and glazed over. "Before we got to the building...a man was hurt, so badly hurt. I helped him to an ambulance. I told my guys to go ahead."

Audrey stood with him in his darkness.

"A minute later the tower came down." His voice gave way to sobs before he lowered his face to his palms. "I should have been in there with them." He continued to sob.

Audrey knew he was in mental and physical shock. The gash on his face was open, and he was losing a lot of blood.

"I'm…I'm so sorry, sir," she said, her words feeling so small. "You are badly hurt; let's get you—"

"I'm not leaving," his voice suddenly hardened, his eyes fixated on the pile before them.

"Okay. You stay right here. I am going to get someone to come help you," she said.

Tucking the pictures back into the front pocket of her uniform shirt, Audrey spotted a triage center being set up. There were no patients. No activity. Audrey walked up to a woman in scrubs with a stethoscope around her neck, wearing a thin paper mask. She looked like she had just walked straight out of the emergency room.

"There is an injured officer, right over there." Audrey pointed. "He has a bad gash on his face and is bleeding badly, but he won't leave," she explained.

The doctor nodded, grabbing a handful of supplies, and hurried over toward him.

An EMT was pulling supplies out of a duffel bag, setting up a treatment area for the injured. It was eerily empty. There was no hustle of incoming patients. There was no activity at all. Audrey thought briefly about showing him the pictures of

Hannah, but she knew there was little chance that anyone had seen her sister. If they had, there was little chance they were still alive to tell.

"Moretti!" Gaston suddenly screamed from the edge of the pile. Audrey hurried over to the group assembled around Gaston.

"Did I not make myself clear? I said we stay together! We are not here just for your sister," he growled, glaring at her. "Everyone who was in those towers has a sister, brother, mother, father. Your sister is no more special than anyone else."

Audrey hated him. She wanted to punch him in the face.

"Easy!" O'Shea spoke up with disgust.

Audrey didn't care to explain herself to Gaston. She turned to O'Shea instead. "I was getting help for an injured port authority officer. He was hurt really bad. He lost his entire squad," she said quietly to O'Shea, with a lump in her throat.

"Listen up!" Gaston shouted. "Our goal is to find as many survivors as we can. The commander wants us on the pile. Buckets are coming. We are going to form a line and fill the buckets with debris and pass them back for the team behind us to sift through. That team will be looking for personal items—rings, wallets, shoes—any sign that we may be close to someone as we dig."

There was a mountain of steel, ash, concrete, and debris in front of them. Only the skeleton of one of the towers remained—three bent, twisted steel protrusions. The thought of using buckets to clear away the mountain of debris to find survivors was the most daunting task Audrey could have ever imagined.

"When the buckets arrive, we get to work. Oh, and forget your radios. The frequencies are all jammed up, and the antenna is down. Your radios are bricks," Gaston said. Turning to Audrey, he growled, "So don't wander off again."

The emotions inside of Audrey were building like a pressure cooker, and Gaston was pushing his luck. Audrey saw the look in O'Shea's eyes as he looked out over the destruction. When he turned to look at her, the sorrow on his face revealed that he didn't believe Hannah could have survived—that anyone could have survived.

"I know you don't think she is alive," Audrey said, "but...I can feel her. So please don't say you are sorry yet."

O'Shea nodded, acknowledging her request. He quickly changed the subject. "I was talking to one of the guys over there from the twentieth precinct. He said we can crash there any time we need to." O'Shea looked over at Audrey, assessing her. She was only half listening, deep in her own thoughts. "He also told me heavy equipment is coming in from local construction sites to help clear some of the big stuff. Workers are leaving their jobs from all over, bringing their equipment," he said, trying to sound hopeful.

Audrey suddenly turned her attention to O'Shea. With the help of heavy equipment, they would be able to get to survivors faster. "Okay then, let's do this," she said with determination.

A pickup truck with a bed loaded with orange buckets pulled up in front of them. The tires of the truck stirred the ash into the air. Audrey could feel the heavy dust enter her lungs again. She looked down at the old, tattered mask in her hand. It would do her no good.

She dropped her mask at the edge of the pile, grabbed a bucket from the truck, and climbed up onto the smoldering mountain of debris. With every step, the debris shifted under her feet. Her boots caught on cables and twisted sharp metal, causing her to trip with every step. The steam rose up from the smoldering pile and stuck to her face.

"Helmets on!" someone yelled from behind her. "These buildings aren't secure. Stay alert!"

It was something Audrey had not considered until that moment. Another building collapse was very possible, but there was no turning back. She lifted the big, clunky helmet over her head and continued to climb up into the destruction.

CHAPTER 23

Audrey tried to keep her balance on top of the shifting rubble. Her team had become part of one of the many bucket brigades working vehemently to clear debris and rubble from the pile. Their job was to fill up five-gallon buckets with debris, and pass it backward to a team of investigators to sift through.

Firefighters had brought every tool they had on hand, such as crowbars and shovels, to dig with, but quickly realized the best tools were their bare hands. The skin on Audrey's hands had quickly become raw from digging barehanded through the rubble and ash. Her arms ached from lifting the buckets full of heavy debris, one after another.

Police dogs assisted in the search on top of the pile, but hours went by without any sign of survivors. Every so often there would be shouting and a flurry of activity from hopeful rescuers who had uncovered a shoe, or had spotted an arm in the rubble. Hope turned to sickening despair as those discoveries lead them only to body parts, not survivors. The remains were then bagged up and labeled for the medical examiner, a gruesome and heartbreaking task.

Audrey desperately needed a break. Her arms ached, her mouth was dry, and her lungs felt heavy. Cases of water were dropped off by local businesses and thoughtful civilians. Audrey took a moment to take a swig of water from one of the dust-covered bottles. It tasted horrible with the ash that had coated the inside of her mouth.

Just then, two firemen carrying an empty stretcher stumbled and shifted as they passed by their brigade. They were en route to somewhere up ahead. Audrey couldn't tell if sweat or tears streaked their flushed faces, but they looked pained, distraught. They came to a stop where two other firefighters stood. As Audrey watched from afar, she noticed one of firefighters talking on his radio. They were no longer moving as quickly as they'd been before, and appeared to be waiting for someone to arrive. Several police officers showed up, and immediately dropped to their knees in prayer. Moments later, the police officers placed a body on the stretcher and covered it with an American flag. The officers hoisted the stretcher up and began carrying it across the pile, as the firefighters walked alongside. As they passed by, Audrey saw the limp arm of an NYPD police officer dangling off the stretcher. The short sleeve of his uniform shirt was ripped and charred.

Tears sprung to Audrey's dry and irritated eyes, and a lump burned in her throat. One by one, each person in the brigade saluted the fallen officer as he was carried across the pile.

Audrey let her body collapse onto the debris. She was losing hope.

Suddenly, there was a rush of commotion a few feet away.

"We have something!" someone shouted up ahead, further into the pile.

Audrey instinctively started climbing toward the commotion, when suddenly Gaston stepped in front of her. "What the hell do you think you're doing?" he scolded.

Audrey's boots slid in the loose rubble as she tried to come to a stop.

"I go first," Gaston said. "If anyone is going to rescue someone, it's going to be me. I am first in command of this unit."

Audrey felt a bolt of disgust shoot through her veins. Gaston pushed past Audrey, scrambling his way over to the commotion.

The afternoon was fading into early evening, and they had not yet found a survivor. Her body shook with rage toward Gaston, and nervous anticipation at the thought of pulling a survivor from the rubble. Her knees wobbled as she climbed unsteadily to catch up to the crowd gathering ahead.

"We need all hands over here! We've got something! Dig!" a rescuer yelled urgently.

As Audrey got closer, she saw what the commotion was about. Protruding from the cleared rubble were a pair of legs— one foot bare, the other with a tattered, dusty, dark-colored trouser sock.

"Help is here," one of the rescuers talked to the person buried in the rubble. "Can you hear me?"

Gaston pushed past everyone and started digging, pulling, and grabbing at the debris with his bare hands. His hands worked furiously, clawing at the ash and rubble. A stretcher was on scene and ready to escort the victim to the hospital. Audrey's heart raced at the thought of pulling their first survivor from beneath the wreckage.

Suddenly a sound came from Gaston she had never heard before. His face instantly drained of color, his eyes wild with horror as he stumbled backward, losing his footing. His breathing was audible and distressed. She saw one of the rescuers throw the crowbar he had been using to dig. He let out a pained roar as he hung his head low.

Then Audrey realized—they had not found a full body.

Making a sign of the cross with his hand, one of the rescuers pulled the bottom half of the victim's body from the rubble. Audrey wanted to turn away, but she couldn't. The horrific sight was burned in her mind forever. Audrey thought she was going to vomit, and her head spun so fast that she thought she would pass out. She had never seen anything so horrific.

Audrey could not keep her mind from thinking the worst—*there are no survivors.*

The victim's remains were gently placed on the stretcher. O'Shea lowered himself to the ground to say a prayer. Audrey knelt numbly next to O'Shea. Too horrified to look up again, she kept her eyes low to the ground. Gaston, chest still heaving, sat on the rubble with his knees pulled up to his chest, breathing wildly.

Suddenly, a siren began to wail through the air. Something urgent was happening. Audrey immediately felt that they were in danger.

"Building seven is about to collapse! Evacuate now!" a loud booming voice yelled over a megaphone.

Audrey and O'Shea each grabbed a handle of the stretcher, helping the other two rescuers carry the remains off the pile. Gaston had already headed halfway to safety up ahead, never once looking back for the team.

With each step, they stumbled, sliding and shifting until they finally reached the edge of the pile. Audrey and O'Shea handed the stretcher to a crew who was waiting to log the remains.

Audrey tried to catch her breath. The burning in her lungs was so intense that it felt as if she were breathing in fire. She doubled over, choking and hacking, more ash entering her chest with each cough. She then noticed a man next to her, wearing khaki pants and a dress shirt, with a clipboard in his hand. He was frantically pointing at one of the buildings.

"Move back! Everyone move back! Building seven is going down!" he screamed.

Audrey looked out at the buildings surrounding the pile and noticed they all had flags perched on the rooftops. The flag on top of building seven was shaking wildly.

Just then, a vibration started under her feet. It got stronger by the second. The man in the khaki pants screamed, "It's coming down! Take cover!"

Building seven began to crumble right in front of their eyes. O'Shea pulled Audrey down low, covering their heads. The force of the collapsing building sent a new cloud of ash over them.

Breathing it in was unavoidable. The ash felt like sand and grit inside of her lungs. She and all the others were standing at the edge of the pile, violently coughing, gasping for air. When Audrey finally could breathe again, she stood to look out through the haze over the pile. Building seven of the World Trade Center was gone.

As she looked around, she spotted Gaston standing impatiently next to their ERT van across the street. O'Shea was by her side, but the rest of the team was congregated at the van with Gaston. Something was happening.

Audrey squinted through the dusty haze, trying to understand what was going on. Gaston looked wild. He yanked open the back door of the ERT van, frantically motioning for the guys to get in.

In that moment Audrey realized what was happening. Gaston was giving the orders to leave!

Gaston then turned his attention to Audrey and O'Shea. "Let's go!" he screamed from across the street.

Audrey's heart sank. They couldn't leave yet! She looked up at O'Shea with desperation in her tired eyes.

"Let's go see what this is about," O'Shea said calmly, trying to reassure Audrey.

Walking briskly to the van, O'Shea came to a stop with the rest of the guys, all who had refused Gaston's orders to get in the van.

"What the hell is going on, Gaston?" O'Shea demanded.

"We're leaving," he said. "Get in the van now!" he screamed directly at Audrey this time.

Nothing else mattered to Audrey anymore. Hannah was alive, she could feel it, and she was not leaving.

She took one step toward Gaston staring directly into his dark cowardly soul. "I am not leaving," Audrey said, her eyes piercing through his cold, soulless eyes.

"Recruit Morretti, if you don't leave right now, I will personally make certain you never become a cop, ever!" he snarled.

A hot flash of rage started in her feet and rose up through all of her limbs. Audrey took one more step closer to Gaston. With her face only inches from his—her eyes on fire—she slowly repeated herself. "*I said...I* am not leaving," she growled, squaring off with him.

Gaston tried to straighten up, his face turning red with anger and embarrassment. Audrey was not backing down. Gaston suddenly unraveled. "Look around you! This is not a rescue mission. There are *no* survivors. Give it up. Your sister is dead!" he blurted out.

Audrey snapped. She picked up a mangled, twisted piece of steel by her feet. Gripping it horizontally with her clenched fists, she thrust it forward across his throat, letting out a roar that came from the deepest part of her soul. Pushing him backward, she pinned him up against the van, firmly pressing the bar to his neck, causing him to gasp for air.

She got within inches of his face again. "I...am...not... leaving," she growled.

Gaston choked and gasped; his eyes wide with surprise. "You are finished, Moretti," he choked out.

Audrey released the steel bar from his neck and threw it hard to the ground. Wiping the sweat from her forehead, she turned and started to walk back toward the pile. "It was worth it," she sneered.

Audrey knew that was the end of her career. She had snapped. Even though Gaston had it coming, she was aware of the consequences she would face when she got back to the department. She found herself completely alone, at Ground Zero, with an unrelenting feeling that Hannah was still alive.

She needed a moment to collect herself. Plopping her worn-out body down on the hard, ash-covered sidewalk, she lay back into a pile of debris. Her academy uniform was ripped and torn, covered in soot.

The sun had descended, and the evening sky was taking over. She had nothing left. Exhausted, she closed her eyes and prayed that when she opened them again, it would have all been a nightmare.

Her eyes were startled open by the sound of O'Shea's voice. "Looks like you won't be the only one without a job when we get back," O'Shea said, looking down at her.

Audrey couldn't believe he was standing in front of her.

"We all told Gaston to go to hell. The guys went back up on the pile," he said. "That coward is probably already halfway back to Connecticut."

"You stayed," she said in disbelief.

"Of course I stayed. I would never leave you here alone."

Audrey felt a wave of guilt come over her again. She had been so wrong about him.

"Let's go to the precinct, get something to eat, and wash up a bit," O'Shea suggested, knowing that Audrey needed a break.

"I have to keep searching," she protested.

"You can't help Hannah if you don't take care of your-self. How useful will you be if you collapse from exhaustion?" O'Shea pointed out.

Audrey knew O'Shea was right. She knew she needed food, water, and a mental break.

"Okay," Audrey agreed, "but we come right back, okay?"

"Deal," O'Shea said, reaching down to help her to her feet.

CHAPTER 24

Hannah had no idea how much time had passed when her eyes opened again. She woke to the sound of water dripping down from above. The clothes on her body were wet, and she was cold and shivering. Hannah could not understand where the water was coming from. Nothing made sense to her. She had no answers, only confusion. The pain that had returned in her leg had caused her to become delirious.

Hannah had also become painfully aware of the deep hunger ache in her stomach. She couldn't remember the last time she ate. She was not even sure what day it was. Her mouth was so dry that it hurt. The intense thirst completely consumed her.

Something had changed since she was last awake. She couldn't see anything in the pitch blackness, but her body had a little bit more room to move. The rubble around her had shifted. Her leg was still pinned, but she had room to wiggle her upper body slightly, and her left arm had even more room in the air pocket. She wished she could see what was pinning her down and crushing her leg.

Hungry, thirsty, and hopeless, her body was shutting down. *I'm going to die here.*

She wished that she had answers before she died. Most of all, she wished she had a chance to say goodbye. Hannah started to accept her fate. She began to say her silent goodbyes, feeling the life inside her body drift away.

"Hannah," a voice spoke.

She wanted to talk, but she was no longer conscious.

Who are you? Why are you talking to me? Don't you realize I am dead?

"Hannah, stay with me. You cannot give up," the voice said.

I can't. There is no hope.

"You have to fight. He needs you to fight," she heard the voice say.

Who needs me to fight? Who are you?

Hannah felt like she was floating—free, painless.

So this is what it feels like to be dead.

Images started to appear in Hannah's mind. Like a movie playing on a screen in front of her, she was suddenly looking at herself on the dirty floor of the subway station. A hand was stretched out to help her. She reached out, instantly getting pulled to her feet. She was face to face with Travis, staring into his deep, sparkling blue eyes. They were in the subway station where they'd first met. He pulled her along, running hand in hand. They flew up the subway stairs, reaching the warm summer morning air. She knew the scene well.

Hannah felt warm and wonderful. She was with Travis again.

The wonderful memory continued to play out in front of her. They rounded the first corner onto a narrow side street, he turned back to smile at her. "My name is Travis by the way," he said over his shoulder.

"I'm Hannah," she replied.

"I know. Hannah with the pink emergency kit," he teased.

She followed behind him as he led the way through the bustling streets of Manhattan until the towers appeared in the distance. Suddenly, Travis stopped. He looked ahead at the towers and then back at Hannah. His face was no longer plastered with his bright smile. He looked anxious and sorrowful.

"You have to stay here," he said.

Hannah stood curbside, looking confused. "What do you mean?" she asked.

"I'm sorry. I can't take you any further. He needs you here, and I…am needed there," he said, tucking a blonde strand of hair behind Hannah's ear.

"What? Why?" she asked frantically. "Who needs me here? I don't understand! Please take me with you!" she begged, tears streaming down her face.

Travis let go of her hand and began walking toward the towers. As he faded into the distance, Hannah cried out, pleading for him to stay. "Please, come back to me," Hannah heard herself whisper, bringing herself back to consciousness. It was dark and cold again. She was no longer under the blue summer sky with Travis. She had no idea what was real anymore.

I am still alive.

Replaying the scene in her mind, she thought about Travis's words. She felt the fight inside of her come alive again. There was something bigger than she understood just yet. She knew she had to survive, but how?

Suddenly, she gasped with realization.

Hannah with the pink emergency kit!

Of course! The emergency kit! In her briefcase! Using her left hand, she reached her fingers around the dust and debris to find the handle. She used her left arm to pull it toward her body, locating the latch on top.

Feeling around blindly in the pitch-black darkness, she popped open the latch and rummaged around inside of the briefcase. Her hand brushed over the bottle of water she had stuck in her briefcase.

Hannah pulled the bottle of water up against her side, and used her left hand to twist the cap. The water and ash had mixed into a paste-like substance, causing the cap to slip between her fingers. Finally she felt the cap release. It was a tight squeeze, but she was able to turn her head and maneuver her arm enough to get the water bottle to her mouth. Hannah swished the water around in her mouth, clearing the grit from her tongue and teeth. After a couple of rinses, she took the best sips of water she had ever tasted in her life.

Rummaging blindly through the briefcase in the darkness, past papers and folders, she felt her cell phone. She used her fingers to pry it open, but not even a dim light appeared on the screen. The battery was completely dead.

Hannah pulled back the elastic pocket on the inside of the briefcase and felt the shiny material of the emergency kit Audrey had made for her. She pulled it out and positioned it against her body, working the zipper across with her left hand.

The first thing Hannah pulled out was a little push-button keychain flashlight. After pressing the button between her thumb and forefinger, the dungeon she was trapped inside was revealed for the first time. There was more space in the air pocket to her left than she had first thought. Shining the light down toward her legs, she saw what was crushing her leg. A large metal beam with a block of concrete still attached was wedged up on top of her right leg. She tried to move her leg again, with no luck. The movement shot a jolt of pain into her bone and up to her head.

Hannah shined the tiny light around the rubble, searching for the person who had been talking to her earlier.

"Hello?" she called out to the voice. She saw no one, and no one answered back.

Hannah shined the little light into the small, pink zippered pouch. There was a protein bar, a thin paper mask, and… a whistle.

A whistle!

In that moment, Audrey's emergency kit didn't seem so silly after all.

No one knew she was under there, but if she could make enough noise, maybe someone would find her. She now had food, water, and a chance at being rescued.

With all of the breath she had in her lungs, Hannah began blowing the whistle.

———

Audrey and O'Shea had arrived at the precinct a little past seven o'clock p.m. Their uniforms were dirty and torn. An officer had found some extra cargo pants and NYPD T-shirts, and escorted them to the locker rooms to shower and change.

The hot shower had never felt so good to Audrey, as she took extra time to let the warm water fall over her aching body. Her skinned fingertips burned while she dried her body with the starchy towel. She slid into the dry-cleaned cargo pants, which were way too big for her, so she rolled up the top waistline and cuffed the bottom of each leg. Pulling the T-shirt over her head and smoothing it down over her body, she caught a glimpse of herself in the mirror. Her stringy, wet blonde hair dripped onto the floor.

She stood for a moment, studying her reflection in the full-length mirror and the shirt with the letters NYPD across the upper left chest. So many officers had made the ultimate sacrifice that day. She was proud to be part of such a heroic profession, but suddenly, she recalled the scene with Gaston. "You're finished, Morretti!" his words echoed in her mind. Regardless, looking at her reflection in the mirror, she saw a cop. It was in her blood, and no one could ever take that away from her.

Audrey pulled her wet hair back into a tight ponytail and proceeded to the patrolman's lounge. If she didn't know otherwise, she would have thought she was walking into a party. Dozens of pizzas, donated by a local pizza place, were stacked up on the table at the back of the lounge, alongside boxes of donuts, bagels, cases of water, bottles of soda, and a half-dozen boxes of coffee.

O'Shea was already in the lounge, sitting in an oversized chair, chugging a bottle of water, when Audrey entered. She was anxious to get back to the search, but she knew she had to eat something. Despite her stomach feeling twisted in knots, she grabbed a plain bagel and a bottle of water, plopping down on the couch across from O'Shea.

There was silence for a few minutes while they replenished and refueled their depleted bodies. Audrey thought back to early that morning and what she had planned to say to O'Shea. She could never have imagined the day would take such an incredibly devastating turn. He had proven even more to her that day how wrong she had been about him. Audrey felt more sorry and guilty than ever. She had to say something, and now was her chance.

"Thank you for staying," she said.

"You don't have to thank me," he replied.

"Well, I do owe you an apology. I judged you, and I got it wrong. I thought you…you know, with the rumor and all, were trying…"

"Ah, now it makes sense," O'Shea said, pausing for a moment. "Listen, I had heard about you, the whole broken nose thing. I had so much respect for you that you didn't give up. That's all. I heard how Preston snapped over the rumor, but I promise you I was not trying—"

"I know," Audrey cut him off. She didn't want him to feel like he had to explain himself any further.

Audrey's head was throbbing with exhaustion. The food in her belly suddenly made her sleepy. She propped her elbow on the armrest of the couch and leaned her head to her hand.

"How about some coffee?" O'Shea offered.

"Sure," Audrey sleepily replied. "Two creams, one sugar, please."

"I bet you that fool Gaston made it back home in twenty minutes. He couldn't get out of here fast enough," O'Shea said as he fixed Audrey her coffee. He continued talking with his back turned. "I've got to tell you, that might have been the best thing I have ever seen, the look on his face when you jacked him up," he rambled on. "He had it coming. Seriously, he deserved every—" O'Shea turned back around to bring Audrey her coffee, realizing she had fallen sound asleep on the couch.

He placed the coffee down and then looked around for something to cover her with. Locating an extra duty jacket, hung over the back of a chair in the lounge, he lowered it over her gently. He sat down in the chair across from her, letting his eyelids slowly fall, until he too had drifted off to sleep.

———

The sound of the whistle echoed inside of the tomb Hannah was buried in. She had been blowing incessantly on the whistle for what felt like hours. Hannah was aware that the sound was likely muffled by the mountain of debris between her and the outside world. With little air left in her lungs, she was getting weak.

Hannah reached for the protein bar and fiddled with the wrapper until she felt the stale bar emerge between her fingers. Everything in her body ached, even her teeth. She took small bites, alternating with small sips of water. Every so often she thought she saw light coming through the rubble above, only to realize she was seeing things that were not there.

Where is that person I spoke to earlier? Why isn't he talking anymore? Did he die? Was he even real?

"Hello?" Hannah called out, feeling silly that she was talking to the air again. "Are you still there?"

Silence.

Hannah was not sure how much longer she could keep hope. She didn't know if she could gather more breath to blow on the whistle. Was anyone even searching? The pain in her leg came in waves, and she welcomed the numbness that came along with shock. But the pain was returning again with a vengeance, and she wanted to give up.

"Blow the whistle, Hannah. You have to keep blowing the whistle," the voice said.

Barely conscious, Hannah wondered if she was hallucinating. She clicked on her tiny flashlight, searching for the man talking to her. She shined it in every direction, only to find emptiness inside the dusty cave she was trapped in.

"Hello? Are you there?" she called out.

Silence.

With the last remaining breath she had, Hannah placed the whistle in her mouth, blowing short bursts with her last, weak shallow breaths.

CHAPTER 25

Hannah thought she heard something. Running out of breath, she was silent, and still beneath the rubble—slowly fading away. She was tired of the tricks her mind was playing on her.

But there it was again—muffled voices talking in the distance. Suddenly one of the voices sounded clearer, closer. "Can you hear me?" the distant voice called out.

Hannah was tired of talking to voices that didn't respond. She took a shallow breath and blew one last burst into the whistle instead.

"We hear you!" the voice said, sounding clearer.

Hannah then felt dust and debris falling around her. A moment later, there were more voices and suddenly, a lot of frantic chatter. It was coming from above.

"Can you hear us?" The voice said clearly, loudly.

More debris shifted, raining down around her. Hannah then saw a bright light above.

This is it. I am dying. That must be heaven.

"We hear your whistle! Help is here! We're going to get you out of there!" the voice said. "Can you hear us?"

It was so real, but she didn't believe it.

Hannah called out weakly, "Are you real?"

The voice from above laughed with joy and relief. "Yes, I am real! I assure you, I am real! We're going to get you out of there. Just hang on, okay? Stay with me."

Hannah couldn't believe what she was hearing. The bright light above was getting bigger, wider. Debris shifted all around her. Was she really being rescued?

Hannah prayed it wasn't a trick her mind was playing on her. She began to cry at the thought that she would live to see her sister, Travis, and her family again.

The light above exploded from above, revealing the silhouette of a man. He called down to her. "Are you hurt?" he asked.

Yes," she replied feebly. "My leg."

"You're going to be okay. We have a lot of help here. Just promise you will stay with me," the man above said.

Hannah began to softly cry. "I promise," she said.

"What's your name, dear?" he called from above.

"Hannah," she replied in a frail voice. "Hannah Moretti."

———

O'Shea was awakened by a flurry of cops scurrying through the lounge. The door in the lounge slammed open into the sally port, and one by one, officers jumped into patrol cars. There was clearly something urgent going on.

"Hey," O'Shea called to one of the officers running by, "what's going on?"

"They found a survivor under the rubble. She has a pulse and is talking to rescuers right now," he said, winded with excitement.

"Did you say 'she?' Do you know anything more? How old she is, anything?" O'Shea frantically asked.

"All I know is that she had a whistle, which is how they heard her."

"Do you mind if we jump in?" O'Shea asked, thinking quickly.

"Yeah, come on. We're all heading down there; you can hop in with me. My name is Manny."

O'Shea reached down to Audrey, shaking her vigorously to wake her. Her eyes opened slowly and groggily.

"They found a survivor, Audrey. A female," O'Shea said. "Rescuers heard a whistle under the rubble."

Audrey blinked a few times as she processed the information. *Whistle…*

"Hannah," she said, suddenly jumping to her feet.

———

The patrol car flew through the streets of Manhattan, the siren screaming loudly into the silent night. Red-and-blue lights flickered onto buildings and storefronts as they passed by. Manny was heavy on the pedal and didn't show much concern for sharp turns.

Audrey peered through the cage divider that separated the front of the patrol car from the back. The cage was where prisoners usually sat, but she gladly volunteered. She needed to be alone with her thoughts. The time on the dash of the patrol car read 10:47 p.m. Audrey realized that they must have been asleep for about an hour in the lounge.

"Thanks for the lift," O'Shea said to Manny, breaking the awkward silence in the patrol car.

"No problem," Manny replied.

Manny turned his head slightly to O'Shea and lowered his voice so that Audrey wouldn't hear. "If you don't mind me asking, your partner seems to have the weight of the world on her mind back there," he asked.

O'Shea looked over his shoulder. Audrey was deep in her own thoughts, peering out the window.

O'Shea quietly responded, "Her sister was in the South Tower."

"Ah. Shit," Manny said.

Manny looked up in the rearview mirror at Audrey.

"You okay back there?" he asked.

Audrey shrugged her shoulders, still peering out the window.

"Listen, we are family here. Whatever you need, you just say the word," Manny said.

Audrey appreciated his words, but her mind was too consumed. She nodded silently, staring off blankly.

Arriving at Ground Zero under the dark sky was much different than during the daylight hours. It was a surreal sight. Huge fluorescent lights shone down onto the pile, illuminating the mountain of rubble brightly against the blackness of nighttime.

Audrey yanked on the door latch before the patrol car had even come to a stop. So anxious to get out, she forgot that the doors were locked in back. O'Shea jumped out quickly from the front passenger seat to free her.

Audrey raced up on top of the pile. O'Shea and Manny followed close behind.

"Up ahead, one o'clock," Manny called out, pointing ahead and slightly to the right.

Audrey saw a cluster of lights shining down onto the area where Manny had pointed to. Dozens of people had crowded around. As Audrey climbed and stumbled across the pile closer to the area, she was overcome by a powerful sensation. She felt her sister's presence, even swearing that she smelled her perfume. Her senses were heightened to a level like never before.

She reached close enough to hear shouts between rescue workers frantically coordinating a strategy. A large group of tired police officers, firefighters, and civilian volunteers had gathered. Audrey could not see through the wall of bodies of the people who had gathered at the scene. She ducked and weaved, trying to catch any glimpse of what was happening, but the crowd was too big. Everyone wanted to witness the rescue. She was not going to be able to get any closer. Suddenly she felt someone grip her upper arm.

Manny shouted to the crowd, "Coming through! Move to the side, please!" Turning to Audrey, he said, "Come on, kid. My guys are up there." He pulled her through the crowd, with O'Shea close behind.

They finally reached the interior circle, past the wall of spectators. A man was down on his knees, calling into a small, narrow tunnel and shining a heavy duty Maglite down into the darkness.

"What's the update, Johnny?" Manny's voice boomed.

"She's buried down there good, but there is an air pocket down below. We just can't get to it. The canal is too narrow for any of us to fit. We are getting the crane over here now to try and clear some of these big pieces, but we're worried about shifting. It could crush her or anyone who tries to go down to get to her."

Audrey felt her heart race.

"She went silent a few minutes ago, but she was able to give us her name," Johnny said.

Audrey's body started to shake. "What…is…her name?" Audrey's voice shook with each word.

"It was hard to make out, her voice was weak, but sounded like Anna or Hannah… something 'etti'." he replied.

Audrey gasped, bringing her hands to her mouth. She pushed past everyone.

"What are you doing?" Johnny asked, surprised.

"I'm going down!" she answered.

O'Shea jumped in, his face fraught with apprehension. "Wait, Audrey, think about this for a minute—"

Audrey stopped him midsentence. "Look at me. I'm small. I can get to her. I can't just let her die down there!"

There was a moment of silence as the men looked nervously at each other.

"Let her down," Manny said to Johnny, who was still kneeling by the narrow opening.

"But the crane will be here in five minutes," Johnny replied, protesting the risky move.

"Let her down," Manny said again.

Johnny stood to face Audrey. "You understand the risk you are taking, right?" Johnny asked. "It's not stable down there, especially when that crane starts moving the big stuff."

Audrey nodded and looked at O'Shea. "I have to do this."

There was nothing anyone could say to make her change her mind.

Johnny handed Audrey his Maglite, and she began her descent into the canal. There was barely enough room, even for her small frame. She shimmied and slithered down, kicking her feet to widen the path as she went. Her head disappeared several feet below the opening. Suddenly her feet were dangling in the open air. Realizing she had reached the air pocket, Audrey twisted and flailed her body until she slid down into a cave-like opening. She clicked on the flashlight and gasped at what the light revealed.

Audrey was next to Hannah's limp body, buried under the rubble. She could barely recognize her sister. Her once beautiful blonde locks were snarled and matted, twisted in gray knots. Her face was covered in soot and ash. But it was Hannah, no doubt. Audrey knew her hands, the curve of her cheekbones, and there was no mistaking the birthstone ring on her finger that Audrey had given Hannah for her eighteenth birthday. Hannah's briefcase was close by her side. Though covered in ash and soot, Audrey immediately recognized the pink emergency kit. Scanning the confined space, Audrey noticed an empty bottle of water, a protein bar wrapper, and...*the whistle.* Audrey hastily grabbed the whistle and shoved it into the cargo pocket of her pants. It was clear that Hannah had fought so hard to survive.

She picked up her limp hand and placed two fingers on her wrist, the way she had been taught in medical response training in the academy. Her pulse was barely detectable. She had to get her out of there immediately. She shined the flashlight out further around the confined space. Hannah's leg was clearly pinned by a large steel beam and concrete slab.

"I've got her! I need that crane here now! Her leg is pinned!" Audrey called up.

"The crane's here! We're sending it in now. Cover your head!" Johnny called down.

Audrey suddenly felt debris violently shift from above. Ash and smaller debris rained down. She covered Hannah's body with her own, and started to talk softly into her ear. "Hannah. It's Audrey. I'm here. We are getting you out of here. Stay with me. Please stay with me," Audrey pleaded, holding Hannah's limp hand in hers.

There was no response.

I need to keep her with me.

Keeping her fingers on Hannah's pulse, Audrey began softly singing into Hannah's ear their favorite childhood song.

Suddenly, she felt Hannah's pulse strengthen. Audrey kept singing until the rainstorm of debris stopped pouring down over them. The hole above had opened up wide. The fluorescent lights flooded down into what had become an open crater. Debris had shifted, and the light revealed that Hannah's body was just feet from a crushed NYPD police car. Audrey looked up to the light, the dust giving a smoky appearance to the air in the bright lights.

Two EMTs began to descend down into the hole, bringing medical supplies and a spinal board.

"We have to get this beam off her leg!" Audrey screamed up to Johnny.

"Okay! Heads up!" Johnny called back down. "The crane is coming back in!" Audrey watched as the crane's arm swung in. The crane hook clenched down on the steel beam, and the arm began to lift it from Hannah's leg. To Audrey's horror, the beam separated from the concrete slab, which remained on top of Hannah's leg. She was still pinned.

"We're losing her pulse," one of the EMT's urgently said.

Audrey looked at the mass of concrete on top of her sister's leg. She knew it had to weigh hundreds of pounds. There wasn't enough time to wait for the crane to return. Time was running out, and seconds mattered. Her sister was fading away.

"Get ready to put her on the board!" Audrey yelled to the EMTs.

Audrey climbed over to the concrete block on Hannah's leg and squatted down, placing her hands underneath the slab.

"On the count of three, pull her out!" Audrey commanded. She never once thought about the strength she would need to lift the concrete block off Hannah's leg. "One, two...three!" she called out.

Summoning every bit of strength she could find, she planted both feet as firmly as she could on the uneven ground. Electricity flowed through her body and into her muscles. Audrey pushed up on the mass of concrete with strength she'd never felt before. Suddenly, the block lifted just enough to free Hannah's leg.

"Pull!" Audrey screamed to the EMTs.

They quickly slid her body out and onto the spinal board. Audrey let go of the block, falling immediately to the ground from exhaustion. She panted, trying to catch her breath as she watched the EMTs strap Hannah's limp body to the board. She crawled over to Hannah's side.

"Stay with me, Sis," she whispered in her ear.

CHAPTER 26

Wednesday, September 12, 2001
12:45 a.m.

Audrey paced back and forth through the cold hospital corridor. O'Shea sat on a hard bench along the wall, with his head resting on his fists. A tired doctor entered the corridor, her neatly combed, straight brown hair rested just barely atop her shoulders. She pulled the wire-rimmed glasses off her face with one swoop of her hand.

"Audrey?" she called out.

"Yes, I'm Audrey, Hannah's sister," Audrey replied nervously, walking briskly toward the doctor. She tried to read the doctor's face.

Is she about to tell me that Hannah didn't make it?

"Your sister suffered a crushing injury to her leg. Due to the amount of time her leg was compressed under the rubble, her body has gone into a type of shock we call Crush Syndrome or rhabdomyolysis," she informed Audrey.

Audrey listened anxiously, wishing the doctor could talk faster. Her words felt painfully slow. O'Shea had come from the bench to stand next to Audrey as the doctor continued.

"Often this type of injury results in renal failure, but right now her numbers look okay. We will need to keep a close eye on her though. She is getting IV fluids and pain medication, and we'll be closely monitoring her heart over these next few days."

The doctor paused for a moment, looking mystified. "Your sister is a very strong young lady, Audrey. It is a miracle she survived."

Audrey let out the breath she was holding. "Can I see her?"

"Hannah is being admitted into the intensive care unit. She's responding well to the intravenous medications. If this progress keeps up, we can hopefully move her out of ICU shortly. We just have to sit tight for now," the doctor said. Seeing the exhausted look in Audrey's eyes, she added, "You have been through a lot. Try to get some rest. We will notify you the moment you can see her. I promise."

Audrey knew there was nothing she could do but wait. "Okay. Thank you, doctor."

O'Shea guided Audrey over to the cushioned chairs in the waiting room, and they took up residence in the two chairs next to each other. He put his arm around her, pulling her close so that she could rest her head on his shoulders.

———

Wednesday, September 12, 2001
8:00 a.m.

The smell of fresh coffee wafting nearby woke Audrey up from her sleep.

"Ow," she mumbled, half asleep, grabbing at the sharp kink in her neck.

She had slept upright and contorted in the waiting room chair all night. O'Shea pulled a cup of coffee out of the cardboard tray and placed it on the side table next to her. Reaching into a white paper bag, he pulled out a warm breakfast sandwich wrapped in foil, and handed it to her.

"Thank you," Audrey said. She placed the sandwich in her lap and picked up the coffee on the side table. She shivered, wrapping her hands around the steaming cup of coffee. The hospital waiting room was cold and comfortless.

"Do you need anything else?" O'Shea asked Audrey before he sat down.

Audrey shook her head. "No, thank you," she said quietly.

She couldn't imagine what it would have been like had he not stayed with her. His presence was comforting. His quiet strength gave her the support she needed.

O'Shea settled into his chair and took a big bite of his breakfast sandwich.

Something had been on Audrey's mind since being down in the rubble with Hannah. There was no way she should have been able to lift that concrete block off of Hannah's leg. The slab was hundreds of pounds of solid concrete. But when she squatted down and began to push up, she felt an impossible strength flow throughout her body. The slab lifted almost effortlessly, as if someone, or something, was helping her.

Audrey unwrapped her breakfast sandwich and took a small bite. She was silent for a few minutes, trying to think of a way to explain it to O'Shea without sounding crazy.

"Down in the rubble last night…I had help," Audrey said softly. "I can't explain it. I don't even know what I am saying really, but someone, or something, helped me lift that concrete block off of Hannah."

O'Shea listened, letting Audrey sort through her thoughts out loud.

"I'm strong, but not that strong. It came up off of her like nothing."

"I understand exactly what you're saying, Audrey. I was there to witness it, along with Manny and all of the other rescuers." O'Shea's eyes met Audrey's and she knew that he believed her.

Audrey had been so preoccupied with her thoughts that she hadn't noticed the phones ringing in the background at the registration desk. She suddenly realized that her parents didn't even know she was in New York City. She jumped to her feet and rushed over to the counter.

"Excuse me, could I please use your phone?" Audrey politely asked.

The heavyset woman behind the counter picked up the large rectangle phone and slid it across the counter.

Audrey knew when she told her parents about Hannah, they would want to come right to the hospital. But traffic was still restricted coming into the city and the trains were

not running. She needed to reassure them that she was with
Hannah and that she would be okay until they could get there.

Audrey dialed her parents' number. Her mother answered
before the phone even rang.

"Mom, I'm in New York. I'm with Hannah in the hospital.
She's badly hurt, but I'm with her."

There was too much to say, and there were things no one
would believe, so Audrey simply said, "Mom, miracles are real."

———

"Audrey, you can see your sister now," a nurse, who appeared in
the waiting room, called over to Audrey. "She's in room 215 on
the eighth floor." She smiled compassionately.

Audrey jumped to her feet and looked down at O'Shea.
Her eyes told him that she needed to go alone.

O'Shea nodded. "I'll be right here," he reassured her.

Every step between the waiting room and Hannah's hospital room felt like an eternity. Audrey picked up her pace when
she got off the elevator, scanning the wall placards for room
8-215. She did not know what to expect when she got there,
and she didn't know what condition her sister would be in.

The door to room 8-215 was slightly ajar. Audrey paused a
moment to take a deep breath. She slowly pushed open the door,
revealing the most beautiful sight—her sister, alive. Hannah was
reclined back in her hospital bed, wearing a drab, blue-gray hospital gown. She was hooked up to dozens of tubes and wires. Her
hair, which would have normally been curled into large, perfect,
bouncy curls, was stringy and pulled back into a ponytail. The

usual vibrant glow of her skin and sparkle in her eyes was pale and dull. Nonetheless, she looked beautiful to Audrey.

Hannah slowly turned her head. For a moment, when she first caught sight of Audrey, the sparkle returned to her half-closed eyes.

"Audrey," she said in a slow medication-induced voice.

Audrey ran over to her bedside. Careful not to hurt her, she leaned over to give her a gentle hug. "I'm here, Hannah. You're going to be okay," she said, pulling back to look at her sister.

"Where's Travis?" Hannah asked groggily. "Is he here? Can I see him?"

Audrey was not sure how much Hannah knew about what happened.

Hannah started to get worked up. "I need to see him. Will you please go get him?" she pleaded.

In an effort to keep her sister calm, Audrey gently stroked her hair. "Shhh... Okay. I'll go see if I can find him."

Hannah's eyes closed slowly, and she drifted off to sleep.

Audrey stayed by Hannah's bedside. The minutes turned into hours as a constant flow of nurses came in and out of her room, replacing IV bags and checking monitors.

"She's going to be pretty out of it for a while," one of the nurses, who saw Audrey patiently waiting for hours by Hannah's bed, said. "She'll come back around when we cut back on her pain medication a bit."

It was getting late into the evening. Audrey understood what the nurse was trying to tell her.

"Take a break," the nurse kindly suggested. "I think tomorrow she will be a bit more herself."

Audrey kissed Hannah's forehead and looked at her face peacefully resting.

"Rest, my beautiful Sis," Audrey said softly, "I won't be far."

Audrey returned back down to the waiting room to find that O'Shea was not there. She searched all over the lobby and corridors and could not find him anywhere. Audrey checked the cafeteria, but when there was no sign of him, she got worried.

She walked toward the hospital front entrance. Through the revolving glass door, she spotted O'Shea. He was sitting on the curb of the emergency room drop off. It was an odd place to sit. Audrey pushed through the revolving doors, carefully examining him from afar. He was very still, staring off into the distance. She approached him slowly, studying him.

"Hey, are you okay?" she asked, joining him on the curb.

"Huh?" he jumped. "Oh yeah, I'm okay. I just needed some air."

He didn't seem all right to Audrey.

"Are you sure? Something seems off." She looked him over.

O'Shea looked at her, and then looked away. Audrey could tell he had something to say.

"Hey." She put her hand on his shoulder. "What is it? You can tell me anything."

"It's just...I'm sitting here, and there should be tons of ambulances pulling up, and doctors running out to help save victims. But here we are sitting on the curb. I haven't had to move once. No ambulances are pulling up. We sat in that nearly empty waiting room all night, and there was hardly anyone there." He went silent for a moment before his eyes filled with tears. "Every time I close my eyes, I see body parts in the rubble, wallets, shoes, hair…I can't get those images out of my mind, Audrey," he confessed, his voice cracking. "I should be stronger than this, but I'm not."

Audrey turned, wrapping her arms around him. Holding him close, she let him sob into her shoulder. O'Shea's chest heaved as he let out the pain of the horror they had witnessed. He quieted after a few moments and sat with his head hung low. Audrey kept her arm wrapped tightly around his shoulders.

O'Shea wiped his eyes and straightened up. "I'm sorry. I didn't mean to break down," he said apologetically.

"Please, don't apologize," Audrey said. "We saw more than anyone should ever see. You are allowed to break down."

The sun was going down behind the city buildings, and off in the distance, rescuers continued to search tirelessly for survivors. As the night came, the city was quiet—solemn and grieving.

———

Thursday, September 14, 2001
6:30 a.m.

The light from the rising sun pierced through the window blinds into the hospital room, waking Audrey up from her sleep. The daybreak did nothing to wake Hannah. Audrey snuck down the hall for a quick vending machine breakfast.

Still groggy from her terrible night of sleep in the hospital chair next to Hannah's bed, Audrey reached into the pocket of her cargo pants and pulled out a couple of wrinkled dollar bills. Feeding the bills clumsily into the machine, she scanned the contents behind the glass. Her nerves prevented her from desiring anything in front of her. She considered a Snickers bar for breakfast, but settled on a blueberry muffin and a bag of pretzels.

Audrey propped herself up against the cold hospital wall, near the vending machine. Halfway through her bag of pretzels, she noticed three nurses enter Hannah's room. There was nothing unusual about it at first, as it was time for their morning rounds. Figuring they would be in there with Hannah for a while, she plopped down on the floor to finish her breakfast of convenience.

Audrey looked around the corridor. The bright fluorescent lights above were harsh on her eyes. The walls were painted a lifeless light gray. She could see all the way down to the end of the hallway to a large window looking out toward the city's skyline. It was quiet except for the beeping and blipping of blood pressure machines and monitors emanating from patients' rooms.

She couldn't wait to tell Hannah the good news. Traffic had opened up into the city, and their parents were on their way to the hospital. Audrey knew Hannah was struggling emotionally, just as much if not more than physically. But Audrey was feeling the effects of the trauma too, and she felt mentally and physically depleted. She was grateful to have reinforcements coming.

Audrey's attention was suddenly diverted back to Hannah's room down the hall. The three nurses had come out of Hannah's room and were gathered outside of Hannah's door. They were huddled together, discussing something quietly.

Audrey observed from afar for a moment, but something about the expression on their faces, the flipping through papers on a clipboard, made Audrey hop to her feet and start walking toward them.

As Audrey approached, the nurses suddenly went quiet.

"I'm Hannah's sister. Is everything okay?" Audrey asked.

Two of the nurses shifted nervously. The other nurse stepped forward, guiding Audrey away from Hannah's door. She appeared older and more experienced than the other two, who were standing frozen in the background.

"I'm Mabel, one of Hannah's nurses." She extended her hand toward Audrey.

Audrey shook Mabel's hand, scanning her round face for clues. She was a stout woman with billowy red hair, which stopped firmly just below her ears.

"We had to run some more tests," Mabel informed Audrey.

"What kind of tests? Is something wrong?" Audrey asked, the concern in her voice rising.

Carefully avoiding Audrey's questions, Mabel replied, "Doctor Burke will be in shortly to speak with Hannah."

Audrey felt unsettled. Clearly there was something wrong.

Mabel lowered her voice and leaned into Audrey. "By the way, your sister insisted on turning on the television. I'm not sure that's a good idea, if you know what I mean." Mabel's eyes looked sad and concerned. "She's watching the news coverage and asking for someone named Travis."

"I'll take care of it," Audrey said. "Thank you."

Audrey quickly entered Hannah's room to intercept her from the television. Hannah was propped up, staring straight ahead. Her attention was completely affixed on the television screen. Audrey prayed that she hadn't seen too much. But when Audrey glanced up at the screen, to her horror, video clips of the bodies falling from the top floors of the North Tower were playing on the screen. Audrey immediately lunged for the remote to turn it off, but it was too late. Hannah had already seen the footage. She was silent. Her eyes focused on something in the distance, as if she could see through the hospital walls and out into the city.

Audrey waited with bated breath for Hannah to say something. After a few moments, she turned to look at Audrey. Tears streamed down her face. She didn't ask for Travis. She didn't ask any questions. Instead, her eyes revealed an acceptance and certainty that broke Audrey's heart.

"Travis is dead," Hannah said.

Audrey jumped in. "We don't know that for sure. Maybe—" she started to say, but Hannah shook her head.

"No. There were jumpers, Audrey. They landed all around me in the plaza. People were trapped... Travis was up there..." Hannah's voice trailed off.

Hannah began to cry. Soft whimpers escalated into deep sobs. Audrey carefully climbed into bed with her sister, holding her close the way she did as kids whenever Hannah had had a bad dream. Audrey reached over to the nightstand for the box of tissues. Pulling a tissue from the box, she gently wiped Hannah's face.

"You saved me," Hannah said.

Audrey reached into her cargo pocket, and pulled out the whistle. "I didn't save you. You saved yourself. You are so strong, Hannah."

Hannah was silent for a few minutes, safe in her sister's arms. She lifted her head to look Audrey in the eyes. Her eyes filled with tears that brimmed over the edges of her eyelids.

"Everything in my mind tells me Travis is dead...but...I *feel* him with me," Hannah said. "I just don't understand."

Audrey wished there was something she could do to make it all better, but for the first time in her life, she couldn't make things hurt less for her sister. All Audrey could do was lie by her side and comfort her. Hannah drifted off to sleep, her head nuzzled under Audrey's chin.

———

Three short knocks on the door of the hospital room startled Audrey.

"Hannah?" a male's voice called from the doorway of the hospital room.

Audrey's heart started beating fast. The nurses' huddle earlier in the morning was still at the forefront of her mind.

"Yes, come in," Audrey called, gently shaking Hannah to wake her.

Hannah slowly opened her eyes.

"I'm Dr. Burke," he said warmly.

Hannah's face was swollen and puffy from crying.

"I have some results I would like to go over with you," the doctor said, glancing over at Audrey. He cleared his throat. "You may want some privacy."

Hannah realized the doctor was suggesting that Audrey leave the room.

"No, it's okay. She's my sister. Anything you have to say you can say in front of her," Hannah said.

Dr. Burke took a breath, looking slightly apprehensive. "Very well." He lifted the front page on his clipboard to read off of the page underneath. "Your levels are looking good. Your kidneys didn't suffer the type of damage we often see with this type of injury, so that is great news. Hydration is up, and the swelling in your leg is coming down." Dr. Burke then paused.

Hannah didn't understand what the hesitation was. It sounded all like great news, but there was clearly something more.

"Hannah…is there any chance you could be pregnant?" Dr. Burke asked.

Hannah was taken aback by the question. "No," she scoffed, quickly dismissing the question, "there's no chance—" Suddenly, the night of her first date with Travis flooded her memory—the sake, inviting him up to her apartment, stumbling, becoming entangled with each other in her bedroom. Hannah's mind raced, calculating the impossibility of the one night with Travis. "It couldn't be…" Hannah mumbled.

Dr. Burke looked down at Hannah with a confirming look in his eyes. Hannah realized the question he had just asked her a moment before was not a question at all. Dr. Burke was *telling* her she was pregnant.

Hannah reached down and placed both hands on her abdomen. She felt Travis's presence rush through her body. She knew in an instant—she was pregnant.

CHAPTER 27

Tuesday, September 18, 2001
12:00 p.m.

It had been a week since the horrific events of the previous Tuesday. New York City had begun to open up again under a new normal. Trains had started to run on a limited schedule, and people slowly and cautiously returned to work. Audrey's and Hannah's parents hadn't left Hannah's side since they'd arrived. It was time for Audrey to return home to face her fate.

O'Shea and Audrey caught the 12:02 p.m. Metro North train from Grand Central Station back to their Connecticut shoreline town. Still in the same NYPD T-shirt and cargo pants they had worn all week, they were looking forward to getting home.

As the train clanked and clambered along the tracks inside the long, dark tunnel leading out of Grand Central Station, Audrey quietly looked at her reflection in the black window. She was not the same person she was a week ago.

Like O'Shea, she grappled with the images stuck in her mind of body parts, personal belongings, death, and destruction. She also struggled with the growing feeling of guilt that her sister had survived, while so many people had lost their loved ones. Her emotions vacillated as she sat next to O'Shea on the unforgiving maroon-and-blue vinyl seats of the Metro North train. The train soon emerged from the dark tunnel, and they were out on the open tracks. The light flooded the train car, causing Audrey to squint.

"We should probably let the department know we are on the way back," O'Shea said.

Audrey had dreaded that moment. She assumed Gaston went right back to the department to write her up. As a probationary recruit, Audrey knew she could be fired for just about anything. Choking out a supervisor would surely be enough cause.

Audrey nodded, staring out the window at the trees whizzing by. She was not sorry for what she did to Gaston. No matter what she faced when she got back, she would make no apologies for it. She would also stand by Preston's actions. Scott deserved what he got too. If that meant she and Preston would no longer have a future as police officers, she would have to accept that. But she refused to back down from what was right.

"Excuse me." O'Shea turned to a man sitting across from them on the train. "Could I borrow your cell phone for a moment to make a quick call?" he politely asked. "My phone is dead."

The man looked at the NYPD sprawled across the chest of the T-shirt O'Shea was wearing and immediately reached for his phone. Handing it to O'Shea, he said, "If there is anything else I can do for you, please…let me know," he said, "and thank you for your service."

O'Shea was at first caught by surprise but then realized they were still wearing the NYPD clothing.

"Oh, we aren't NYPD officers," O'Shea said.

"Are you officers somewhere?" the man asked.

"Yes, we're on our way back to Connecticut from Ground Zero," O'Shea replied.

"Well then, you are true heroes," the man said. "I am grateful for everything you do. The man then leaned forward to address Audrey too. "Thank you for your service."

Being thanked for her role as a police officer meant the world to Audrey, and she was determined to fight to achieve her dream.

Audrey held her breath as O'Shea dialed the extension to the sergeant's desk at the police department.

"Hey, Sarge," he said, "it's O'Shea. Just letting you know myself and Recruit Morretti are on our way back."

Audrey could not hear what was being said on the other end of the phone, but she felt a pit in her stomach.

O'Shea nervously glanced over at Audrey. "Yes, sir," he responded into the phone, "I will tell her."

He hung up the call and turned to Audrey. "The chief wants to see you in his office as soon as we get back."

Audrey's heart sank. She was in deep trouble.

———

Audrey was a sight to see as she walked through the halls of the police department on her way to the chief's office. She was in desperate need of a long, hot shower, new clothes, and a good hair-brushing. Audrey rounded the corner and saw Eileen sitting outside of the chief's office, looking anxious. She jumped to her feet at the sight of Audrey.

"Oh, my dear"—Eileen scanned Audrey once over—"I'm sorry you had to come right here. I'm sure you just want to get home. I can only imagine what you've been through. Come on. They are waiting for you."

"They—?" Audrey began to ask, but Eileen had already opened the door to the chief's office.

In front of the chief's desk stood a woman dressed in a navy-blue business suit and matching navy-blue pumps. Her narrow face and high cheekbones were framed by wispy layers of dark brown hair. Audrey guessed she was somewhere in her early fifties.

Confused, Audrey stood awkwardly, having no idea what was going on.

"Recruit Moretti," the chief spoke, "this is Mayor Farraday."

Audrey felt her knees weaken. Gaston had gone crying to the *mayor*! She was in deeper trouble than she'd thought.

Mayor Farraday stepped toward Audrey and extended her hand for a handshake. "Hello, Audrey."

Despite the mayor's warm demeanor, Audrey felt paralyzed. She shook the mayor's hand but was unable to speak. Her mind was racing.

The chief cleared his throat. "Recruit Morretti, I have been made aware of what happened in the city."

Audrey felt the blood drain from her face. "I can explain—" she started to say, but the chief cut her off.

"I received a call yesterday from a Sergeant Manny Ramirez with NYPD Twentieth Precinct," the chief continued.

"Manny?" Audrey blurted out.

"Yes. Sergeant Ramirez," the chief responded. "I am aware that you risked your life to help rescue a victim trapped under the rubble. He said you were instrumental in the rescue process, and without your efforts, the victim likely would have died before the crew could get to her."

Audrey was in shock. It was not at all the conversation she had expected. Her voice felt shaky as she tried to speak. "That was my sister," she said, her voice cracking with emotion.

"I know," the chief said, a smile spreading across his face. "I think it's safe to say that letting you go into the city was the best decision I have ever made in my career."

Mayor Farraday stepped forward, looking at Audrey with admiration and respect. "Audrey, we would like to honor you at graduation next week with the Bravery Meritorious Action and Life Saving Award."

Audrey could not believe what she was hearing. *Graduation!* She would not only be graduating the academy but would also be awarded one of the greatest honors a police officer could receive. She felt immense relief come over her, but it was quickly replaced with a crushing feeling of guilt. She could not graduate the academy without Preston. Suddenly Audrey's face changed.

"Is everything okay?" Mayor Farraday asked, looking perplexed.

"I'm honored. I truly am, but...I cannot graduate this academy if Preston—I mean, Recruit Briggs—doesn't graduate too. He deserves this job just as much as me, if not more," Audrey said.

The chief cleared his throat again. "Recruit Brigg is under investigation for conduct unbecoming of an officer."

"That's just it, sir. Preston was just *defending* me. One of the guys was spreading a terrible rumor about me..." Audrey started to explain.

Mayor Farraday's eyes narrowed. "What *kind* of rumor?" she asked, suspecting she already knew the answer.

Audrey looked embarrassed. "That Preston and I were—"

The mayor cut her off. "Say no more. I know where this is going." She stepped toward Audrey and looked her in the eyes, woman to woman. "If I had a dollar for every rumor and innuendo during my career simply because I'm a female, I'd be rich. It is unacceptable, and I will not tolerate it on my watch."

The mayor then turned to the chief with squinted, angry eyes. "Immediately reinstate Recruit Briggs to the police academy. As for the recruit who is behind the rumor, I want all of his information on my desk by tomorrow morning."

Audrey fought back tears. She would be graduating the academy after all, and Preston would be right by her side.

———

Audrey turned the key in the lock to her apartment and pushed open the door. Lucy barely looked up from where she sat on the counter licking her paw. She clearly had been personally offended by Audrey's absence.

"I know, I know. I've been away, and you are mad at me," Audrey said, scratching the top of Lucy's head.

Audrey looked around at her apartment. Everything looked exactly the same as when she had left the morning of September 11 yet everything had changed. Audrey felt unsettled and anxious. It was a subtle feeling that had persisted since the day of the attacks. Underlying all other emotions, and always present. She had developed a persistent tightness in her chest, unsure if it was a result of the ash she'd breathed in for days or post-traumatic stress.

Audrey placed her dead cell phone in the charging station and went straight to the shower. The hot water ran, steaming up the bathroom. She tiredly undressed, taking note of the scratches and bruises on her bare legs. She hadn't felt any pain at the time, but she knew the scrapes and bruises were from forcing a path down the narrow tunnel to Hannah. She stepped into the shower and let the hot water rain down over her body. For the first time in a week, she was alone. She quickly found that her mind was a prison full of horrifying images and traumatic emotions.

As Audrey began to decompress, the events of the past week played out in her mind. From the moment Eileen had walked into the academy room announcing that a plane had crashed into the World Trade Center, Audrey could have never imagined what would unfold from there. The unimaginable had happened so quickly.

Like a tidal wave, emotions overtook Audrey. She lowered her body onto the shower floor, wrapped her arms around her knees, and cried uncontrollably.

CHAPTER 28

Saturday, September 29, 2001
2:00 p.m.

The auditorium was packed wall-to-wall with family members and friends of the graduating recruits. It was not the way Audrey had envisioned graduation day. Her parents and Hannah would be missing from the audience. She knew her parents needed to be by Hannah's side while she recovered in the hospital. Still, she couldn't help but feel sad that no one was in the audience for her.

Audrey paced backstage as she waited for her graduating classmates to line up for the ceremony. Preston suddenly appeared in front of her, looking handsome and official in his uniform. The first act of transitioning from recruit to officer was shedding the khaki academy uniform and donning the official navy-blue department uniform. The formal ceremony uniform also included white gloves and a five-point hat. Audrey's hat was too big for her head and kept sliding down onto the middle of her forehead. Preston pushed the brim of her hat up with his white-gloved hand, so he could see her eyes.

"We made it," he said, beaming with pride.

"It wasn't pretty, but we made it," Audrey replied.

Audrey noticed one of the pins on Preston's collar was crooked. She instinctively reached out to fix it. Preston lifted his chin to let her unpin and straighten it.

"There," she said, patting the front of his shoulder.

Preston smiled down at her. "Thanks, Audrey. You're like the big sister I never had."

Audrey smiled back. "I guess I have family here today after all."

One by one, their classmates joined them backstage. Ethan, Jonathan, and Ray filed in line behind Audrey and Preston. Scott was the last to arrive, staying distant from the rest of the group. As promised, Scott had received a personal invitation to the mayor's office for a special conversation. He was a changed person after that day, having little to say the last week of the academy.

It was time to line up in preparation to cross the stage. Audrey shifted into position in front of Preston. Her heart soared with pride as she anticipated crossing the stage. She tried to push away the loss she felt that Hannah was not there.

She felt a tap on her shoulder from behind. Audrey turned to find O'Shea standing in front of her, holding two dozen red roses. Her face lit up in surprise. She didn't expect him to be there.

"I'll be in the front row, cheering for you," O'Shea said.

Audrey was overcome with emotion. She hadn't seen O'Shea since they had been home, but he had never once let her feel alone through the entire ordeal. She should have known he would be there.

"These are for you." O'Shea lifted up the flowers. "I'll hang on to them for you until after." He nervously shifted, realizing the entire academy class was watching.

Audrey pushed up on her toes and kissed him on the cheek. O'Shea blushed.

"Good luck," he said, smiling proudly. He then skipped down the short flight of stairs, from the side of the stage, back into the audience.

Preston winked at Audrey and gave her a double thumbs-up of approval. Audrey knew in that exact moment that she would one day marry O'Shea,

Suddenly, the sound of bagpipes filled the auditorium. One at a time, they would be called to cross the stage to receive their official police badges.

Before the curtain opened, Audrey reflected on everything she'd endured to reach that moment. She had persisted through so much opposition from Gaston and his failed attempts to keep her from that very day.

Shortly after handling Scott, Mayor Faraday learned how Gaston had left his squad in New York City. While delving more into the actions of Sergeant Gaston, she also learned that he had treated Audrey in an inequitable manner over the course of the police academy. He received an invitation to her office, just like Scott had. Mayor Faraday had a special assignment for Sergeant Gaston. He was assigned to pin each badge on every graduating recruit at the ceremony that day, including and, especially, Audrey.

Audrey would revel in the moment when Gaston would be forced to pin her badge on her uniform in front of everyone.

The curtain suddenly pulled back, giving Audrey a full view of the packed auditorium. O'Shea was sitting front and center, just as promised.

One by one, the recruits stepped forward, crossing the stage when their name was called. Audrey was next in line. It was the moment she had been waiting for her entire life.

"Officer Audrey Moretti," the chief announced.

Audrey felt Preston pat the back of her shoulder as she took a step forward. She proudly walked across the stage, glancing down into the audience. O'Shea was clapping proudly for her.

Audrey came to a stop in the middle of the stage in front of the podium. Gaston stood in front of her, holding her official badge. He looked like a scolded puppy, and she knew it killed him to bestow such an honor upon her. Looking dejected and humiliated, he pushed the tall silver pin's post through the holes of her uniform shirt.

"Before we continue with the presentation of the badges, we would like to take a moment to honor Officer Moretti this evening," the chief said to the audience. "As you are all aware, the events of September 11 ᵈevastated us, both as a nation and on a personal level. It is a date we will never forget."

A somber hush fell over the audience.

"When our young recruits cross our stage, they are heading into a new career that will test their bravery, honor, and resilience. Officer Moretti has already proven all of these attributes. Tonight we would like to honor Officer Moretti for her bravery and resilience. Audrey was instrumental in recovering a victim under the rubble at Ground Zero. That victim was her sister."

The crowd gasped.

"Tonight we present Officer Moretti the Bravery Meritorious Action and Life Saving Award, the highest honor that can be achieved in police work," he said.

The chief picked up a large beautifully lacquered plaque. Audrey's name was engraved on a shiny gold plate that was mounted on the front of the award.

"Sergeant Gaston," the chief said, handing the plaque to him, "you may now present this award to Officer Moretti."

Clenching tightly his jaws, Gaston took the plaque from the chief's hand. After he handed the plaque to Audrey, the audience erupted with applause. Gaston begrudgingly pulled his feet together and held his white-gloved hand up to his five-point hat to salute Audrey.

Audrey's fought back tears of pride as she walked off the stage, with the plaque tucked under her arm. A moment after she stepped off the stage, she heard words that made tears stream down her cheeks.

"Officer Preston Briggs," the chief announced into the microphone.

————

Saturday, December 15, 2001
9:00 a.m.

Hannah moved slowly across the living room floor of the quaint New England Cape she had grown up in with Audrey.

The house hadn't changed much over the years, and the familiarity and comfort was what Hannah needed most during her recovery. The bedroom Hannah had shared with Audrey was still the same as when they'd left home. The same pictures hung on the walls of the living room. The kitchen table was the same one they had sat around for so many dinners together.

Her recovery had been slow and painful, but each day she regained strength in her left leg and increased her endurance. She had undergone hundreds of hours of physical therapy in the months after being released from the hospital. But it was the emotional recovery that took the greatest toll. Hannah couldn't bear to return to her apartment in Manhattan. She never wanted to return to the city again.

The months since the attacks had been emotionally grueling. Each night she would lie awake, wishing Travis was still alive somewhere out there, even though she knew in her heart he was not. She spent hours torturing her mind, wondering where he was when he had died. The not knowing haunted Hannah the most. Was he trapped? Did he jump? Vivid images of horrific scenarios constantly flashed through her mind, tormenting her to no end.

Hannah suffered from nightmares, anxiety, and bouts of depression. She wondered how she would ever be able to take care of a baby, when she couldn't even manage her own existence.

It had been three months since the horrific day of the attacks. There wasn't a day that went by that she didn't think about Rosemary and Eli. Each time her thoughts turned into tears. Hannah felt crushingly guilty for surviving. At first, she secretly hoped that Rosemary and Eli believed she too had died in the attacks on September 11. She couldn't bear for them to know that she had survived and Travis had not. But as time went on, she realized it would be selfish of her not to share with them the news that she was carrying Travis's child. And the day came when she had to face them. Hannah had to reveal the truth—a truth that she knew would ultimately bring hope and joy to their decimated hearts, the way it had for her.

Later that morning, Hannah would arrive at the doorstep of Travis's apartment, the same doorstep she had crossed to meet Rosemary and Eli for the first time—one of the happiest days of her life. She would stand at their front door, revealing that she was alive when Travis was dead. She would have to endure their shock, pain, and, possibly, anger at the sight of her. Would they embrace her? Or would she instead be the representation of everything they had lost?

Hannah sat down on the loveseat in her parent's living room, waiting for Audrey to arrive after her midnight shift. Audrey had made it through three months of field training under the wing of seasoned officers. Having the least amount of seniority as a new officer, she was promptly assigned to the midnight shift upon completing her field training rounds.

Hannah placed her hands on her newly emerging belly. The small, round bump under her clothing was becoming ever-present. Through all of her pain and sorrow, she was amazed at the life growing inside of her—the life that would allow Travis to live on.

There were so many emotions to sort through. One moment she was grateful for the time she'd had with Travis, the next she was angry at him being taken away from her so quickly. She couldn't understand why she was given the gift of true love, only for it to be ripped away from her so suddenly.

Hannah heard footsteps up the front walkway. Audrey unlocked the front door and peeked in the house, still wearing her uniform slacks and a dark blue sweatshirt with her department badge sewn on the chest. It was a cold pre-winter day in New England.

"I left the car running," Audrey said.

Hannah stood up slowly, grabbing the envelope on the coffee table in front of her. The envelope contained a stack of ultrasound images that she'd received from her appointment the day before. Hannah's loose-fitting maternity shirt billowed out as she bent over to clutch the envelope off the table.

"Are you ready to do this?" Audrey gently asked.

Hannah took a deep breath. "No," she said softly, "but it's time."

———

As Hannah stood in front of Travis's apartment, his absence became more palpable than ever. She had to accept that he would not be on the other side of the door when it opened. Hannah had no idea what to expect when Rosemary would open the door and see her standing there. Her hand shook as she reached out her index finger to press the doorbell. Audrey stood next to her.

Hannah heard the dong of the bell chime inside the apartment. She felt her knees quivering under her. Several seconds

later, Hannah heard footsteps approaching on the other side of
the door and come to a stop. She knew someone was looking
through the door's peephole, and it made her want to shrink.

The locks unlatched from the inside, and the door opened
slowly and cautiously. Rosemary stood in the doorframe, her
face blank and unreadable at first. She looked different from
when Hannah had last seen her. The months had taken a
toll. Her once shiny brown hair was now peppered with gray
strands, noticeable wrinkles had formed on her face, and her
once blue sparkling eyes, similar to Travis's, were lackluster.

There was total silence as Rosemary vacantly looked at her.
Hannah did not know what to say. She felt paralyzed.

Moments later, Rosemary took in an audible gasp of air as
if she had not been breathing. "Hannah," she said breathlessly.
Rosemary's expression remained frozen as she stepped forward
and gripped her tightly. She hung on Hannah's shoulders, silent and in shock.

Hannah wanted to speak, but no words came out. Rosemary
took a step back to look at Hannah. She pored over Hannah's
face with her eyes. Within seconds Rosemary's face contorted, and her eyes revealed the deepest sorrow Hannah had ever
seen. Her face became a mural of the indescribable pain and
grief of a broken mother.

"Oh, Hannah," she said, bursting into tears. The lump in
Hannah's throat turned into weeps as she and Rosemary cried
together in the doorway.

Then Hannah heard a sweet voice say her name. A voice she
recognized immediately. She almost couldn't bear to look up.

"Hannah?" Eli said softly, as if he could not believe his own eyes.

Hannah peered around Rosemary to see Eli's face, wide-eyed at the sight of her.

"Hannah!" Eli cried with a gut-wrenching, throaty voice as he pushed his wheelchair forward. Tears immediately fell from his eyes, like fat raindrops from a summer sky.

Hannah ran to him as tears streamed down her face. She crouched down to wrap her arms around him. Rosemary stood in the doorway, her hand covering her mouth. She wept, watching Eli sob in Hannah's arms.

"Hannah, you're alive," Eli cried in disbelief. He pulled back to look at Hannah, his sweet blue eyes glossy with tears. Suddenly, his face changed. "Travis—" Eli started to say, his grief overwhelming him. He started crying again.

Audrey entered the apartment and closed the door behind her. She stood quietly in the entryway, giving Rosemary, Hannah, and Eli space to grieve together.

Rosemary cleared her throat, trying to regain her composure. "We had a small service for Travis about a month ago," Rosemary said apologetically. "We didn't know you...we thought you..." Rosemary struggled to find the right words.

Hannah understood. They thought she had died too. Standing in Travis's apartment, she wished that he would just jump out from the kitchen to surprise her—that it was all just a bad dream.

Rosemary looked sorrowfully into Hannah's eyes. "Come." She reached for Hannah's hand. It was the same way Travis had held Hannah's hand so many times. She led her down the hallway and into the living room. She opened a small drawer inside of the console table—the same console table that adorned the picture of Travis as a little boy, wearing plaid pants.

Hannah recalled Eli teasing Travis about the picture the last time she was there. Now she stood in the same spot, in front of the same framed picture, but there was no laughter, no magical spark of new beginnings.

Rosemary took a small black velvet pouch from the drawer. She carefully pulled open the drawstring and reached in with her fingers. What she pulled out took Hannah's breath away.

Rosemary held up the flattened penny from the World Trade Center—the same one that Hannah had made on the day Travis took her to the observation deck. It was no longer shiny and new, but rather bent and charred.

Hannah looked at Rosemary, confused.

"The medical examiner returned this to us. Travis's remains were found a few weeks into the search. This…was in his pocket." Her voice cracked.

Hannah felt the tightness in her throat again, and her eyes stung with tears.

Rosemary placed the penny in Hannah's hand. "It was his good luck charm; he always had it with him," Rosemary said, holding the penny between their embraced hands. "He loved you so much, Hannah."

Hannah pulled the penny up to look at it. She searched for clues, hoping it would somehow reveal something about Travis's final moments. The penny's imperfect edges and charred exterior only revealed that something terrible had happened, not what or how.

"Do you…know anything more?" Hannah asked, her voice barely audible.

"No." Rosemary shook her head.

Hannah sensed that Rosemary knew what she was asking. She was sure that Rosemary too had been searching for the same closure as Hannah was and had asked the same questions. Where was Travis when the plane hit? Was he in his office on the 104th floor? Did he die upon impact, or was he trapped? Did he suffer?

"There is one more thing," Rosemary said, reaching into the drawer. She pulled out a square, black scrapbook. "He couldn't wait to give this to you. He worked so hard on it." Rosemary smiled through sad eyes as she handed Hannah the book.

Hannah took it into her hands, and suddenly it was as if Travis were standing right there in the room with them. She drew in a breath, as if his spirit had just entered her body and breathed new life into her soul. She slowly opened the scrapbook to the first page.

When You Live Each Day to the Fullest,
Life Can Never Be Too Short ...

She ran her fingers over his beautiful handwriting. Tears overflowed from her eyelids. Travis knew how to live. In the short time that she was blessed to have known him, he had taught *her* how to live. As she slowly turned the first thick, laminated page of the scrapbook, the corners of her mouth pulled into a smile while tears fell from her eyes.

Two photos from their walk across the Brooklyn Bridge had been arranged diagonally on the first page. The first was the photo that Travis had unexpectedly snapped of Hannah's face, capturing her reaction as they began to cross the bridge.

Grazing her eyes over the two photos, and the creatively placed corresponding stickers, Hannah could see how much thought he'd put into making the scrapbook. The second photo was of Hannah and Travis on the bridge, with the towers jetting high into the sky in the background. It was glued onto aqua-blue rectangular card stock and affixed to the page. A caption just above the picture read:

Our Towers

Hannah couldn't look any further. She needed to sit. Closing the book, she walked over to the couch. "I'm sorry. I just need a moment."

As she sat down, she felt the presence of her belly protrude. She took a few deep breaths to gather her thoughts. With each breath, she felt her stomach rise. It was time to share her news. Hannah looked over at Audrey, who was holding the envelope. Audrey walked over and slipped the envelope to Hannah.

Wiping her eyes, Hannah said, "I'm sorry. This is my sister, Audrey."

Rosemary forced a sad smile through her grief.

Hannah took a deep breath, clutching the envelope nervously between her fingers. "I have something to share." She glanced nervously between Rosemary and Eli, her voice soft and unsteady.

Prying open the envelope, she pulled out the stack of grainy black-and-white ultrasound images. Hannah handed the stack to Rosemary, who took them carefully into her hands. She started to flip through them, when her eyes suddenly widened.

Rosemary looked up at Hannah, her face asking a million questions. "Is this..." She looked disbelievingly at Hannah.

Hannah's eyes filled with happy tears. She nodded her head in confirmation. "His name will be James. James Travis Russell," Hannah said, tears spilling down her cheeks. When Hannah had found out that she was having a boy, her mind immediately flashed back to the day in the park with Travis. He had told her that if he ever had a son, he would name him James.

The aqua-blue hue suddenly returned to Rosemary's eyes; the twinkle Hannah had seen so often in Travis's eyes sparkled once again in hers. Color returned to Rosemary's face, and she looked ten years younger with the realization that she would soon be a grandmother—and that a part of Travis would live on.

Eli looked confused. "What's going on?" He looked curiously at Hannah.

Hannah crouched down next to Eli's wheelchair. "You are going to be an uncle."

Eli's face lit up. Hannah unmistakably felt Travis all around her. The room was suddenly filled with magic the way it was the day Travis had brought her home to meet Rosemary and Eli for the first time. It was the magic of new beginnings.

CHAPTER 29

April 2002

The cold, gray Northeastern winter months dragged on, but the promise of spring was just around the corner. Each day that went by, Hannah's body changed and grew. James had grown so much in her belly, and she could feel him moving often. Every time he kicked, it made Hannah smile.

On one of Rosemary and Eli's many visits to Connecticut, James had been extra active. Hannah asked Eli if he wanted to feel the baby move. Despite his initial apprehension, curiosity ultimately won. She placed his hand on her belly, and with the thud of James's strong kick, Eli's eyes widened in surprise and awe. Hannah laughed at his reaction.

Rosemary and Eli visited as many weekends as they could. Through such a horrendous tragedy, the family had grown in size. Hannah's parents opened their home to them any time they wanted, and Rosemary and Eli happily took them up on the offer. Weekend visits were spent cooking, eating dinner together, shopping, and even attending church together. The love that surrounded them had grown, despite the large gaping hole left by the loss of Travis.

Hannah had unequivocally decided that she would never return to the city. Her parents and Audrey had gone to her apartment and moved all of her belongings back home. She knew it would possibly take years for her to get back on her feet, emotionally and physically, especially with a newborn on the way. There would be no father to help in the middle of the night with feedings, diaper changes, fevers, and all of the things that came along with a newborn. Hannah would need the help from her family for a while, but she vowed that she would soon find a place of her own to raise James. More than anything, she wanted to make James proud. Hannah would raise James to become the amazing man that his father was.

But Hannah struggled. During the day when people were around her, she was distracted, as well as when she felt the joy of a kicking and active baby inside of her. In those moments, she believed she was making progress with her grief and trauma. It was the nighttime, however, when anxiety and torment took over.

Intense grief would consume her under the cover of darkness. Unrelenting questions continued to fill her head of what had happened to Travis. All she knew was that the airplane had crashed into the North Tower between the ninety-third and ninety-ninth floors, severing all three stairwells. Everyone above the impact had been trapped.

She wondered incessantly about her friends Marilyn, Don, Miles, and the hundreds of other people who had worked at Berkley and Stanton. Hannah learned that the plane had crashed into the South Tower between the seventy-seventh and eighty-fifth floors. Was there any chance that her friends were still alive? Maybe they'd listened to her and changed their minds about deciding to evacuate. Or had they remained on the eighty-fourth floor when the planes had hit? Deep down inside, she knew the answers. She just couldn't accept it. There was nothing fair or decent about any of it.

Hannah's grief had turned to anger in recent weeks—so much anger that her heart would beat fast and her body would shake. Marilyn had grandbabies she had loved with all of her heart. Don had a wife and two daughters he was putting through college. Miles had just gotten engaged. Travis and Hannah were supposed to have watched them get married on New Year's Eve. Travis should have been there to watch his son grow. So many lives had been destroyed.

Haunting questions still hung over her, like a dark storm cloud. The voice she had heard while she was buried under the rubble, was it a real person? Was she imagining it? Was it Travis somehow communicating with her? What about the vivid vision she'd had of Travis leading her toward the towers, only to tell her she could not go with him? "He needs you here, and I am needed there," he had said in her dream. She now understood "he" was James. Did Travis come to her somehow even after death? Why was he needed at the towers?

And then there was Abina. Hannah thought often of her and the brief time they'd spent together in the stairwell. She had no idea what had happened to her after the ambulance had taken her away.

Of all the haunting questions in her mind, there was one that brought her to a place so dark, leaving her so riddled with intense guilt. If she hadn't helped carry Abina out of the stairwell that morning, past the dozens of people filing orderly down the stairwell, would she have been in the building when it collapsed? Had those precious few moments made the difference between Hannah living and dying? Were the people who had moved to the side to allow her to help carry Abina out of the building able to escape before the collapse? The smallest of factors that morning had made the difference between life and death. These unanswered questions, survivor's guilt, and unexplainable anomalies continued to torture Hannah.

As time slowly moved on through the dark, cold winter, Hannah felt Travis's presence slipping away from her. She had felt Travis with her so much in the beginning, when she was buried under the rubble, during her time in the hospital, and at his apartment that day she'd gone to see Rosemary and Eli. Hannah hadn't felt him with her since that day. She worried time would take him further from her.

Would those few weeks they had spent together be enough to withstand the passage of time? Hannah wished for Travis to come to her in her dreams, just so that she could see him. But each morning, she woke up with no recollection of any dreams, no visits from Travis. Her heart ached, thinking he may never come to her again.

One gray, cold early April night, Hannah had waddled her way to the top of the creaky old stairs of her parents' home to retire for bed. She felt the strain on her knees and low back under the extra weight of her pregnancy. Maneuvering herself into bed, she propped herself up against the headboard and covered her belly so that she was snug under the warm blankets.

Hannah fixated on the bright full moon outside her bedroom window. As she stared at the light of the perfectly round orb in the sky, Hannah pretended that Travis was somehow looking at the same beautiful glow. She decided not to wait for him to appear in her dreams that night. She began to talk to him.

"I miss you so much," Hannah said into the dark, empty room.

"I haven't felt you in a while. Are you still with me?" Hannah looked around for any sign of him. Nothing appeared, no voice returned her conversation. She sat there, alone and consumed with grief.

"I need to know that you are still with me." She broke down in tears. Giving herself a moment in the dark silence to compose herself, she continued again, "James is growing so much. He's always kicking. I think he is going to be so much like you." Tears rolled down her face. She wiped them away and focused on the intricate markings on the moon. If the wonders of the moon and stars existed, she had to believe it was possible for Travis to hear her.

"I don't know how I am going to do this without you," she wept, thinking about how James would grow up without a father. It wasn't fair.

Hannah closed her eyes and cradled her belly, grasping for any connection to Travis. "Please, come to me," she whispered, her face pulled tightly. She wished more than anything that when she opened her eyes, Travis would be standing there by her bed. There was nothing but darkness in the room, except for the glow of the moon. Hannah looked out the window, feeling alone and empty.

Suddenly she saw something that made her eyes open with surprise. Soft, gentle snowflakes had begun to fall from the sky. There had been no forecast for snow. Hannah rose from the bed and stood at the window. The moon seemed even brighter, and the flakes fell softly and gently, similar to the way Travis had once whispered in her ear.

She then remembered the day Travis had taken her to Central Park and the butterfly that had landed on her hand. *"Someone from heaven is visiting you,"* he had said.

The sudden and unexplainable snowfall was an undeniable sign that Travis was still with her and James. She smiled up at the sky. "Thank you," she said to Travis, somewhere nearby.

––––––––

Friday, June 15 2002
The day James was born was a beautiful sunny June morning. He had decided to arrive four days early, which did not surprise Hannah in the least bit. If he was anything like his father, he would be ready to take on the world and experience new things.

The first resemblance of Travis was noticeable the moment James was handed to Hannah. She peered down at him through tears in her eyes. James had Travis's unmistakably blue, sparkly eyes.

Over the years as James grew, so much of Travis emerged. James loved adventure, and he charmed everyone he met with his big smile and flashy eyes. He was a miracle that had come from the most tragic of events.

Hannah and James settled into a small home of their own, not far from Audrey and their parents.

Rosemary and Eli never missed a birthday, holiday, or special event. James's birthday parties were big extravaganzas, celebrating the joy of James's birthday, but also the life of Travis that lived on through him.

One night when James was five years old, he pulled a small black book from under his pillow at bedtime. It was the scrapbook Travis had made Hannah. She had never looked past the first page. It was too painful. She had hidden it away in a box in her closet.

"I'm sorry I snooped," James said shamefully, "but will you look at this with me?"

Hannah wrapped her arms around James, pulling him up onto her lap. "Of course," she replied, hiding the dagger of pain she felt in her heart. Sometimes being a mother required more strength than what felt humanly possible.

Hannah opened the first page and immediately felt the tightness in her throat.

"Whoa!" James exclaimed at the site of the Brooklyn Bridge with the Manhattan skyline in the background.

Hannah smiled. "Your daddy took me for a walk over the Brooklyn Bridge."

Her eyes settled onto the picture with the Twin Towers in the background. She didn't tell him the towers were no longer there. In fact she didn't mention the towers at all. She would tell him everything when the time was right. Until then, she would protect him from the harsh truth, as long as she could.

James was captivated by the pictures of his parents on the pages in front of him. As painful as it was for Hannah to revisit those memories, she hoped that James could see the love they had shared in those moments.

Hannah apprehensively turned to the next page. What she saw flooded her heart with bittersweet emotions. A beautifully hand-drawn picture of Brooklyn Bridge Park was sketched across the two open pages. In the middle of the park, Travis sketched a beautiful carousel—the carousel he told her would one day reside there. Hannah felt tears stinging her eyes. She wondered if the carousel ever did make it there but it didn't matter. They would never get the chance to return and ride it together. The raw pang of sadness and anger that came with terrible loss gripped Hannah, as if no time had passed or healed her heart. Grief had no rules.

"Whoa, where is this?" James asked. "I want to ride that carousel!"

Hannah looked at James; his eyes were wide with wonder and excitement.

"That's Brooklyn Bridge Park," Hannah explained. "The carousel wasn't there yet; that's why your Daddy sketched it in. We were supposed to come back to…" Hannah's voice trailed off. She didn't want to upset James with what should have been.

James placed his hand gently on her arm. "It's okay to be sad, Mommy." James's blue eyes looked up at his mom. "I get sad too sometimes. Don't worry. I will take you there one day. We will ride the carousel together."

Hannah shouldn't have been surprised. He was Travis's son, after all. She smiled through her tears and pulled James in close.

"You are amazing. Just like your daddy," she said, kissing his soft, warm forehead.

As difficult as it was to revisit those moments, she knew James was longing to know more about his father. Maybe he was also searching for who he would one day become.

"After we crossed the bridge that night, we sat on a bench in this park right here." She pointed to the sketch. "We got the biggest slices of pizza you could ever imagine. Your dad folded his pizza in half when he ate it! When I had teased him about it, he said that all New Yorkers eat their pizza that way. Then he told me he had a lot to teach me. "

James chuckled.

Hannah turned to the next page. The photographs Travis had taken at Central Park were spread across the pages. She ran her fingers over the picture she'd taken of Travis on the Bow Bridge.

"This is the day your daddy helped a little boy who was having a seizure in the park," she said, recalling the scary incident.

James's eyes flew open. "Like...a superhero?"

"Yes, just like a superhero," Hannah said. "He was so brave, just like you. He also loved adventure, just like a little boy I know." She playfully tapped James's nose, causing him to giggle.

Hannah turned to the next page. She gasped when her eyes fell onto the photograph affixed to the page. She immediately recognized it as the souvenir photo they had taken before going up to the observation deck. With their arms stretched in the air, they were superimposed to look as tall as the towers. Hannah had never given the photo a second thought, but evidently, Travis had gone back to purchase it.

"And this is when your dad took me to the top of a very tall building to look out over Manhattan," she said, making no mention of the South Tower. "I was so scared, but not your dad! He wasn't scared of anything."

"Mommy?" James asked. The look on James's face had suddenly turned sad. "Why did Daddy have to die?" His eyes filled with tears.

His words cut through Hannah's heart like a knife. How could she possibly answer that question when she herself still did not understand? Hannah searched for words, but none came. She had no answers. There was no making it right; no justice to it at all. James waited for his mom to answer.

"I don't know," Hannah replied softly, wishing she had more to say. She hugged him tightly. "I can tell you though, that Daddy is always with us," she reassured him.

James looked confused.

"But...how? I can't see him. I can't hear him," James responded sadly.

"This is how." Hannah pointed to the picture of the butterfly on her hand in Central Park. Brushing James's soft blond hair away from his face, she explained what she had learned from Travis that day.

"When a butterfly lands on your hand, or a cardinal suddenly swoops right in front of you, or even a sudden, unexpected snowfall or a rainbow after a storm...these are all signs from Daddy. You just have to look for him in different ways."

Hannah thought back to the unexpected April snowfall. She wished more than anything for James to feel his father, the way she had that night and so many times since.

"If you keep your heart and mind open, you will find that Daddy is all around you," Hannah said.

James sleepily lay down on his pillow. "I want to help people, like how Daddy helped that boy. Do you think I'm brave enough?" he asked.

"I know you are brave enough, my dear. You are going to save the world one day," Hannah said.

James smiled. Reaching for the scrapbook, he closed it and pulled it close to his chest. "Can I keep this?" he asked as his eyes slowly closed.

"Of course," she whispered, watching him drift off to sleep, clutching the scrapbook to his heart.

CHAPTER 30

August 2010

Approaching the ten-year anniversary of 9/11

Ι t was a hot August day in Connecticut. The air was heavy and humid. Hannah sat in a small booth with tan vinyl seats, waiting for Audrey to arrive for their lunch date. James had recently turned nine years old, growing too fast for Hannah.

It had been almost ten years since the attacks on 9/11, and both Hannah and Audrey still suffered from both emotional and physical scars from that day.

Despite the terrible events ten years earlier, blessings had surely come along since that fateful day. Audrey and O'Shea had gotten married three years after the attacks in a small sea-side ceremony. With two secure and stable jobs in the police department, they were excited to start their own family. But health issues had progressed in Audrey, as she suffered from unexplained coughing fits and intermittent shortness of breath.

Audrey had done her best to downplay her condition, but Hannah had been hearing increasing stories of debilitating illnesses developing in Ground Zero first responders. There had also been a sudden emergence of cancer in those who had been exposed to the toxic dust and ash.

Adding to Audrey's heartbreaking health issues was her struggle to get pregnant. There was no way of knowing if her infertility issues were a result of the effects at Ground Zero, but she had her suspicions. O'Shea and Audrey tried for years, but every test they took showed the same heart-crushing "negative" result. They had accepted that having a family was not in their cards.

Audrey breezed in through the door and plopped herself down on the squishy, tan vinyl booth seat across from Hannah. "Man, it's hot out there." She unraveled a napkin and desperately tried to fan her face with it.

The way Audrey frantically picked up her glass of ice water and slurped it down made Hannah pause. "Are you okay?" she asked suspiciously.

"Me? Yeah, I'm good—just hot, thirsty, and starving!"

But Hannah knew her sister, and she was acting strangely. Hannah studied Audrey curiously. "Okayyyy," she said skeptically. She pushed a menu across the table to Audrey. "How about a couple of sushi rolls to start?" Hannah asked casually.

Audrey clutched her hands together, pulling them up to her mouth as if trying to hold in her words. Her eyes twinkled as they looked directly at Hannah. "No sushi for me today," she blurted out. "No sushi for me for nine months!"

Nine months, no sushi…that can only mean one thing…

Hannah's eyes flew open. "Are y-y-you…?" Hannah stuttered.

Audrey's face exploded into a smile, nodding her head excitedly.

Hannah immediately burst into tears, jumping up from her seat to wrap her arms around her sister. "You're pregnant!" she bellowed.

"I'm about four weeks along," Audrey said, smiling wildly.

Hannah wiped her tears from her face. "I'm so happy for you. Mike must be so excited!" she said.

"Oh, you should see him. He has already made a list of names. He is convinced it's a girl. He wants to name her Addelyn." Audrey placed her hand on her belly. She picked up the ice water again swigging large sips. "I'm so thirsty!"

The waiter arrived at their table to take their order. Hannah's eyes were blurry from her tears of joy.

Audrey quickly perused the menu. "I'll have the chicken and broccoli lunch special," she said.

"Make that two," Hannah said, handing the menus back to the waiter. He scribbled down their orders on his notepad and hurried back to the kitchen.

Hannah and Audrey had so much to catch up on, but Audrey's happy news took center stage. Hannah could relate to the physical changes and discomforts that came along with pregnancy, but emotionally, Hannah's pregnancy had been far from ideal. She had spent the entire nine months of her pregnancy grieving the loss of her baby's father and the love of her life. Hannah was so happy that Audrey had O'Shea, and they would get to experience the pregnancy together.

Audrey took another swig of her ice water. She suddenly looked intently at Hannah. "How are you?" Her tone was serious.

"Fine, good," Hannah replied immediately. "James is excited to go back to school in a few weeks. Fourth grade! Can you believe it?"

Hannah rambled. She was avoiding what Audrey was really asking. The ten-year anniversary of 9/11 was approaching. It had been all over the news, and Hannah had done all she could to avoid it.

The new memorial would be unveiled that year in honor of the ten years that had passed. Two beautiful infinity pools had been constructed in place of each tower. The names of every person lost on 9/11 were etched into the granite walls surrounding the pools. Hannah had never been back and had no intentions to, even with the new memorial.

Audrey reached her hand across the table, gently covering Hannah's hand with hers.

"The ten-year anniversary," Audrey softly said.

Hannah looked away, avoiding the conversation.

"Have you thought about maybe attending the ceremony this year? The memorial is said to be beautiful. It may—"

Hannah cut her off. "I can't go back there," she said curtly, her face hardening. She looked distantly past Audrey. "I don't know how I could ever face that again."

From the very first anniversary, Rosemary and Eli had attended each year. Each year Hannah declined their offers to accompany them. She always felt ashamed that she couldn't bring herself to go. But now with the new memorial and it being the ten-year anniversary, she felt even more guilt.

The memorial services grew each passing year into a beautifully perfected ceremony. The names of all those who died were read out loud by family members. Moments of silence interjected the readings at the exact times the planes had crashed and each of the towers had fallen. Hannah had tried to watch it the first year on television, only making it through a few minutes before she had to shut it off.

In fact she had avoided television completely on the anniversary every year since. She couldn't handle seeing clips of news coverage from that day—the very images of the horrors she'd experienced in person.

"We will all go with you," Audrey offered. "O'Shea and I, Mom and Dad. Rosemary and Eli will of course be there. You won't be alone."

Audrey paused, but she couldn't avoid the topic any longer. "I also think it would be good for James to go," she said nervously.

Hannah looked up in surprise at Audrey. "No. Not yet. He is too young still to know," Hannah protested.

Audrey sighed. "He is nine years old, Hannah. Kids talk. He knows more than you think about that day. You can't protect him from the truth forever. Wouldn't it be better if he learned about it from you?" Audrey asked.

Hannah's eyes filled with tears. "That's just it. I don't know the truth. I don't know how Travis died. Ten years later, I have no answers for my son, for me," Hannah said, her voice cracking. "Even if I could handle going back, I worry that it is too much for James."

It was one of those moments she wished for Travis to appear. There were so many times she needed Travis to help with those big parent decisions.

Audrey allowed Hannah a moment to think. Hannah was staring down at her ice water, fiddling with her straw.

The waiter appeared at their table. "Sashimi platter for two," he said, placing it down on the table in front them.

"Oh...um...no, that's not our order," Hannah politely said. The waiter looked around the restaurant, confused. There were only two other occupied tables. He picked up the platter and tried each table, both groups of diners shaking their heads in response.

The waiter returned to Hannah and Audrey's table, still holding the platter in his hand. "No one else ordered it." He shrugged his shoulders. Not knowing what to do with it, he placed the platter down on their table. "Here, it's on the house."

The sashimi platter in front of her was so similar to the one Travis had shared with her at Haru's Sushi Palace ten years before. Hannah smiled. The beautiful platter unexplainably showing up at their table was Travis telling her to come to him. Hannah suddenly changed her mind.

"Okay," she said to Audrey, "we will go to the ceremony."

———

Sunday, September 11, 2011
Ten-year anniversary of 9/11
Hannah watched as James studied himself in the full-length mirror of their hotel room in New York City. Dressed in a navy-blue suit, he looked more like a young man than a nine-year-old boy. Hannah could clearly see Travis when she looked at him. His hair had gone from fine blond, little boy strands to

thick, lush, golden-brown waves, just like his father's. Hannah squatted down in front of James and straightened his bow tie.

He was quieter than usual, even for an early morning. Hannah could tell he was anxious. She too was fighting back the uneasy and apprehensive feeling in her stomach. It was the first time returning to the city since the attack ten years earlier. The 9/11 Memorial Plaza, where the ceremony would be held, was just a few blocks down from their hotel—the same place where the World Trade Towers had once stood.

It would look so different from what she remembered a decade before. The last images of the towers were still etched in her head. The burning balls of fire wafting out of the windows of the upper floors, the sight of bodies falling, and the dirty, debris-cluttered fountain still haunted her.

It was the place where Travis had died. It was the place where she almost died. She could not believe she was returning there. There were still so many questions left unanswered, and time had not healed even the slightest bit of pain.

James had been invited to be part of the reading of the names at the ceremony. He would also have the opportunity to say a few words in honor of his father, as would other children of victims—children who were either too young at the time of the attacks, and some, like James, who had not even been born yet. They were old enough to speak of the loved ones who had ripped from their lives—loved ones they never got a chance to know.

James shifted in his brown dress shoes. Hannah studied him closely. "Are you sure you want to do this?" she gently asked. "If you are too nervous, you don't have to."

James shook his head. "No, it's not that. I am ready. I have practiced all the names, and I know my speech."

But Hannah could tell something was on his mind, something heavy. "Then what is it, honey?" She took his hand into hers.

He paused for a minute and shifted his eyes downward. "It's just that...I know Dad died on 9/11, but...how exactly did he die?" James sheepishly asked.

It was the question that Hannah had dreaded the most. She had hoped that by the time he was old enough to ask, she would have an answer, but that answer never came.

Hannah took a deep breath. "Do you want the truth? Even if the truth isn't what you hope to hear?" she asked.

James looked nervous. He nodded silently.

Hannah reached for his other hand, kneeling face to face with him. "The truth is that I don't know. I don't have that answer. I wish I could tell you more, but I truly don't know." Hannah hung her head. "I don't think we will ever know, honey. I am sorry."

James looked deflated. He was searching for the same closure she had also been searching for. Hannah pulled him toward her, wrapping her arms around him. He hugged her back for a moment, and then she felt him tense up.

"Do you think he jumped?" James blurted out.

Hannah pulled back in surprise. She had been very careful about what she had revealed to him about that day. She tried to protect him from knowing too much about the horrors that had occurred—the jumpers especially. She suddenly realized that he knew more than she had thought, just like Audrey had warned her.

"Where did you hear about that?"

James shrugged. "Kids talk."

Ugh! Audrey is always right.

Hannah pulled James over to the stiff hotel couch and sat next to him. "I am not sure what else you have heard from your friends, but I don't want you to hear things that are scary from the kids in school. People were trapped on the upper floors," Hannah's voice cracked with emotion, "and yes, some jumped. I don't know where your dad was when everything happened. All I know is that the airplane hit the upper floors of the North Tower, and everyone above was trapped; your dad worked on the 104th floor."

James looked down at his feet with tears falling down his cheeks. "Dad was so brave. I bet he helped a lot of people that day."

"I bet you are right, kiddo. I bet you are right," Hannah said.

CHAPTER 31

Hannah clutched James's hand tightly as they walked the busy sidewalks toward Memorial Plaza. Hannah looked around while passing through the city blocks, struck by how different the once familiar area looked—how different the city felt.

She was briefly brought back to her younger years, when life was full of dreams and promise. Once a young, vibrant girl with stars in her eyes and a dream to work on Wall Street, she now didn't recognize herself in the reflection of the storefronts they passed. But for a moment she was a young woman again, in love and floating on the clouds.

Hannah spotted Audrey and O'Shea, her parents, and Rosemary and Eli, waiting for them up ahead.

"Nanna! Eli! Uncle Mike! Auntie Audrey! Grandma! Grandpa!" James exclaimed, bolting from Hannah's hand.

Hannah had a moment of reprieve from her nervous anticipation, seeing the joy on James's face. Despite growing up without a father, James had a full and wonderful family, surrounded by so much love. Even Uncle Preston had become a part of the family, always present at important family events. Preston, pretty much a big kid himself, was James's favorite video game buddy.

Eli, who had grown into a young man over the years, looked handsome in his dress shirt and bow tie. He had affixed an American flag to the back of his wheelchair, proudly representing his country. It was a cool, early morning in Manhattan, the sun peeking through the clouds, warming the air in intervals.

Rosemary bent down to James's eye level. "Are you ready, kiddo?" she nervously asked.

"I'm ready," James confidently responded.

Rosemary's eyes lifted worriedly, meeting Hannah's. Hannah nodded, confirming that James was ready.

"Your dad will be so proud of you. He will be watching down today," Rosemary said.

People mulled by sullenly as they approached Memorial Plaza. Hannah could not avoid it any longer as they stood on the edge of the plaza.

Audrey took Hannah's hand, rubbing her back reassuringly. "I am right here with you," she said as they took their first steps into the plaza.

Hannah's first sight of Memorial Plaza was overwhelming. It could have been a different place altogether than where she had once worked with Travis and her coworkers. There were no towers like the ones she'd once known, and there was no dust and debris like she had last seen. The destruction had long been cleaned up, replaced with two enormous infinity fountains, each pool placed exactly where each tower had once stood.

The plaza was dotted with perfectly manicured tufts of green trees, further beautifying the grounds. As Hannah moved closer to the fountains, she was drawn in by the beauty of the cascading waterfalls. The sunlight glistened on the water. The sound of the rushing water calmed and comforted her.

She stood at the edge of the first pool, her hands resting on the polished stone perimeter. Hannah noticed the grooves carved into the stone underneath her fingers. She gently ran them along the stone, over the names of those who died right there at the World Trade Center.

Looking up across the pool, an enormous American flag hung from the roof of the building across the way. She looked around, taking in the beauty of the plaza, as if visiting a place she had never stepped foot on before. Despite it being the exact physical location, it wasn't the same place she once knew, and it never would be.

Hannah peered over the stone ledge, letting her eyes follow the flow of the waterfall down to a second waterfall below, where the water ultimately disappeared. The pool was the exact size of the tower's footprint, exactly where it had once stood. The design fully encompassed how she felt. The rushing water would never fill the pool—the same way the hole in her heart from losing Travis would also never be filled.

At the same time, the way the water continued to flow, even after disappearing from sight down below, gave Hannah such a sense of peace and healing. Travis may have disappeared out of sight, but he would live on forever.

Hannah's attention was suddenly pulled to her right. A woman had just approached the stone wall next to her. Upon seeing a name etched in bronze, she threw her body on top of it and wept. She held a framed picture of a man in her hand.

Hannah looked around the perimeter of the reflecting pool. People mulled around, clutching framed pictures of their loved ones, dabbing their eyes with tissues, and embracing each other in grief. Some had etched with a crayon the names of their loved ones on a piece of paper. Roses dotted the wall among the names, placed lovingly by those left behind. Somberness hung heavily in the air. With the opening of the memorial, it was the first time family members had an official physical place to go and grieve—a place to go to honor those they had lost.

Hannah knew Travis's name was somewhere along the wall, etched beautifully in bronze, but she wasn't ready to see it just yet.

There was a heavy police presence throughout the plaza. Officers stood watch with long guns at the ready. James was captivated by the police officers pacing by on patrol. He stopped wide-eyed to look at one of the officers with a police dog.

"Come on, buddy," Hannah said, gently nudging James along, "let's go find our seats."

As presenters, they were seated up close to the stage. James would be summoned when it was his time to go to the podium.

Audrey sat down next to Hannah and was using her program to fan herself. Though the air was not hot, she was dealing with raging pregnancy hormones.

The sudden skirl of bagpipes summoned the meandering crowd to take their seats. The mood was somber as the shrill sounds from the bagpipes pierced through the air. There were news cameras in every direction. The flickering sound of news camera shutters could be heard mixed in with the sound of the bagpipes.

The ceremony began with the angelic sounds of song by a children's choir, and then a moment of silence to commemorate the North Tower being struck—8:46 a.m. The calm and silence that marked the moment was a direct contrast to what Hannah had witnessed from the conference room that morning ten years earlier.

After opening remarks, pairs of presenters began reciting the names, one at a time. James shifted nervously in his seat as Hannah held his hand.

It was time for James to go up and position himself on stage. Hannah watched in awe as her son was escorted to the podium and staged next to the second presenter. He looked so little behind the podium. He pulled the microphone down low to reach his mouth. As small as he was, he had an enormous presence on stage. He found his mom in the audience and gave a thumbs-up, unshaken and steady. Hannah clutched Audrey's hand and held her breath.

The set of presenters before James had just finished, and the news cameras panned to James and the woman standing next to him at the podium. They took turns, slowly announcing the names they had been assigned. James had practiced incessantly, ensuring that he pronounced every name correctly. His little voice was sure and confident as he read each name out loud.

James suddenly paused, taking in a breath. Hannah knew he had reached his father's name.

"And my dad, Travis F. Russell," James announced, his voice cracking.

Hannah could see James fighting back tears but he bravely continued.

"I didn't get a chance to meet you. But everyone tells me I am so much like you. Mom, Nanna, Eli, and I all miss you so much. Though I can't see you, Mom tells me you are always with me. I promise to always make you proud," James said through tears.

Hannah could hear sniffles from the crowd all around her. Tears poured down Hannah's face as her heart burned with grief. James returned to his seat, falling instantly into Hannah's arms. He buried his head under her arm and cried.

Hannah finally felt James's body relax. He pushed back into his seat, resting his head on her shoulders. It had taken so much out of his nine-year-old body, emotionally and physically.

"You did amazing, my little man," Hannah said, dabbing his tears with her tissue.

Clouds had moved in, covering the sky with a shroud of gray, matching the mood underneath it. Hannah looked up at the sky as she listened to the list of names being read out loud. Soft notes from a flute played in the background. The sound of rushing water from the fountains could also be heard, reminding everyone in the audience that their loved ones were, and would always be, there with them.

Looking up at the sky where the towers used to be, she remembered something Travis used to say to her.

Look up. Maybe you will see me.

Those words once playful and silly had become haunting.

Hannah searched the sky, remembering where the towers once reached far up. No matter how silly those words had been, she had still looked out the window of the eighty-fourth floor to the top of the North Tower, searching for a glimpse of Travis in the window on the 104th floor.

Now she sat looking up at a gray and empty sky, with no hope of seeing Travis's face smiling back at her. There were moments that Hannah could not bear the sadness. That very moment was one of them. Her grief was tangible; the loss hung on her, covering her, like the floral dress she wore on her body.

Hannah hadn't noticed that there was a pause in the reading of the names until she heard the sweet strum of a guitar playing over the speakers. It was soothing, beautiful, and familiar. She listened closely, trying to place where she had heard a similar sound. Then she heard the unmistakable voice of James Taylor, gently singing a melancholy song in perfect harmony with his acoustic guitar. His voice wafted through the air and swirled around Hannah. Suddenly, she was dancing with Travis on the rooftop. She closed her eyes and let herself be transported back to that night—the night before their lives were forever changed, as they innocently fell asleep, listening to the same soothing voice of James Taylor playing over the CD player.

She abruptly opened her eyes, becoming aware of the unbelievable coincidence of James Taylor performing live at the ten-year memorial—of all days, of all artists, of all events...

Hannah looked up at the sky, smiled, and whispered, "I see you."

———

It took over three hours to read through the names of all the victims who had perished at the World Trade Center. Hannah sat through the entire ceremony, intently listening to each name, waiting and bracing herself. When she heard the names of Marilyn, Don, and Miles read out loud, her stomach tightened, and she doubled over in sobs. It was the first time she was forced to acknowledge the finality of the loss of her friends. Hannah felt heart-wrenching sadness and debilitating survivor's guilt. She wished she had physically dragged Miles and Marilyn into the stairwell that day. She wished she had screamed at Don when he turned back.

Nearly everyone who had remained in her office that morning had perished in the attacks, including Berkley. Months after the attack, Berkley and Stanton had offered its employees who had survived to work at the sister location in New Jersey. It was an offer that Hannah had definitively declined.

The conclusion of the ceremony was marked by the somber performance of "Taps" by trumpeters throughout the plaza. Those still left in the audience cried, embraced each other, and held up photos of those they had lost.

Hannah knew what they needed to do next. They needed to find Travis's name on the wall. It was such a seemingly small task, but would bring with it a tidal wave of grief.

Hannah placed her arm around James's shoulder and started slowly toward the memorial pools. Rosemary, Audrey, and O'Shea walked alongside Eli's wheelchair as it maneuvered through the crowd. They walked along the perimeter of the North Pool, slowly sifting through the names inscribed in bronze along the way. Finally, about halfway around, she saw it: TRAVIS F. RUSSELL, beautifully etched into the stone.

Rosemary hung her head and placed her hands over his name as she cried. Hannah could not imagine the visceral pain of losing a child. She moved up behind her and placed her hand on Rosemary's shoulder. Eli had pulled up next to his mom, and James wrapped his arms around Hannah, burying his head again in tears. Ten years later, it was still so raw.

They stood at Travis's name for over an hour, telling stories of him, laughing, and crying. The afternoon was winding down, and the air was getting chilly. Rosemary looked tired. There was only so much a grieving mother could take in a day. Hannah was exhausted too.

It was time to go. As they all started to slowly disperse from the wall, Hannah noticed James standing quietly in front of Travis's name, following the letters with his finger.

Hannah turned back, joining James at the wall.

"Hey, you okay, buddy?" she asked delicately.

James shrugged, his face long with sorrow.

"I don't want to leave. It makes me feel closer to him being here, seeing his name," James said.

Hannah spotted a crayon on the stone wall someone had left behind.

"Well," Hannah replied, "I have an idea."

Unfolding the memorial program, she sprawled it out over Travis's name.

"We can bring his name home with us," Hannah said.

She started gently scribbling back and forth over his name, each letter starting to appear on the paper.

James's eyes widened.

"Here, you try." Hannah handed the crayon to him.

He rubbed the crayon back and forth, over each letter, until Travis's full name appeared on the paper. He held up the finished product and smiled.

"Thanks, Mom," James said, burying his head into her. Hannah hugged him tightly.

Suddenly, a man's voice interrupted the moment. "Excuse me," the man said, startling Hannah.

Hannah looked at the man speaking to her. He was a heavyset gentleman with red hair and red freckles dotting his face. He was seated in a motorized wheelchair similar to Eli's, but she was sure she had never seen him before in her life.

"Forgive me, but…are you Hannah by any chance?" he asked.

How did he know her name?

"Um…y-y-yes," Hannah stuttered. "I'm Hannah."

The man looked nervous. Hannah did not understand what was happening.

"I've been searching for you for ten years. My name is Carl. Travis and I were dear friends. We worked together on the 104th floor."

Hannah's eyes searched his face, trying to understand why he had been looking for her.

"Oh, hello…um…" Hannah awkwardly replied, "this is James…Travis's son."

Carl's eyes fell onto James. "Oh…wow. I didn't know," Carl replied, looking surprised.

"Well, he came as a bit of a surprise to me too," Hannah said, too much to explain in the moment.

Carl smiled as tears came to his eyes. "Travis has a son. How about that," he said in disbelief.

After a moment, Carl focused back on Hannah. "Travis saved my life on 9/11. Actually, Travis saved many lives that day." Hannah was stunned. "What do you mean?"

Carl looked apprehensively at James. Hannah realized there was something he didn't want to say in front of James. But Hannah knew James needed answers, no matter how difficult it might be to hear.

Hannah looked at James and then back at Carl. "It's okay. You can go on."

Carl smiled at James. "Strong, just like your dad," he said.

James looked up at his mom, smiling bashfully.

"That morning, we had just gotten into the elevator. I forgot my briefcase at the coffee kiosk, and Travis ran back to get it. There were fifteen of us, including Travis, in that elevator when the plane hit the North Tower," Carl recalled.

The elevator... Hannah gasped. She had never imagined he was in the elevator when the plane had struck. She always assumed he was trapped on the 104th floor.

"When the plane hit, our elevator went into a free fall. The emergency cables caught us, but we were trapped between floors with the doors locked shut. None of us had any idea what was going on. Smoke and fumes filled the elevator shaft; we could hardly breathe. It was dark for a few moments until the emergency lights came on. A few of us were hurt, some of us started to panic," Carl explained, pausing for a moment to gain his composure.

"I 'm sorry, I still have a hard time talking about that day. If I hadn't forgotten my briefcase, if Travis hadn't gone back to get it, we would have made it to the 104th floor. We would've been trapped. It's crazy how those few moments…" His voice trailed off.

Hannah's eyes were wide in disbelief as if she were seeing a ghost. Stunned by what he was telling her, she couldn't speak.

"Anyway, in the elevator, Travis stayed so calm. I had been knocked off my chair and had a terrible lump on my head. He checked on me and helped me back into my chair. A woman, Marie, she was due with her first baby any day. Travis really took care of her."

Carl dabbed the sweat off his forehead with a handkerchief from his front suit pocket.

"We felt the building swaying—creaking, twisting—while we were trapped inside that smoke-filled steel box. We thought that was it for us. And it would have been if it weren't for Travis." He paused again to catch his breath.

Both Hannah and James hung on his every word. It was what they had waited so long for—answers to the questions they thought they would never get. They were finally finding out what had happened to Travis in his final moments, and it was nothing like they had imagined.

"We called out for help and banged on the elevator doors, but it seemed no one could hear us. Marie was crying, worried about her baby, and some of us tried to use our cell phones to call out, but it was of no use. Travis stayed calm through it all, reassuring us, giving us hope. At one point, I saw him writing something on a piece of paper he had pulled from his briefcase. I didn't know what he was doing until later," Carl said.

Hannah looked down at James, checking in on him.

"After what felt like forever, we heard the best sound I have ever heard. A loud, booming voice yelled, 'FDNY, we hear you!' Someone had heard us banging, and the fire department came with crowbars to pry the elevator doors open. The elevator was stuck pretty far down from the platform though. Travis refused to go. He stayed back and helped hoist everyone up into the grasp of the firefighters above. He wouldn't leave until everyone was out. Last I knew, they were scrambling to find rope to help lift Travis out.

Hannah pulled her hands to her face. She couldn't believe what she was hearing. James stood still, his bottom lip starting to quiver as he fought hard to fight back tears.

Carl looked into James's tearful eyes. "Your dad saved fourteen people from the elevator that day. Because of him, we have all gone on to live full and wonderful lives. Babies have been born, grandparents have met their grandchildren, weddings have happened, and birthdays have been celebrated. We will never forget the sacrifice Travis made for us and our families. We get together every year to celebrate him; we call it 'Travis Day,'" Carl said. "He's our hero."

With those words, James's posture straightened. His lip stopped quivering and his chin lifted. Tears that had begun to well up in his eyes receded back behind his eyelids. Sadness was replaced with pride. James stood tall as he looked up at his mom.

"Dad really is a hero," James said proudly. "I knew he helped people that day. I just knew it."

Hannah smiled through her tears.

Carl reached his hand out to Hannah. He held a piece of paper folded in quarters. "*Hannah*" was written on the front. She recognized the handwriting right away.

"Right before Travis helped hoist me up out of the elevator, he handed me this note," Carl said solemnly. "I've been looking for you since. I hoped I would find you here today."

Hannah's hand shook as she reached for the note. She slowly unfolded the paper, revealing a handwritten note.

Dear Hannah,
If I don't make it out of here, I want you to know that these past weeks have been the best of my life. It doesn't matter the amount of time spent with someone, but how much love was shared in that time. I will love you forever.
P.s. Remember to look up...maybe you will see me...
Love, Travis

As Hannah read Travis's words, tears rushed down her face, like a waterfall.

"Thank you," she said to Carl, pulling the note close to her heart.

CHAPTER 32

Hannah and James returned home from the ten-year anniversary memorial ceremony different from when they had arrived in the city.

Though she finally learned of Travis's final moments, mysteries still remained for Hannah. Abina's name was not among the names of the victims who had perished on 9/11. Hannah searched tirelessly for her for years after the ten-year memorial. She combed over names and records of employees who had worked at the World Trade Center during that time. There were several victims from Ghana who had died on 9/11, not one was named Abina.

In fact, there was no record of anyone named Abina ever working at the World Trade Center. Was Abina real, or had Hannah imagined her altogether?

Hannah had also learned that there were no victims in close proximity to her while she was buried under the rubble. It wasn't possible to have heard someone talking to her. Hannah still had no answers for the voice she'd heard. She chose to believe it was Travis who had come to her in her darkest hour, keeping her alive.

The incessant beeping sounds Hannah had heard while buried under the rubble haunted her dreams. She would come to find out years later that those beeps came from the "PASS" devices, Personal Alert Safety Systems, worn by the firefighters. The devices are designed to activate when there is lack of motion for 30 seconds, signaling that a firefighter is in dire distress. Though Hannah didn't know it at the time, the silence she had awoken to hours later under the rubble, indicated that the batteries had run out on the PASS devices. She struggled to accept that all of those firefighters had likely perished.

Hannah still grappled with incredible guilt for surviving that day, when so many hadn't. She also blamed herself for Audrey's health struggles. She was vividly aware that had it not been for her sister's heroic efforts, she would have died under the rubble. Audrey never spoke of what she did that day to save Hannah, and she never blamed Hannah for her deteriorating health.

The next year, at the 2012 9/11 Memorial Ceremony, Hannah and James attended their very first celebration of Travis Day. The group of fourteen survivors from the elevator and their families met at the survivor tree in Memorial Plaza the day before the ceremony.

They lit candles and said prayers, told stories of their families and the blessings they were allowed to have because of Travis. They became an extended family to Hannah and James over the years. Hannah could have never imagined that so much good would come after such a dark time in their lives.

Audrey and O'Shea were blessed with two beautiful little girls. Not many knew of the struggles they had gone through to be able to conceive, but Hannah knew what miracles Addelyn and Hope were.

Preston's innocent and guileless personality landed him in the role of school resource officer at the Greenport Elementary School. Working with the kids was the perfect fit for Preston. Even more perfect was his match with Ms. Kim, a sweet, soft-spoken kindergarten teacher at the school.

Preston and Kim got married under a gazebo in the town park, inviting the entire school and their families. A year later, they welcomed a baby boy named Jack, the same year Audrey and O'Shea welcomed Addelyn into the world.

Addelyn and Jack were buddies from the very beginning, just like Audrey and Preston. When Preston had found out about how Addelyn wasn't allowed to join Scout Rangers, he immediately signed up Jack, and then volunteered to step up as the Scout Ranger troop leader. Preston then gladly took Addelyn into his Scout Rangers troop, and encouraged more girls to join too.

Despite all of the blessings and joyous events, Audrey's health had deteriorated more each year.

By the time Addelyn and Hope were of school age, she was dependent upon the use of an inhaler and supplemental oxygen to battle her shortness of breath. Her declining health forced her to leave the police force after fifteen years. The effects of breathing in the toxic ash at Ground Zero had taken a toll on so many first responders, many succumbing to cancer and other terminal illnesses.

As the years stretched on, Hannah watched James grow into a teenager, and, in the blink of an eye, emerge as a man. He had become the exact replica of his father—extraordinarily capable, brave, charming, and adventurous.

The summer of 2021 was the beginning of a bittersweet new chapter. James had graduated high school, and Hannah was soon facing having to let him go. She knew she had to let him fly so that he could do what he was meant to do in the world. But for so long it had been just Hannah and James against the world. He was her everything. Hannah was certain that, somehow, James would carry on Travis's legacy.

Hannah had never been interested in dating again. Deep down, she knew she could never find the kind of love she shared with Travis with anyone else. Her heart was too broken to give to anyone else anyway. She focused solely on raising James to be the best young man he could be.

The approaching month of September would mark twenty years since the attacks of 9/11. The passage of time had both shocked and saddened Hannah. It was a day that was etched in her soul as if it had happened the day before, yet twenty years had passed.

The physical injuries she'd sustained long ago on that day were emerging with a vengeance on her aging body. She could handle the physical pain. What hurt the most was that with the passage of time people seemed to forget. Generations had been born since that horrific day. People went about their busy lives. History was being forgotten, and Hannah sometimes wondered if anyone cared any longer.

She remembered the weeks and months after the attack. It was a common sight to see American flags attached to cars, headlights on during the day to show unity with each other. Civilians approached police officers in passing to thank them for their service. People were kind to each other. They had come together as a nation.

Twenty years later, the country was more divided than ever.

———

Friday, September 3rd, 2021
Audrey sat on the front porch in the early evening, rocking back and forth slowly in her wooden rocking chair. A cool front had come through and the lighter air was more breathable for her lungs, allowing her to take a break from the tube she sometimes wore in her nose to supplement her oxygen.

Her cell phone on the armrest of the rocking chair started to vibrate. It was Preston calling. She swiped right to answer.

"Hey, Preston," she said, sounding winded.

"I've got good news, and I've got bad news," Preston replied.

Audrey thought for a moment. "I'll take the good news first."

"Our Scout Ranger troop has been invited to carry the flags during the twentieth anniversary ceremony next week," he said.

Audrey's face lit up. "Oh, Addelyn will be thrilled." Her heart felt so full of pride. She also felt a pang of sadness knowing she wouldn't be able to attend in person. She was simply not well enough.

"I know you probably can't—" Preston started to say.

"Mike will go." Audrey quickly replied. Plus, Hannah will be there, and Addelyn has the best scout leader in the world… so it's okay."

But she knew she could never fool Preston. It wasn't okay, and there was nothing she could do about it.

"I'll take lots of pictures," he said, trying to make her feel better.

Audrey forced a smile, even though Preston couldn't see her. Sometimes it was just easier to say nothing.

There was a long silence, and Audrey could tell the bad news was coming. She braced herself.

"So, um…I found out some sad news today. I hate to be the one to tell you, but I'm sure you would want to know," Preston said.

Audrey's heart rate increased, causing her to feel short of breath. She wished she had her oxygen nearby.

"I was talking to one of my buddies in NYPD today. He told me that Manny Ramirez died a week ago…thyroid cancer," Preston said regretfully.

Audrey's heart dropped, and she felt a pit in her stomach. Her mind flashed back twenty years to the night she rode in the back of Manny's police cruiser from the precinct to Ground Zero. He was there when Hannah was rescued. He had been there to witness when she lifted concrete block off of Hannah's leg. He had even taken the time to call her chief to commend her bravery. Time had gone by, and they had lost touch, but she always held Manny close to her heart. She had no idea that he was even sick.

The news was not uncommon though, and after twenty years, she had almost become numb to the reports of cancer and related illnesses in those who were at Ground Zero. She wondered how long she had on this earth with the illness that was ravaging her body.

As she sat in silence on the phone with Preston, she recalled how the ash had felt in her lungs, and how her body immediately tried to reject it by coughing it out, but it never left.

When the towers collapsed, the buildings and their contents were pulverized, including electronics, furniture, building materials, and bodies. The ash was a combination of everything inside the towers in dust form, and contained asbestos and microscopic shards of glass, among other toxins.

"I'm sorry, Audrey," Preston said. "I know how important Manny was to you."

"Thanks for telling me." Her voice was barely a whisper.

As she got off the phone with Preston, she felt tears well up in her eyes. Her heart hurt...for Manny, and for the countless firefighters, police officers, EMT's, doctors, nurses, volunteers, and citizens of New York City who had succumbed to illnesses related to 9/11, from the toxic dust they breathed in. The number of fatalities was steadily increasing, and would soon surpass the number of victims who died on the actual day of the attacks.

Just then, the front door opened, and Addelyn and Hope joined Audrey out on the front porch.

"Hi, Mommy!" Hope said cheerily. "Whatcha doin'?"

Audrey quickly collected her emotions, and forced a smile onto her face. "Come here, my girls," she said, pulling them in close. They were the greatest joys in her life, and always made her feel better.

"I just got off the phone with Uncle Preston, and he had some great news." Audrey turned to look at Addelyn. "Your Scout Ranger troop has been invited to participate in the 9/11 ceremony this year."

Addelyn's eyes flew open wide, and she beamed with excitement and pride. For the moment, Audrey left out the bad news that she wouldn't be able to attend the ceremony with Addelyn. She also didn't mention the death of her friend Manny. As a mother, she always tried to protect them. But deep down she knew that one day they would have to face the world without her, much sooner than they should.

Audrey rocked slowly, holding the girls close. Her illness had taught their family to slow down and enjoy the simple moments. The sun flickered though the tall pine trees as it descended for the night, the cool air swirled a small pile of leaves around in the driveway, and they could hear the steady trickling of the stream nearby. Those were the moments Audrey lived for, and she would cherish each one she had left, for however long that would be.

Saturday, September 11, 2021
Twenty-year anniversary
The wail of bagpipes pierced through the air, followed by the angelic voices of the children's chorus. It was all familiar from years past—the opening statements, the moments of silence, and the heartfelt reading of the names.

Hannah knew Travis was happily looking down, seeing how much their family had grown and the love that surrounded James throughout his entire life. As Hannah watched Addelyn march to the side of the stage, the American flag waving in the breeze, she smiled at how much she reminded her of Audrey.

The ceremony was the same yet different. Hannah felt older and on the verge of change. The highlights in her blonde hair had faded, mixing with strands of gray. James was no longer a little boy. Though the pain of their loss was still ever-present, knowing what had happened to Travis had given them a sense of peace over the years.

After the ceremony, they visited Travis's name, like they had every year, and placed a rose stem in the first letter of his name.

The National 9/11 Museum had opened in 2014, but Hannah had never felt ready to go inside. Every year that she attended the memorial, she bypassed the museum altogether.

But that year, on the twentieth anniversary, there was something she had to do. Standing in front of the entrance to the museum, Hannah squeezed James's hand for courage. In her other hand, she held Travis's charred, bent souvenir penny that had been recovered from the rubble.

Hannah stopped to take in a breath as they walked in through the front entrance of the museum. For a moment she felt as if she were back inside of the World Trade Center. It held a familiar resemblance to what it once was, yet it was completely different.

As they rode the escalator down to seventy feet below ground level, they observed two monstrous steel beams that were showcased in the glass atrium. The beams were remnants of the World Trade Center.

Hannah and James walked along slowly, taking in the sights before they reached Foundation Hall. There, she saw what was known as "The Last Column"—the last remaining pillar that had once stood tall and proud at Ground Zero. Dozens of markings on the column represented those who had climbed the pile during the rescue and recovery. The column was a symbol of hope and strength.

It was quiet and somber, similar to the mood at the outdoor memorial. People milled about, observing the displays of what remained of the towers. The inside of the museum encased the exterior of the memorial pools above where the towers once stood. Hannah realized the enormity of the towers' footprint as she walked along the perimeter of the pools from inside of the museum.

They walked past crumpled and charred fire trucks and police cars, and what was left of one of the elevator motors from one of the towers. Hundreds of posters made by family members desperately searching for their loved ones after the attack were displayed along the walls.

Hannah felt the crushing weight of horror from that day returning. She squeezed James's hand tightly for support. They stopped in front of the double glass doors leading into the historical exhibition.

"I'm right here with you," James said, reassuring his mother.

Hannah felt immediately overwhelmed upon entering the room. The walls were packed full of photographs, personal belongings, newspaper clippings, and artifacts. News footage from the day played on televisions mounted on the walls. First person testimonies were shown on a loop. She felt as though she'd gone back in time and was experiencing the day all over again.

Hannah took her time, giving herself breaks as she needed them. She softly wept, moving slowly through the displays with James by her side. As she rounded the corner, she saw a room with dark curtains separating the section from the rest of the room. There was a sign warning of graphic images. James peeked in.

"Come on, let's keep walking," James said to his mother.

Hannah didn't move.

"James, I know you want to protect me, but I have to go through this process," she said. Hannah pushed through the curtains. The images on the screens pierced through her heart.

The jumpers.

Large screens mounted on the walls played footage of those who leapt from the upper floors of the North Tower. Hannah suddenly felt like her skin was inside out, and she could feel every nerve in her body. She relived feeling the booms of bodies landing nearby as she searched the fountain for Travis that morning. Seeing the images on the televisions in front of her broke her. She turned to James and sobbed. He held her tightly until she couldn't cry anymore.

Through her blurry eyes, Hannah looked at her watch. "We should move along."

They entered into the memorial exhibition room. Thousands of pictures were displayed on the walls, honoring each victim who died at the World Trade Center. They walked the room, studying the faces of each life lost. Then they came to Travis's photograph. James reached out and touched it, hanging his head for a moment. Lifting his head, he wiped his eyes. James noticed the kiosk behind them. He found his dad's name and pressed the button.

"Travis F. Russell" was announced over the speaker in the room, followed by a short biography in his memory. Hannah and James stood next to each other, arm in arm, solemnly listening to the names and short biographies of the victims over the loudspeaker.

Hannah checked her watch. It was time to meet with the curator of the museum.

"It's time," she said.

Hannah felt apprehensive, but she knew she was doing the right thing. They made their way back to the entrance of the historical exhibition. A tall woman with short, straight blonde hair, wearing a black pantsuit and a name tag on her chest, greeted them.

"Hannah?" she asked.

"Yes," Hannah reached out to shake her hand. "You must be Cindy."

The woman smiled. "It's so nice to finally meet you. Thank you for reaching out to donate. We appreciate all artifacts and belongings that help tell each person's story. It is important to preserve the history of what happened on 9/11 and donations like yours help us with that mission."

Hannah reached into her pocket and pulled out the souvenir penny. She hesitated for a moment.

"There's one more thing." She pulled out the folded note Travis had written to her in the elevator before the North Tower had collapsed.

"I want to donate this as well," she said, looking nervously at James, hoping for his approval. It was her wish to share Travis's story of love, sacrifice, and heroism.

J . S .   F A R M E R

James nodded.

As Hannah handed the items to Cindy, she felt fulfilled, sharing Travis's story with the world.

"We will take good care of these for you, I promise," Cindy said.

Before exiting the museum, Hannah and James stopped in front of a large wall covered in thousands of blue tiles. Each tile had its own shade of blue, for each victim who died at the World Trade Center. A phrase sprawled across the wall, in big, bold letters, embedded itself deep into Hannah's heart, where it would stay for the rest of her life. The letters were forged using steel that had been recovered from the wreckage.

NO DAY SHALL ERASE YOU
FROM THE MEMORY OF TIME.
-Virgil

Hannah put her head on James's shoulder. Feeling calm and at peace, she sighed. "I am ready to go home now."

James smiled a sly Travis-like smile. "Not quite yet. I have a surprise for you," he said.

CHAPTER 33

James looked up at the towering Gothic pillars of the Brooklyn Bridge in front of them.

"All these years I have heard about your walk across the bridge with Dad," James said. "I've always wanted to take you across again."

Hannah looked at her son in awe. He wasn't much younger than Travis was the day he took her across the very same bridge.

He put his arm around her as they stepped onto the walkway of the bridge.

"You know the scrapbook Dad made for you?" James asked. "After you tucked me in every night, I would sneak my flashlight and look through the pages until I fell asleep." James chuckled to himself. "Silly, I know."

Hannah smiled up at her son. "Not silly at all."

Hannah breathed in the air as they crossed over the river. The wind blew her hair up from below the bridge. The sun was falling slowly from the sky. She was no longer a young woman, though she refused to acknowledge the creaking in her joints and the fatigue that had crept up on her with age.

James no longer needed her to protect him. He had become a man. As they crossed the water, memories of James as a little boy flooded her mind. She remembered how his little hand felt in hers and what his sweet voice sounded like when he sang his favorite songs. She could still feel his little arms wrapped around her neck, and his soft kisses on her cheek.

When they reached the other side, James turned left off the bridge.

"Where are we going?" Hannah asked.

"You'll see."

They walked along the riverfront. The water glistened with the setting sun as the boats lazily sailed by.

Hannah noticed something in the distance. She squinted, trying to focus her eyes on what was up ahead. Suddenly she heard the joyous sound of carnival music. Then she saw a beautifully restored antique carousel, housed in a glass pavilion. As they got closer, she could see people from young to old gliding up and down on the intricately painted horses. Others were enjoying a ride in the exquisitely painted chariots.

She turned to James, her face lit up with surprise and delight. "The carousel! It's here!"

"I promised you I'd take you here one day," James said proudly. "It's called Jane's Carousel."

Hannah couldn't believe her eyes.

"It took twenty-two years to restore the carousel," James said. "It was finally brought here and opened in 2011. Wait right here. I'll be right back." James scurried over to the ticket booth to purchase their ride tickets.

Hannah turned to take in the sight of the carousel. It amazed her how something as simple as a merry-go-round could bring so much universal happiness to all. The familiarity of the classic ride along with the nostalgia of a time long ago intrigued riders of every age.

James returned with their tickets, hooked his arm through Hannah's arm, and led her to the carousel. Hannah stepped up onto the platform, taking in the beauty of the carvings in each horse. She picked a majestic white horse to ride. James hopped up next to her on a royally decorated noble brown horse.

She wrapped her hands around the silver pole and suddenly remembered what it felt like to be young and carefree again. The ride began slowly and the sounds of percussions, organ, and thumps of a snare drum danced on the air. As the ride picked up speed, Hannah felt the whoosh of the breeze flow by her. Each rotation gave them views of the Manhattan Bridge on one side and the Brooklyn Bridge on the other.

Hannah took it all in. Her eyes fell upon a young couple, snuggled up together in one of the chariots. So caught up in love, there was no one else in their world at that moment. Hannah then spotted a little boy up ahead, bravely letting go of the silver pole. "No hands!" he screeched over the music. His mother reacted quickly, making sure he didn't fall and reminding him to hold on tightly. Hannah caught the reflection of James in the mirror of the carousel. He was that little boy not long ago and in no time at all, was all grown up. She then looked up at the white carnival lights above whizzing by, and took in the smells of the Brooklyn food vendors wafting from nearby.

When the ride came to an end, James helped her off her horse and helped steady her. There would never be words profound enough to thank James for the gift he had just given her.

"Now, it is my turn to take you somewhere," Hannah said. "I hope it's still there!"

She led the way around the block toward the small pizza place where Travis had taken her twenty years before. The name had changed, and it looked a bit different, but the pizza place was still there.

Two huge slices were shoved into the oven and, in a matter of moments, handed to them on a paper plate, barely visible under the huge triangle slice.

With their pizza plates in hand, they walked back to the waterfront to the very bench she'd sat at with Travis.

"This is it," Hannah announced. "This is where your father and I sat. It was a night just like this, actually."

Hannah looked up at the sky. A faint half-moon was coming out for the night. The lights on the Brooklyn Bridge had illuminated under the early evening sky. It would soon be dark, and the air was getting chilly. The wind kicked up, bringing with it a random red maple leaf from somewhere nearby. It floated back and forth in the air until it landed directly onto James's plate.

"Excuse me," James said to the leaf, plucking it off his plate.

James shifted anxiously on the bench. "I have something to tell you."

Hannah looked at him curiously.

"I've decided to join the NYPD. I took the entrance exam and I passed. I can join as soon as I turn twenty-one."

Hannah was quiet at first. She always knew he would do so much good in the world. Suddenly it all made perfect sense. She remembered how entranced he was with the NYPD officers patrolling the plaza at the ten-year memorial ceremony. That was also the day he found out his father had died a hero. Looking back now, Hannah realized, that was likely the day James's path in life was formed.

"I'm so proud of you," Hannah said, her eyes filling with tears. "If your dad were here, he would be so proud too."

"He *is* here," James said, holding up the red maple leaf that had landed on his plate moments earlier.

Hannah closed her eyes and placed her head on James's shoulder. She could feel Travis all around. Though his physical presence could not be seen, Travis was never far. He had been with James through every step of his life. And now James would go on to become a hero, just like his father.

Only the powers of the universe knew the fate James would face one day. But for that moment, all was right with the world, sitting next to James Travis Russell, underneath the lights of the Brooklyn Bridge.

ACKNOWLEDGEMENTS

This book is dedicated to my daughters—my inspiration in life; two little humans who showed me who I was always meant to be. To my husband, Shawn, this would have never been possible without your support. Thank you for believing in me.

Life happens, the unexpected will bump you off course at times, but the people who don't let you lose sight of your dreams are the keepers. Addison, thank you for picking up Mommy's half-written book in the middle of it all, and begging me to write more. You sure kept me on my toes! Emma, the excitement in your eyes kept me writing every single day. Debby, my very first reader, my biggest cheerleader, and my dearest friend, I could have never done this without you. Thank you for believing in me, and more importantly, for showing me how to believe in myself. Cari, you inspired me long ago when you wrote your first book. Thank you for your amazing support along the way, and for being one of my first readers, and dearest friends. Mom, I told you I would write a book one day with that laptop!

I had an incredible team to help bring this project together. A special thank-you to my editor, Rosanna Aponte, book cover and interior designer, Danna Mathias, and dear friend, Maria Viteri, for her intuitive and creative logo design.

There are no words great enough to thank the first responders, who so selflessly gave their lives on September 11, 2001, as well as those who have succumbed to related illnesses since. To all of the victims of 9/11, and their families, we will never forget.

ABOUT THE AUTHOR

 J.S. Farmer grew up in a small town in Connecticut. She studied criminology and psychology at Central Connecticut State University. After seven years as a police officer, she shifted her career into the private sector, working as a government security analyst for a defense contractor. During that time, she earned her master's degree in national security and public safety at the University of New Haven.

A native New Englander, she now resides in northeast Florida with her husband, two daughters, and dog Jackson. Her favorite place in the world is the beach, where she enjoys searching for shark teeth, and relaxing in the Florida sun. You can find out more about J.S. Farmer, and her future novels, at www.jsfarmerauthor.com.

Made in United States
Orlando, FL
24 March 2023

31390594R00196